ARITHMOPHOBIA:

AN ANTHOLOGY OF MATHEMATICAL HORROR

Arithmophobia: An Anthology of Mathematical Horror edited by Robert Lewis

This book is a work of fiction. All events, incidents, characters, names, businesses, places, and other entities depicted in these stories are either fictitious or are used fictitiously.

All stories and poems appear here for the first time.

Cover art: Elderlemon Design
Design and layout: Robert Lewis

Published by Polymath Press, a trade name of Polymath Enterprises, LLC. Please direct all inquiries to Polymath Press, P. O. Box 461870, Aurora, CO 80046-1870, online at www.polymathpress.com, or via email to editor@polymathpress.com.

First edition
March, 2024

ISBN(paperback): 978-1-961827-04-2
ISBN (eBook): 978-1-961827-05-9
Library of Congress Control Number: 2024932341

ARITHMOPHOBIA:

AN ANTHOLOGY OF MATHEMATICAL HORROR

Edited by Robert Lewis

POLYMATH
—PRESS—

Aurora, CO

Other Polymath Press titles by Robert Lewis

Case Files of the Rocky Mountain Paranormal Research Society Volume 1
by Robert Lewis & Bryan Bonner
Published September, 2023 by Polymath Press

In the Woods: A Fiction Foundry Anthology
Edited by Robert Lewis
Published November, 2023 by Polymath Press

Contents

INTRODUCTION
Robert Lewis

Mathematics tends to evoke a visceral reaction from most people. Some love it and some are terrified of it. This anthology of horror stories inspired by mathematical ideas is intended for both groups of people. So even if you're not a "math person," don't put this book down just yet. Yes, there's math in it. No, you don't need to be a doctoral-level mathematician (or any kind of mathematician, for that matter) to understand or enjoy the stories. Every story stands on its own as an excellent work of fiction even if you've never taken a math class in your life. But if you *do* have some math background, I think you'll enjoy seeing some familiar names and some familiar ideas. In other words: when I put this anthology together, I specifically insisted on stories in which mathematics was integral to the plot (pun intended) but which would not exclude even the least mathematically-inclined of all readers.

Those of us who find ourselves in the "love it" group with respect to math can easily be captivated by the beauty of a well-argued proof to the point that we risk becoming obsessed. Intellectual history is full of stories of crazed and sometimes anti-social mathematicians. Georg Cantor, who introduced the world to different sizes of infinity, spent much of his life in a mental institution. Try grappling with the infinite at such a deep level and see if you fare any better. But even on a much smaller scale, mathematicians tend to be obsessive kinds of people. I recall one instance in which I discovered the author of a math book I'd read and enjoyed was a professor at a local university. When I went to his office to ask for an inscription in my copy of his book, I at first thought he wasn't there because all the lights were off. How wrong I was! He was right there, sitting alone in a back corner of his unlit office, scribbling equations on a tablet-sized blackboard (the kind schoolchildren used back in the day and which became a staple in Victorian seances). We'll meet some similarly obsessive characters in the pages to follow.

But what of those who are afraid of mathematics? This book is named after just that fear, and it's a real thing. I've worked with a lot of math students over the years, and I can easily understand why people get anxiety when faced with something like a math exam. Math is *hard*, and never let anyone tell you any different. British author and "stand-up mathematician" (yes, that's a real thing, though I question how many of them there are in the world) Matt Parker once remarked that "mathematicians aren't people who find maths easy; they're people who enjoy how hard it is." And it's true. The most interesting and rewarding things any mathematician—whether student, professional, or hobbyist—ever comes across are those that require some real mental effort to unlock. If you find yourself in the category of people who struggle with mathematics, don't fear. You're in very good company. And of course, we'll also meet some characters who share your struggles in the stories you're about to read.

Despite many people's deep and abiding fear of mathematics, I think a lot of people are probably wondering: why an anthology of mathematical horror? I could muster plenty of convincing-sounding arguments. I could say that math horror makes sense because so many people are afraid of it. I could find some historic examples of horror authors who made use of mathematical ideas in the past (H. P. Lovecraft comes readily to mind; in fact, I even made a YouTube video on my *Phobophile* channel explaining in some detail what Lovecraft was really on about when he wrote of non-Euclidean geometries in stories such as "Dreams in the Witch House"). Those arguments are all true, but they're not the real reason for the book you now hold in your hands (or on your screen if you're one of those eBook kinds of people).

The honest to God truth of the matter is: this is just a pet project for me. I wasn't always a math guy. My high school days were spent taking as little math as possible. I was a words guy, not a numbers guy. But when I got to college and started taking math courses taught by some truly excellent professors, I fell in love with the subject (enough so that I shortly found myself standing in the Registrar's office adding a math major to my program). Of course, I was already a horror nerd by then, so I immediately found myself looking for mathematical horror stories; fiction that could scratch the math and horror itches simultaneously. Much to my dismay, there wasn't a whole lot of it. I read Lovecraft, of course, and he had some math-y ideas. And there were a few others. But not nearly enough. So the real reason for this book is that this is the book I've been wanting to read for *years*, and nobody else seemed like they were going to be crazy enough to actually make it happen.

After I put out my call for stories and saw the quality of work coming in, I knew I had my work cut out for me. The authors—both those who ultimately made it into this anthology and most of those who unfortunately didn't—understood exactly what I was looking for and made it incredibly difficult to make my final selections. Like mathematics, though, curating a selection of stories for an anthology is enjoyable precisely because it is difficult.

The end result is, of course, this collection of thirteen stories and one poem. Thirteen stories because the number thirteen itself reminds us of "scary" numbers, and one poem both to wrap things up in a thoughtful manner and just in case any potential readers might be a little *too* stricken by triskaidekaphobia to read the anthology if it contained just the unlucky thirteen. However, lest you think there's nothing creepy about fourteen (if you want to count the stories and poem together), it is the number of pieces into which Set tore the body of Osiris as well as the number of sacrificial victims of the Minotaur in mythology. Turns out, pretty much any number can be frightening depending upon the context.

Never mind their number, though. The most important thing about the works in this anthology is their quality, and I can confidently say that these are exceptional works of literature and represent a wonderful and eclectic mix of visions, both in terms of their mathematics and in terms of their horror.

We begin with "One-Two, Buckle My Shoe" by Elizabeth Massie, a tale of mathematical obsessions taken to dark extremes. Then, in "Splinters" by Miguel Fliguer and Mike Slater, fractal geometries and non-integer dimensions provide the framework for a philosophical discussion of Lovecraftian terror. "Manifold Thoughts" by Patrick Freivald asks us to consider: if mathematical constructs could communicate with us, what might they say and do? Liz Kaufman's story "Real Numbers" introduces us to a student who's become convinced that numbers are watching us disapprovingly and perhaps even plotting against us. Mathematics, history, and religion collide as characters use number theory to unlock ancient secrets in "Eratothenes' Map" by Damon Nomad. "They'll Say it was the Communists" by Sarah Lazarz takes us into more recent history as something strange and frightening begins happening to the teams of women working as "computers" during the Space Race. A stereotypical math problem—the sort we've all probably seen on some exam or other—comes to life in Martin Zeigler's humorous tale, "Trains Passing." Josh Snider tells us of a symmetry-obsessed professor who encounters a supernatural form of symmetry in "Asymmetrical Dreams." The mathematics behind werewolves is on full display in "Critical Mass" by Rivka Crowbourne. "Lost and Found" by Joe Stout shows us that our own math classes might not have been so bad after all, as a lost student finds himself in a strange house where he must take the math exam of—and for—his life. Brian Knight's "A Strange Thing Happened at the Coffee Shop" reminds us that mathematics is at the heart of reality itself—and asks what might happen when someone starts manipulating those equations. A struggling math student tries to use his newfound algebraic skills to solve the mystery of his tutor's disappearance in "Solve for X" by Wil Forbis. David Lee Summers shows us what we might see if we could somehow peer into spatial dimensions beyond our usual three in "A Presence Beyond the Shadows." Finally, "The Ghosts of the Spiral" by Maxwell I. Gold brings the anthology to a close in a poem inspired equally by horror and the Fibonacci numbers.

Initially, I'd thought to provide (either in this Introduction or in an Afterword) a collection of mathematical notes on each of the stories for readers who might be interested in digging a bit deeper. In the end, though, I decided the stories are so good they can speak for themselves. However, I will mention that I've personally double-checked all the mathematics. Some of the stories may take a bit of artistic license with a few mathematical ideas, but all the solutions—where solutions are given—are correct. And if you're interested in some of these ideas, there's no shortage of math books and websites to assist in your tumble down the rabbit hole.

So, at the end of the day, *should* we be afraid of mathematics? I don't think so. One of the authors featured in this very anthology, during our early discussions, mentioned struggling to come up with ideas for a story because math is beautiful rather than scary. I agree. But as beautiful as math itself may be, it can reveal some truly frightening things about our universe. In that context, I think the mathematical theorem and the horror story serve similar purposes. Both can be beautiful things even as they reveal dark truths to us.

With that in mind—and with my sincere thanks to each and every one of you for taking the time to read this book—let's begin our exploration of the strange world of *Arithmophobia*.

ONE-TWO, BUCKLE MY SHOE

Elizabeth Massie

"Janie?" It's Mom. She's calling from down the hall, but I hear her clearly. "Janie, come here, please."

I sigh. I'm in the middle of making hamburgers for lunch and my hands are greasy and a little bloody. I lick the blood off then wipe my hands on my jeans. There is so much to do around here. Though, sure, it was my choice.

"Janie," comes the voice again. She'll keep calling until I go. I slide the frying pan off the burner and turn off the timer. I leave the kitchen, counting my steps.

Don't get me wrong. I love my mother. But she can be a pest at times.

Twenty-four step to her door.

Pushing open the bedroom door, I step inside and close the door behind me. Mom's room is quite dark. The blinds are drawn and no lamp is turned on. The only thing visible is the little clock on her nightstand. The numbers glow faintly, orange. Mom's on the bed, of course. I can make out her shadowy shape lying there. She's a small, frail old woman. I'm a big young woman, tall like my Dad was.

"What, Mom?" I sigh heavily. "I'm trying to make lunch."

"It smells good," she says. There is a scratchy hopefulness in her voice. "Can I help?"

"Mom, you know you can't."

"I'd like to, Janie. Please?"

"No, Mom."

"How long 'til lunch is ready?"

I tap my watch so I can see the time. "Seven more minutes."

"What time is it now?"

"I put that clock on your nightstand. You can read clock, Mom."

I can hear her turn her head slightly. "Eleven forty-two."

"Eighteen minutes until noon."

"So supper will be ready—"

"At eleven forty-nine."

"You're so smart. I always hoped you'd be smart. How many seconds, then?"

Numbers. Always numbers.

"Four-hundred twenty."

"Okay. Good" A pause. "Please, let me help you."

"You can't. You know you can't. Please stop interrupting me."

Mom doesn't say anything. She knows she can't get up. She knows she can't help me, even if she wants to. She's been in bed for three days, seven hours, and forty-one minutes now. I'm taking care of her, much like I took care of Dad. He was an alcoholic. Gone now. Died two months, three weeks, five days, seven hours ago. That's 2,095 hours if you're interested, 125,700 minutes if you're really interested. Everything's up to me here at home. I don't mind so much. I have some freedom. Well, except when Mom gets demanding.

I leave the bedroom, return to the kitchen. Nineteen steps this time. My stride is bigger, so I go back to the bedroom door and do it again. There. Twenty-four steps.

I put the pan back on the burner and turn the timer back on.

I watch the burgers, flip them after sixty-eight seconds, and count to myself as the timer ticks down.

On the kitchen wall is my high school diploma. I wanted to go to college but the money wasn't there. I'm smart, though. I did well in school, especially science and math. My mom was never very smart, but she knew it was important to *be* smart. She didn't teach me much, but she did teach me about math, starting when I was not quite two years old. She'd repeat that little rhyme:

> *"One, two, buckle my shoe,*
> *Three four, shut the door,*
> *Five six, pick up sticks,*
> *Seven eight, lay them straight,*

ONE-TWO, BUCKLE MY SHOE

Nine ten, a big fat hen."

From my earliest years, Mom taught me that the only things that are eternal, the only things that never end, are numbers. You can count your entire life and you'll never reach a final number. Animals—including people, of course—die. The world will crumble away. Dreams can be crushed. The sun will burn out. But numbers live on forever. The whole idea fascinated me. It still does. Imagine my joy when I learned everything could be expressed in numbers.

Mom repeated the rhyming verse to me every night through elementary school, changing the words sometimes to suit the occasion. When I misbehaved, it was this one:

"One, two, buckle my shoe,
Three four, shut the door,
Five six, pick up sticks,
Seven eight, feel their weight,
Nine ten, switch her again."

And the sticks were right there and they hurt. I did my best to behave.

Mom also impressed upon me that the most important thing a person can do in a lifetime is to learn. Learning makes the maze of life easier. It keeps you from getting stuck somewhere. Mom never finished high school; spent her first forty-one years working at the mill. Then she met Dad, whose name was Bob, and immediately got pregnant. The two were married seven weeks before I was born. That's forty-nine days—seven squared—or 1,176 hours. Dad kept drinking. Mom kept working. Quit when she was sixty-five. She's always had high hopes for me. "You gotta learn all you can, Janie, so you can get out of here," she'd say. I never forgot that. I never will.

"Janie?"

The burgers are ready. I slide the pan off the burner and line two plates with paper towels. Then I scoop the burgers onto the plates. Ketchup and pickles from the fridge, buns from the cabinet.

I look up at the diploma again. There is dust on the top and the glass is smudged with cooking grease. I miss school. I especially miss the science fairs. I won all of them in middle school and high school, showing off my math-based experiments. I crafted experiments on probability, volume, and time. That was the best part of school. I have my ribbons in my room, tacked to the wall.

And though I couldn't go to college, I still do my math experiments. It makes life tolerable. I've worked with ants, spiders, worms, mice. Each one carefully set up, each one carefully monitored and recorded. How long? How many?

How often? How slow? How fast? So many questions to pose and to answer.

I put the burgers on the bun. Mom likes ketchup and pickles. I just like ketchup. I put on the condiments and take the meals down to her room.

Twenty-four steps.

As soon as I step inside, I hear her say, "Janie. I'm worried."

I don't reply. I put both plates on the nightstand then get the lap trays from top of the dresser. I put Mom's plate on one tray and place it on her chest. Then I return to the kitchen, fill two glasses with water, then twenty-four steps back to Mom. I close the door behind me and sit on the chair near the head of the bed.

"Time to eat, Mom."

"Thank you."

I put my plate on my tray and hold it in my lap.

"You are a very smart girl," says Mom. "You know how proud I am of you."

"I do. Thanks."

"I know you work hard here and you work hard at the store."

I forgot to mention that I have a part time job at the dollar store. I hate it so why talk about it? We need the extra income. Mom's Social Security isn't very much. That's basically it.

"Janie?" says Mom.

I let out a breath. "What?"

"I would love to stay with you and help you a while longer. Please, Janie?"

I ignore this. She knows she can't. I take a bite of my hamburger. It's pretty good. Lots of ketchup. In the shadows I can see Mom's hand go to the tray, then to her mouth. After a moment, she says, "This is tasty."

I take another bite. I can smell that Mom has urinated the bed. I wasn't on time with the bedpan for this one. Not my fault; she didn't call me to help.

"Mom, you pissed."

"Yes."

"Why didn't you call me?"

"I don't want to be a burden. I want you to be happy."

"You aren't a burden. You are very important to me. You know that. I've told you over and over. Dad was important to me, too."

"But Janie, you—"

"Eat your hamburger. I'll clean you up in a bit."

I can hear Mom take a bite and chew.

"You know," I say, picking meat from between my back molars. "Once I share my experiments with a university, I'm sure they'll give me a full scholarship.

4

Won't that be great? When I get a scholarship and then a degree, I'll have my pick of jobs in math or science. I'll make lots of money."

Mom chews, says nothing.

"You were great, Mom, teaching me about numbers, about math. I give you lots of credit for the success I'm going to have."

Mom swallows. "Janie, please listen to me."

I take another bite of my hamburger, get ketchup on the tip of my nose. I wipe it off, lick my finger.

"Janie. Listen—"

I look at my watch. "It's almost time. Fifty-three seconds to go. Let me get your plate out of the way. I'll give it back to you in a moment."

Mom makes a funny groaning, grunting sound. It's almost as if she no longer thinks math and science are important.

I put her tray on the floor, click on the lamp on the nightstand. The glow makes Mom close her eyes and look away. She says, "Janie, please listen to me." I pull the bedspread back, exposing her ankles, which are lashed to the footboard with ropes. The scent of urine is stronger now, but I'll deal with that later. Mom's arms and hands remain unshackled. My focus, though, is on the red braided cord at her neck.

It took some figuring to rig this up. Four days ago (96 hours; 5,760 minutes), I told Mom there was a big nest of mice—eleven to be precise—in the wall of her bedroom. I traded rooms with her, saying I would get rid of the mice and then she could have her room back. While Mom was busy elsewhere, I took care to set up my experiment just as it should be. Found sturdy ropes for the ankles. I considered something for her arms but that would make more work for me in the long run, feeding her and all. As to the red cord, I drilled two holes, seventeen inches apart, in the mattress up near the headboard, where her pillow would be. Then I drew both ends of the cord through the holes, running down to the bedframe. One end was secured to the frame. The other end was threaded out to the side. I knotted that end to the spoke of a small spigot wheel handle that was screwed to the leg of the nightstand. When I turn the wheel handle, it will tighten the cord.

The following day, I told Mom the mice were gone and she happily returned to her room. After we shared our evening meal in the kitchen and after she'd watched a *Perry Mason* rerun in the living room, I gave her a cup of tea with a bit of chloral alcoholate (don't ask where I got it; I have my sources). She was out within the half hour: twenty-eight minutes, thirteen seconds to be exact. I hoisted her from the couch and carried her to her bedroom.

Thirty-seven steps.

I lashed her ankles with the ropes. I slipped her head beneath the red cord and adjusted it so it was loose around her neck but tight enough so she couldn't sit up or pull out.

She awoke the next morning with a scream. I kind of expected that. I brought her a bowl of warm oatmeal with honey but it didn't calm her down. So, I sat in the chair by the bed and explained it to her.

I reminded her of my math experiments, the ones with the insects, the mice and rats and squirrels. I confessed to her that Dad didn't drown in the tub on his own. He was an experiment, too. He was drunk in the tub, singing some stupid song. I climbed in and sat on his chest, pushed his head under, and timed how long it would take a man of his age (sixty-seven), his weight (one-hundred seventy-two pounds), his height (six feet, one inch) and his weakness for spirits (on average, a six-pack of beer followed by a half of a thirteen ounce bottle of rye daily) to drown. I'd researched drowning. I'd found reports that had basic information on how long it could take people of certain weights to drown. But I hadn't found any actual human experiments on the matter. Dad wriggled and struggled, tried to knock me off, as was to be expected. But he was unconscious after two minutes, forty-six seconds. After another minute and a half, he convulsed. I pulled his head up, watched as he went blue. He convulsed again. I felt for his pulse, and at exactly nine minutes, seventeen seconds, his heart stopped for good. I let him go, climbed from the tub, took some photos, and recorded the results.

While I was telling Mom this, I could see she wasn't pleased. Her eyes began twitching and her hands began clawing at the red cord.

"Oh, Mom, don't do that," I said. "You know the importance of math and science. You taught me that numbers are eternal and everything else is temporary. And you were right, Mom. Put your hands down. Don't mess this up, now. Let me explain my new experiment."

Mom continued to grab at the cord. "Let me go, Janie!"

I shook my head. I quoted her old rhyme:

"One, two, buckle my shoe,
Three four, shut the door,
Five six, pick up sticks,
Seven eight, feel their weight,
Nine ten, switch her again."

There were several thin but sturdy sticks I'd placed in the corner for a situation like this. I picked them up and whipped Mom's hands, hard enough that it clearly made an impression, both on her psyche and on her hands. She put her hands to her side and bit her lip.

I then told her what was going to happen. I was going to tighten the cord enough so it was just touching her neck. Then, I would turn the spigot wheel handle a quarter inch twice a day. The plan was to see, with that amount of turn daily, how long it would take to crush her windpipe and kill her. My little home-made garrote. Mom whimpered. That really wasn't unexpected but the greater good, right?

However, I didn't tighten the cord up against her neck right away. Because, in all honesty, my experiment wasn't what I'd told her. It wasn't just to see how long it would take for her to die from strangulation, which would be vaguely interesting. I primarily wanted to find out how many times a person of her age (sixty-six), weight (one-hundred thirty-nine pounds), and height (four feet, eleven and two-thirds inches) would plead, threaten, and bargain to save their life. It's now been three days, eight hours, and nineteen minutes. She has pleaded to be released thirty-four times. She's only threatened twice. She has bargained nineteen times, offering to help me do other kinds of experiments instead of this one, to help me clean and cook. Fascinating. I've recorded it all.

I glance down at her feet. There are gouges in the flesh where she's tried to wriggle free. I feel bad about that. That wasn't part of the plan, but it is what it is. I hand Mom's lunch tray back to her but she only stares at the plate on her stomach, at the half-eaten hamburger.

"Mom, I'm going to start tightening the cord now. Thank you for taking part in this. I owe it all to you. I will attend the university. I will make a mark in the world."

I can tell Mom wants to scream but she is afraid I'll slash her hands again. She does plead once more, however. "Janie, listen to me, please. This isn't the best way to—" Guess I'll have to record the number of pleads as thirty-five.

"Not another word," I say, and I turn the spigot wheel handle until the cord touches her neck. I smile. Then I turn it a quarter inch. It tightens, but not enough to keep her quiet. She whispers, "Janie, please don't!"

Thirty-six pleads.

I kiss Mom on the forehead and take her tray and mine back to the kitchen. Twenty-four steps.

This evening, I'll do the second tightening. I wonder when Mom will begin to strangle. It won't be long, but still I'm curious. Math and science are so exciting, so thrilling. Learning is the best thing in the world.

As I wash our plates, I look up at my diploma on the wall. Once Mom is dead, I'll hang her in the basement. Say she was devastated over the loss of my Dad and hanged herself. Dad was an easy explanation; a drunk, drowned during a bath.

I wipe the plates dry and put the pan in the sink.

I remember what Mom said when she found Dad dead in the tub. "I can't live without him," she'd cried. "Oh, Bob, if only we could be together again."

I nod to myself. Seems my experiments will take care of that. Two birds with similar stones, right? I hear Mom weeping down the hall. At least that doesn't qualify as another plead, threat, or bargain.

Smiling, I scrub the pan.

SPLINTERS
Miguel Fliguer & Mike Slater

(The auditorium is almost full, and the audience is getting restless. House and stage lights are dimmed. A deep, theatrical voice booms from the P.A.)

Nuclear chaos; quadrillions of subatomic particles colliding; matter and antimatter, quarks and antiquarks; creation and destruction; spacetime ripping apart, melding with itself in inconceivable configurations; galactic superclusters collapsing and rebirthing. And everything happens at the center, the place where everything began. And in an infinite universe—oh, and it is, more infinite than we can possibly know—*all points are the center.* Yet it also happens in the space *between* the dimensions we know.

(The voice pauses. Rafter spotlights slowly come up as the audience applauds. The Professor stands at stage-center, a small wireless microphone clipped to the lapel of his slightly wrinkled suit. An unmarked plastic bottle rests on a tall bench by his side, condensation sliding in lazy rivulets down its flanks.)

Hello! Welcome to my talk. Thank you so much for coming. It's good to see so many young faces in the crowd, coming on a weeknight to a campus auditorium looking for *science*!

(Applause.)

Thank you, thank you. Tonight, we're going to discuss Chaos and Order. For the past couple of days, I've been trying to set my ideas in order in preparation for this talk. Still, I'm sure Chaos will take us through a few unexpected detours. As we'll see later, that's the nature of Being.

Let's begin with the basics. We're all familiar with dimensions. For example, a dot can be thought of as having no dimensions at all. A straight line drawn on a pristine piece of aluminum foil, it's just one-dimensional, right? Disregard for a moment the thickness of your drawing implement, and imagine you're wielding an ideal, zero-dimensional pen. And since the foil's thickness is much smaller than its other dimensions, you could disregard it too, and visualize the foil as a two-dimensional plane, with a one-dimensional straight line written on it with your zero-dimensional pen. Alright?

Let's move one step further. If you pile several sheets of foil, like a block of printer paper sheets, you now start to see…volume, that's right, thank you. The three dimensions. Thickness is not negligible anymore, so when you hold that block in your hand you can now visualize its depth in addition to its length and width. That's the three-dimensional space we're all used to. Perhaps you've heard about four-dimensional constructs like the tesseract, which can be thought of as a cube with vertices, edges, and faces over four spatial dimensions. But we won't explore those higher realms now, for what I want us to do is to visit those strange dimensions *in between*.

What if I told you that *non-integer* dimensions are a thing? Okay, I see some people nodding in the audience. Think about it. Imagine you're trying to write a straight line on another two-dimensional piece of foil, but this time you suffer from a neurological malady, and your zero-thickness pen trembles in your hand so you end up with a meandering doodle. How many dimensions does it have? Not one, because it spreads across the two dimensions of the foil, yet it's not a 2D flat surface itself. It lies between one and two dimensions. What the hell?

Now, for those few incredulous faces in the crowd, I'll tell you what. Take that sheet of foil with that unsettling doodle and crunch it into a ball. Squeeze it tight, make it as spherical as possible. Now it's not a two-dimensional object anymore, since it extends itself over the three dimensions of space. It has width, height, and depth. But neither is it a solid object like a steel bearing, because no matter how tightly you crunch and compress it, tiny folds and creases remain inside it and on its surface, and so this object doesn't fill the spherical space completely. So it's not exactly 3D. It's an unholy abomination, lurking in the spaces between two and three dimensions. Five hundred years ago, someone would've been burned at the stake for the idea, right?

Compress and squeeze as much as you want, you'll never turn it into a true solid object that fills the spherical space. You can only build an approximation, with a number of dimensions very close to three. If instead you just give the foil a couple of crunches without applying too much pressure, the resulting dimension will be closer to two, and with every new squeeze the number will slowly creep up, yet it will never reach three. Just like with that doodle. If your illness is not too serious you could trace a sort of smooth wavy line with a dimension closer to one, the dimension of a straight line. But if your hand tremors are excessive, you will end with a complex, fuzzy doodle with lots of zigzags and loops, closer to the two dimensions of the sheet. I know, I know, I'm oversimplifying it, but bear with me.

In the 1930s, a German mathematician called Felix Hausdorff worked out the formula to calculate the dimension of those strange objects which are not exactly 3D, 2D, or 1D. We're not going to delve deep into the math of the appropriately named Hausdorff Dimension; you can look for it on the Internet. Not now, please; let go of your phones. I'll just say it's a formal way to evaluate what we just discussed, and it applies both to theoretical mathematical constructs and to the objects we deal with in reality, in nature. Real objects that we hold in our hands, yet they're not exactly 2D or 3D but something in between, a non-integer number of dimensions, which can be either a *rational* number or an *irrational* number (which you'll recall is a number that can't be represented as fraction or a ratio of two integers). Somewhere deep inside your kitchen drawer lurks an object with, let's say, square-root-of-eight dimensions. Not to mention the weird stuff in your fridge. Have you ever had a close look at a piece of Romanesco broccoli? Now *that* is something out of H.P. Lovecraft. You're familiar with Lovecraft, right? The guy was a prophet, I tell you. I bet he knew a lot more than what he unveiled in his stories....

The human body isn't exempt from that dimensional weirdness. We think of our bodies as three-dimensional organisms, and for most practical purposes we indeed are. But our lungs, our bones, our heart with its vascular system—we'll return to that one in a while—everything inside us is built out of *self-similar* structures. Things that look pretty much the same no matter the scale you examine them. There are many self-similar structures in nature, and a classic example is a coastline. When you look at a coastline from different altitudes, the nooks and crannies and bays and peninsulas tend to look the same no matter the scale.

On this subject I recommend the works of Benoit Mandelbrot. Check him out, he coined the word *fractal*. Yes, I see heads nodding. His work is math-heavy but highly didactic and quite a fun read.

To me, the most interesting organ in this regard is the brain. Because inside the brain, the dimensions aren't even homogeneous. They vary from the inner core where it's closer to a solid three, outward to the cortex where the creases and canals provide a large surface inside the restricted space within our skulls.

(The Professor pauses. A smile curls on his lips, as if he's enjoying a cherished memory.)

Have you seen a picture of those beautiful fractal brain hemispheres? Or better yet, the real deal on the operating table? They always remind me of the *Ylem*, the primordial *thing* that was present at the Big Bang before time and space even existed. It was there before there was a *there*. Some say the *Ylem* was a soup of inconceivably high-energy neutrons, but I have other ideas. I think we'll take a little cosmology detour now.

(After another dramatic pause, the Professor resumes in a theatrical voice.)

In the Beginning, about six thousand years ago....

(The audience laughs. The Professor grins, pleased they understood his little joke.)

In the Beginning, there was Darkness. The face of the Lord moved across the waters and said, *"let there be light!"* And there was Light. Such light. The Universe exploded into being. Matter and antimatter co-annihilated, almost, *almost* taking with them the infant Universe.

But we are here. Now, thirteen-point-eight billion years later, we are here. Why? How? Well, apparently there was a slight imbalance; ever so little more matter than antimatter. And it is apparent because we are here now.

Here. Now. *Here* is a strange place. And *Now* is a strange time. Every one of you, of course, will tell me that the Universe that we can perceive comprises no more than four percent of the whole. Right? Just the tip of the iceberg. All the matter we can see or guess at adds up to four percent of what *must* be there. *Dark matter!* It's the only explanation.

(The Professor reflectively pauses. He uncaps the bottle and takes a couple of sips.)

That popular hypothesis has a tiny little problem: namely, that to make the math work we must assume that ninety-six percent of the Universe is made of something we can neither sense nor detect, but we know it must be there. In other words, we must take *on faith* that our scientific hypothesis is correct.

(The Professor indicates his derision with a snort.)

I'd bring the theology students in the room into this next, but it is a long tangent. Suffice it to say, they're amused by the fact that physicists and cosmologists will in the same breath tell them that we've no idea what ninety-six percent of the Universe is made of…but there can't be a God. Heaven forbid!

(The audience laughs.)

They smirk, yet they don't suggest to you that maybe Dark Matter is made of angels or some great, fractal consciousness' surface, universally contemporaneous and omnipresent. They're quiet. *They* respect other religions.

(After another pause, he scans the crowd expectantly.)

There are other explanations, my dear *hard science* acolytes. We've already been discussing one. Stay with me; I'll get there.

Remember our friend, Mr. Tinfoil Ball? Now take that tightly, densely compacted ball of foil, and unfurl it. Pull it. Stretch it. Iron it. Polish it with patience and elbow grease. Do whatever it takes to get it back to the pristine, smooth, two-dimensional sheet you pulled from the roll. Can you succeed? Let's test it. I shall spill across your newly flattened sheet a vial of indigo ink to see how well you have done. What shall we find?

(He gestures a theatrical wave of command. An unseen intern activates a till-now quiescent projector lurking in the hidden reaches of the auditorium ceiling. Spidery webworks of luminescent purples pulse to life against a backdrop of utter blackness.)

Ah, look! An exceedingly fine structure still remains. Behold, there it is. You cannot flatten the sheet again after such rough treatment. Not completely. The ink reveals the minute-scale impressions left by the events of the past.

But wait! I see your narrowed eyes and parted lips. You there, my biology seniors and neurology majors. You will tell me this is a neuronal network. I've done a substitution, and I'll not get one over on you so easily, eh?

(The Professor nods at the scattered replies from the audience.)

Oh? My esteemed cosmologists, do you have other ideas? It's a Dark Matter survey map, you say?

(The Professor paces along the stage in silence for a long moment. His left hand begins a slight tremor, and he puts it in his pocket.)

You are both deceived by your disciplines, even as you are informed by them. It *is* a dark matter map…but I am here to tell you that it also *isn't*. Yes, it is the output of a simulation conducted on a supercomputer by merging hundreds of thousands of astronomical observations, painstakingly uploaded into a model designed to plot the hidden geography of the Universe. And yet, the same expert cosmologists and astrophysicists who create and use these magnificent diagrams routinely miss the point of what the diagrams tell them. For you see, this one is not a map of dark *matter*, it is a map of dark *topology*. It is the hidden *geometry* of the universe, not geography. Galaxies do not fly apart under their rotational velocity due to dark matter haloes; they are bound in place by the fine-scale contours of space itself.

Space has texture, that's what I am telling you. The ink in the crinkles of the tinfoil is the matter we know. All of it. Space itself, at the Planck scale, has a fractal texture. And it got that way…how? You already know.

Statement A: Matter can neither be created nor destroyed.

Statement B: Matter and antimatter co-annihilated in the first instant of the birth of the Universe.

Contradictory, isn't it? That cyclopean detonation, all that matter, all that antimatter—of which what we have left is the barest echo of all that was—is preserved in the texture of the fabric of space itself. Like a coin pressed into the foil, it left an impression that cannot be ironed out. Not in 13.8 billion years, not in 13.8 trillion.

(A brief pause, then the Professor seems re-energized.)

A while ago we were discussing God. Now I'd like to take a little side trip and talk about Kabbalah. Specifically, the Lurianic creation myth, so named after Isaac "The Lion" Luria, a sixteenth-century Jewish scholar and mystic. He proposed the idea of the *Ein Sof*, literally the *Endless* or the *Infinite*, which was, for want of a better term, God before becoming God. In modern terms we would say it was the steady-state pre-universe, without space, without time. Think of it as the pristine, untouched sheet of foil, if you will. Now, follow me with this.

In the Beginning, the *Ein Sof* inhales and contracts unto Himself, thus crunching the perfect foil sheet into the primordial ball. Then, not unlike a glass-blower, He exhales inside a series of vessels *created by the same exhalation*, that are supposed to contain His divine emanations: the ten *sefirot*. Maybe you've heard the word before?

The first three vessels withstand the divine Breath and therefore become the higher, spiritual realms. But the lower vessels shatter and disperse the sparks of God's essence across space and time, creating the material world and everything it contains, as space and time themselves unfold.

Now, if the consequence of that imperfect spreading is the texture we discussed a while ago—the unfurled sheet of tinfoil still retaining the memory of the crumpling imprinted on itself—then Creation, and us as part of it, is a *failure of the Divine*. God created the world by breathing into containers that broke down. Incompetence from Him, or perhaps one of his lab assistants. Those things happen. But He saw that mess unfolding at his Holy Laboratory, and yet *He didn't stop the experiment*.

(A long pause. The Professor half-turns to look into the dark beyond the curtains.)

Luria, and the Kabbalah scholars who followed him, clearly understood this tiny inconvenience. So they proposed that mankind could, through prayer and good deeds, achieve the *Tikkun Olam*, the rectification of the vessels' primordial screw-up. Essentially, praying for the foil sheet to become pristine again, but also ironing and polishing the spacetime creases through charity and loving thy neighbor. Well, look around us. Is it working?

(The Professor gestures towards the back of the room. The slide projector, which had been dormant for some time, suddenly returns to life.)

There are as many arrangements of the *sefirot* as Kabbalist schools exist, and

15

they all look like what we would today call relationship graphs. Consider this slide. Isn't it interesting how those ancient diagrams overlaid the *sefirot* trees with illustrations of the human body? See how each one of the ten *sefirot* gets mapped to a different organ like the brain, the heart, and the kidneys? What this image is telling us…. Yes, I see some of you, mouth agape in sudden realization. The creases in the texture of the Universe, the imprints of God's primordial lab disaster, are reproduced, down to the Planck level, *inside us*.

(A pause. The Professor can't see the audience past the first few rows of the darkened auditorium, but he can hear a rising murmur that rolls and sloshes at him from the back of the room.)

And how could it be otherwise? *As Above, So Below*, the ancient motto of Hermeticism, still rings true. No wonder our vascular network has a fractal structure—so does the fabric of the Universe itself.

(While the Professor pauses for effect, the projector goes on standby.)

I'm going to quote a very old, very neat passage. "The Old Ones were, the Old Ones are, and the Old Ones shall be. Not in the spaces we know, but between them, they walk serene and primal, undimensioned and unseen." Between the spaces we know. Undimensioned. Pretty cool, right? This comes from the *Necronomicon*, a book originally written around the year 700 by Abdul Alhazred, a polymath poet from Yemen. Now, the consensus among scholars is that the *Necronomicon*, Abdul Alhazred, and the Old Ones are all fictional, a product of the brilliant imagination of H.P. Lovecraft. In fact, that quote first appeared in Lovecraft's *The Dunwich Horror* in 1929. Well, fiction or not, Lovecraft—or Alhazred—was clearly onto something here.

Whichever one you prefer to imagine wrote this bit, he spoke of nuclear chaos at the center of everything. A daemonic sultan, spewing forth the lifeblood of the universe, surrounded by monstrous pipers whose cosmological ululations keep the center quiescent, a slumbering force of creation and destruction. Sounds familiar? If the universe had blood, what would it be?

(Several audience members shout their answers.)

Yes! Correct, thank you. Hydrogen. To paraphrase a Frank Zappa quote, the second most common element in the universe, after stupidity.

(Some of the audience laughs, others nod their heads. There's a wry smile both in the Professor's words and on his gaunt face.)

But! If enough of it coalesces? No, not stupidity! Hydrogen. Get serious! What do we get? Fusion! Suns! And enough of those? Galaxies! And in the center? Yes, a lurking monster. Always ready to devour, bottomless, inescapable, eternal. And yet, it creates. All those structures are bound by the inaudible thrumming of unseen, amorphous, shifting fields, magnetic and *alive*: binding plasmas and thrashing pseudopods of heliotropic destruction flung blindly off of stars and their corpses. Without these unsung heroes, we would not exist. The Sun would have lashed this little blue marble into a barren stone without them. Without the magnetic fields and twisted, invisible geometries that surround and shape the flaring, mindless rage of active galactic nuclei, the whole universe might have been scoured clean not just of life but of its mere possibility. Imagine one of these mind-numbingly gigantic voids of matter and energy, but fully awake and unconstrained. All would be nothing, and nothing would be All. This is what the Mad Poet called Azathoth. His ancient erudition would have told him that *"aza"* means "uncountable," and *"Thoth"* was, of course, the god of knowledge of his pagan ancestors. Uncountable cosmic mystery. Unknowable, and death itself to approach. Azathoth.

(The Professor seems to fold in on himself for a moment. His left hand trembles again, fluttering over his heart, and he thrusts it in his pocket, bending at the waist a little in a sort of bow towards the puzzled audience. With a deep inhalation, he straightens and goes on.)

Let's talk for a moment about the ghastly, maddening *sight* of Azathoth. Descriptions in the *Necronomicon* and other scholarly texts speak of an amorphous mass of uncountable thrashing, formless limbs made of the very substance of darkness, eternally sleeping under the lull of hideous cacophonies played by Its flute-wielding servitors. But who has actually *seen It?* We are supposed to believe those accounts from witnesses near the center of Existence, who stared at something that lurks in the cracks and crevices between dimensions, yet conveniently shows Its form in the human visible spectrum? A little preposterous, if you ask me. But! What if what they saw was just a shadow, a projection over our 3D space, of something inconceivably and infinitely more horrible, dwelling in those "inaccessible" higher dimensional spaces?

Let me illustrate that with an analogy. Imagine a swimmer's hand coming out of the water surface, and you're watching it from above, in slow motion. First, you see five ellipses, as the fingers start to emerge and intersect the water plane. As the hand rises, the ellipses get bigger and start to merge. And then there's only one weird shape. If you watch the whole swimmer from above, you see similar shapes—head, arms, feet, torso—growing and shrinking, sometimes disappearing completely only to reappear some distance ahead. Yet we have no idea of what the hand, or the swimmer, actually looks like. And why is that? Because we're only seeing a 2D fragment or slice of the unknowable whole.

We, of course, lack the perceptual apparatus for spatial dimensions greater than three. But subtract one to all dimensions involved, and the problem remains. Visualize a cube, spinning randomly in space. If you cover one of your eyes, or eliminate depth perception through another artifice, you only see a floating, shape-shifting polygon, just a projection over your view-plane. Again, since we humans are unable, for now, to perceive a fourth spatial dimension, if we see something shapeshifting before our very own eyes, couldn't we conclude that what we're seeing is only the projection of a higher-dimensional entity moving through a reality we cannot fully perceive?

(The Professor grows increasingly agitated, almost toppling the bench with the bottle.)

You all have read Lovecraft, my friends. You know what a *shoggoth* is! Biomechanical shape-shifting entities, designed and bred by an ancient race that came from the unplumbed gulfs of space millions of years ago and settled on what is now Antarctica. How did they travel here? Lovecraft did not elaborate, but I'm sure they were able to bend spatial dimensions as easily as we bend a piece of licorice. And they of course *knew* how to make 3D projections out of the hyper-dimensional horrors they found on their way here.

(The Professor sits on the bench and produces a pill from his pocket. He downs it with a long gulp from the bottle, catches his breath, and continues his lecture.)

And that brings us to the problem of *where*. Azathoth is omnipresent, yet we are told It dwells in the center of the Universe. What does that mean? The center, my friends, is a point in spacetime. And a point, as we discussed earlier, *has no dimension*. So Azathoth lays within those strange fractal spaces between dimensions, and that's how Its tendrils can reach us. They don't have to traverse the unplumbed gulfs of intergalactic space, just take shortcuts through the fractal dimensions in between. We will return to this in a moment. But first: tentacles!

(Sparse audience laughter.)

Oh, I can see many of you perking up your ears. This topic never fails to cause interest. How can I keep babbling about Lovecraft and Azathoth without mentioning tentacles? I guess you're expecting me to switch gears now and start talking suggestively about *hentai* and teenage Japanese girls…with slides if possible….

(The audience yells and hoots.)

But let's get serious, my naughty friends. Tentacles are symbols, fundamental ones, deeply imprinted in our psyches, and there lies the root of our fascination with them. Have you seen those videos of octopuses escaping from fish tanks or even closed jars, through the narrowest crevices? Just like that, Chaos is always blindly probing for openings into our reality, not unlike a Lovecraftian monster's feelers approaching an unsuspecting high schooler's panties.

(Some of the audience hoots, joined by a few screams of "we want slides!")

Ok, ok, calm down. Chaos comes to us in waves. But also it comes from *within us.* And…and the chaos within us gestures outward. Chaos Magick? *Oh, come on, Professor. Surely you will not raise that ridiculous confabulation of* Star Trek *level quantum babble and Wiccan pseudo mythology?* No. Not quite. But a few of you are familiar with the *reality* of quantum entanglement, and the rest have at least heard of it. How can the center of all things reach us here, on the fringe of an unremarkable galaxy in a backwater supercluster, surrounded by billions like it? Because distance is, fundamentally, an illusion. All distance. Any distance. And when the source of the illusion, the dreaming mind of Chaos reaches out, it's from *within.* You. Us. Me. We are entangled. Azathoth reaches you through *you.* You are not separate from nuclear chaos. We postulate entanglement to explain phenomena we cannot understand intuitively. *Oh look, this photon over here that we've entangled with that other one moving in the opposite direction can affect the other. Isn't that remarkable? It should be impossible. No signal can reach* that *one from* this *one, so they* must *be* entangled.

Meh. The word means nothing. Do you want to know what is happening? They are not separate photons at all. They're one thing, partially obscured by the limits of our pitiful sensoria. As Lovecraft told us: "We live on a placid island of ignorance in the midst of black seas of infinity, and it was not meant that we should voyage far." Indeed, Howard, indeed.

Ah, but can I explain my pronouncement? Yes. Reason with me. Imagine. Let my thoughts and yours entangle.

You all have seen a party clown blow up balloons and tie them into fanciful shapes of animals and hats, yes? Good. Imagine that we steal one of his bright yellow balloons. In the next room lies a bathtub full of jet black water. We blow the balloon up but make no shape. It is a three-foot-long latex banana. We tie it off and, holding the center, we thrust it beneath the water. Bobbing and sending out ripples across the blackness, the ends break the surface. These are our "entangled" photons.

A stranger enters the room. We ask what he sees. "Why, two bright little yellow orbs, partially submerged, two or so feet apart." Remember the swimmer example we discussed a while ago? Same thing. We hand the stranger a pin and ask him to choose one of the orbs to pop. He does, and to his unsophisticated, uninitiated surprise, both orbs vanish. He is dumbfounded. He has only affected one orb! Aghast, he leaves to report to his fellows the magical pin which destroys what it has not touched. If only he could see below the surface of those black waters, he would be so comforted to know that it was always only one object. It was merely the connection he could not perceive. And what he destroyed was so very much larger than what he could merely perceive. Mmm, perhaps he would *not* be comforted by that.

(He inhales deeply, followed by a sigh of outward breath.)

Chaos waves…they forever crash on the shores of our reality, unpredictably of course. What kind of Chaos would it be if you could predict it? And the relentless waves lap at the foundations of the puny sandcastles we build on the beach. Sometimes we manage to reinforce them; oftentimes a sudden wave destroys it all. Our smidgen of Order and structure is so fragile, and Chaos is always looking for a way to kick sand in our faces. Azathoth can't help it and doesn't care.

Our struggle against Chaos attempts to introduce a little Order into everyday decay. We hope unconsciously that our connection with the center is a *two-way* quantum highway so we can inject a measure of Order back through it. A little

20

bit of Yang light amidst the dark Yin of the *taijitu* symbol. Apollo in triumph, restraining Dionysus for a while, caulking and painting a damaged wall. *Cleaning our rooms,* as a wise man once summed it up. All this is indeed quite noble, yet isn't it also laughable? I mean, don't we realize we're up against a Universe hell-bent on turning us back into our constituent particles? Think of a microscopic krill, waving its infinitesimal limbs, struggling against a current that will carry it inexorably into the maw of a blue whale, to be digested and dissolved into basic nutrients. That's pretty much how it goes.

And with regard to Chaos within Order, and Order within Chaos, as the Yin-Yang emblem suggests, we know from life experiences that the first proposition is indeed true. In everyday situations, if life has somehow managed to grant us a respite of happiness and peace, there is always, *always*, blind chance ready to screw up our best-laid plans. Contrast this with the opposite idea of a seed of Order trying to mitigate Chaos in our lives. What people could call a lucky break. Think about the odds for each half of the *taijitu* to happen. Think about the fact that Chaos can *afford* to be blind and idiotic—qualities that Lovecraft, or Alhazred, aptly applied to Azathoth—whereas Order necessitates sight and thought. Not that I am implying an intelligent design and denying the possibility of spontaneous Order. Given enough time and amino acids, *Life will always find a way,* as they say. It will prevail and return unexpectedly, like tendrils of light Yang sprouting from the darkness of the Yin. This Order itself is the product of Chaos, as in the Primordial Reducing Atmosphere. Carbon, hydrogen, nitrogen, and oxygen floating blindly and insensate in a storm-racked sky, and a chance bolt of lightning fuses them into the first amino acids. *Zap!* It's *alive!*

In the mythos of many cultures, incidentally, the act of creation always emerges from the intersection of dynamic Chaos and static Order. Turning what is *not* into what *is*. Like striking two pieces of flint together, then sparks fly at their fractal boundary, and *boom*! Where there was nothing, now there's a fire. A symphony. A steam engine. A well-tended garden. A blueprint for Auschwitz's shower rooms. A weaponized strain of a respiratory virus. Oh, perhaps you were under the misimpression that creation is inherently good?

Whether good or evil, creation is only an ephemeral reprieve from primal Chaos. What is Death itself but the embodiment of the final victory of Chaos over the temporary Order of life, matter, thought, action, creation? But I digress....

(He pauses again, lost in his thoughts for a few seconds.)

Isn't it evident that the deck is stacked against Order? That there is a massive imbalance in favor of Chaos?

God. God, whatever denomination you may favor, is, or should be, a more-or-less active force for Good, Order, Yang, Reason, Apollo, whatever you want to name it, always grappling with the blind idiot Azathoth, Chaos, Yin, Dionysus. Struggling for dominion over reality, and over *us* as the only sentient part of it. For as Solzhenitsyn wrote, "the line dividing good and evil cuts through the heart of every human being." But that line is not clear cut, my friends. It is a fractal, and its boundaries are fuzzy. Chaotic. It is the trembling doodle we spoke about a while ago, that exists in the space between dimensions. And this explains why you might believe yourself to be a good person, a loving husband, a caring parent, a model citizen, a peaceful individual who wouldn't hurt a fly, and then something happens and one of Azathoth's tendrils reaches up from within. Its messenger and servant, the Crawling Chaos, slithering across the spacetime textures left by the Demiurge's failed lab experiment. And Chaos insinuates itself as something tiny and harmless at first, and maybe not even within *you* but two generations earlier, like a slight transcription glitch in your grandfather's DNA that eventually snowballs across time into a full-blown nightmare and throws your world into madness and despair, and the *taijitu* in your heart becomes as black as the Pit, and you want to set the world on fire, or contemplate how to make everything disappear with a bullet or a noose. As if you were certain that this world is all there is.

(The Professor pauses for another drink, but the bottle is almost empty. He drops it to the floor and looks backstage. Under his withering gaze, a terrified aide comes running and leaves a fresh one on the bench. He uncaps it with unsteady hands and drinks several long gulps.)

Azathoth, the dealer in the Universe's Casino. It always wins in the end. That, in a nutshell, is all you need to know to understand what's going on in the world today.

(Suddenly he seems tired, his shoulders droop a little as he surveys the attentive crowd.)

You're probably familiar with the idea of a divine spark that resides inside each human being. Of course, we're not talking objective science here. We're dealing in the language of myth, narrative, symbols. One interesting corollary of this idea is that no one is beyond redemption, for embedded inside one's being is a fragment of the Creator's radiance, scattered in the Beginning when the Vessels shattered. How did it end there? Beats me. When Daddy planted a seed inside Mommy's tummy....

(The audience again laughs.)

Don't be too quick in laughing, my friends, for therein resides a core argument of where life begins. But if you expect me to approach that subject tonight with a ten-foot pole, think again.

(More laughter.)

But let's assume for a moment that the divine spark is real, and propagates itself in every generation, perhaps through a layer of firmware beneath the DNA replication code. And we all go walking around this world, conducting our businesses, loving our friends and families and pets, being kind to each other, but also stabbing each other in the back, robbing widows and orphans, gleefully going after our neighbors with hammer and tongs and artillery and suicide vests. What if there is indeed a spark inside each of us, but it doesn't come from that scattered divine essence? What if there is a better, darker explanation? I think some of you in the audience have already figured it out, judging from the horror in your expressions. Yes, we all have a spark, a *Splinter of Azathoth*, lodged precisely in the fractal line between Good and Evil that passes through every human heart, as Solzhenitsyn aptly put it. In our heart of hearts, we *are* Azathoth.

(The audience remains in stunned silence. A few people begin to chant, tentatively at first, then louder: "We are Azathoth, we are Azathoth!" The Professor looks in their direction, amused and interested. He grins mischievously.)

Oh, come on. If you're going to do it, do it right. It's *"Iä Azathoth! Iä Azathoth!"*

(The chant recedes in confusion.)

Yeah. A chicken in every pot, and a splinter of Chaos lodged in every heart.

(Laughter drowns the last vestiges of chanting from the audience.)

Isn't that a better explanation of the state of the world around us? And of reality itself? And of Being? No need to postulate a God who created us, gave us free will, commanded us to be good to each other, and then left us to our own devices, to be eventually judged and sent to Heaven or cast into the Lake of Fire. Or perhaps to be redeemed anyway, irrespective of whatever atrocities we committed in life. Occam's razor says there's a much simpler explanation. Random Chaos rules from within us. Azathoth reigns everywhere. And I mean *everywhere*. Who can say death is truly the end? How can you *know* that you're not going to wake up in the afterlife, stuck like a pinned butterfly within a spectral realm akin to the spaces between dimensions we know—but this time *forever*—trapped next to Azathoth and Its deathless flutists at least until the heat death of the universe. Ah, but everything fades out when the physical body disintegrates, you say. With no brain left to process the experience, how can there be any experience at all? With your heart turned to dust in your grave, you object, there is no splinter of Chaos to torture your soul anymore.

I wish I could share your optimism, my friends, but unlike most of its practitioners (with the exception of the esteemed Dr. Hameroff), I know how anesthesia works. Brains are full of carbon microtubules. They didn't really appear to serve much purpose. Were they structural? Metabolic detritus? What were they for? Neurologists wondered for decades. Dr. Hameroff, an anesthesiologist, noticed that molecules of the most commonly used modern anesthetics gather at the ends of these structures. They clog them up, and consciousness goes away. That's what anesthesia does. It leaves the body functioning perfectly fine but turns off the mind. How? Most biologists will say, "we don't know." But we do. We just don't understand what it means to say that the connection to the mind has been severed. One day, we'll connect the quantum dots. Where do those microtubules lead, Doctor, if not into the manifold of compactified dimensions? But I digress…if I'm actually even here.

(He pauses, reflects for a moment, then paces the stage.)

And think of those abominable servitors with their abhorrent fluting, lulling Azathoth to keep It sleeping, dreaming, for if the music stops, It wakes up and the Universe ends. So the music of the servitors is what holds the Universe together, like the strings that glue mesons together and keep reality from unraveling. Had Lovecraft lived enough to learn about string theory, he would have ditched the flutes and turned the servitors into cellists. The guy had a sense of humor, you know.

(While the audience laughs, the Professor takes a long pause. He has clearly lost his train of thought. Mechanically, he grabs the bottle and takes a few sips, gazing away. Audience members whisper in the darkness, confused and slightly worried. But soon he collects himself.)

Alright, with all that said, what could possibly be the point of that Cult of Azathoth that has been making the rounds recently on the news? As a matter of fact, on my way here to the auditorium I stopped by the campus cafeteria and saw no fewer than three flyers on the billboard, all from different groups announcing weekly gatherings to worship Azathoth.

(A few enthusiastic yells from the audience.)

Oh, we have some of them in the house tonight. Great. Anyway, I took a tear-off stub from each flyer, for research purposes of course. But doesn't it seem completely pointless to worship an entity essentially unaware of any existence outside Itself? At least most religions have concepts of their respective deities interacting with mankind, of course not always in a positive way, but hey, it's something. Azathoth gives us nothing. So what's the return on investment of worshiping it?

(Pause. The audience seems to be pondering where the meandering lecture is going now.)

After recent personal developments, I've given this problem a lot of thought, and I believe I've reached a plausible justification. Bear with me now.

You have heard about the idea of entropy reversal. Quite simplified, it means that since decay, dissipation of energy, and the direction of the arrow of time itself are consequences of the expansion of the Universe triggered by the *Ylem* explosion, or the *Ein Sof* blowing too hard into too fragile vessels, if that expansion somehow stops, and a contraction process begins, one of the several conflicting hypotheses says we would witness a reversal of all those processes. Decay reversal, rusted metal slowly becoming pristine again, diseases reverting their progress and vanishing. Even eggs unscrambling themselves.

(Several audience members laugh.)

But what would be the implications for Azathoth? Well, remember those monstrous flute-playing servitors, their music being the glue that holds the strings tying the Universe together? Those Sultans of String!

(More laughter from the audience.)

I know, I know, there was only one Sultan, and it was Azathoth Itself. Allow me that poetic license. Now, what if the real goal of the cults is to make the Sultans *stop playing?* The servitors don't seem to be blind idiots like their Master. At least they have some sort of limbs to manipulate the flutes, and mouths and breathing physiology to blow into them whatever passes for air in those unimaginable domains, to create a piping cacophony of sound that somehow propagates across the vacuum between dimensions. Weird. But monstrous as the servitors are, they're still infinitely more relatable to us than Azathoth. And that makes them, at least in theory, receptive to worship, to prayer.

(He picks the contact email stubs from his pocket and shows them to the audience.)

When all other Gods have failed, I say it's worth a shot, becoming the Sultans' fan club on Earth. We already have the club's badge, *the dark splinter* right in our hearts. So we could pray to them for their music to end, for the unraveling of the strings, for the disentanglement of quanta, for the reversal of entropy and decay and Parkinson's.

(The Professor puts the stubs back in his pocket. Again, he grabs the bottle to drink but again, it's almost empty. He glances backstage, but no aide comes forth. Time's running out.)

Which kind of cultists are we? You, out there in the yellow polo—will you run amok with that pin, sticking it in whatever metaphorical balloon will hold still long enough to let you? Just to see if someone else pops?

(Clearly aware of the audience's laughter, the boy looks confused, proud, and embarrassed all at once.)

Which of you will think to reach below the surface and feel the rest of the structure of our balloon, your mind blown open by the fact of its unity? Which

26

of you will drain the tub, willing to let it all swirl away just for a glimpse of understanding?

(He looks out at the audience, hands in his pockets. Some of them shift in their seats, and some begin to clap as they mistake this for his closing words. His mouth opens, and they fall silent.)

Friends, let these be my words of parting. If, as early humanity postulated, there was ever a benevolent deity in charge of things—or, as others say, one that got things in motion and sat to watch the results—I guarantee you, it fled in horror, long ago. No one is at the wheel, and the wind of Chaos propels the rudderless universe towards nothingness. It will expand until all is a cold waste floating in utter darkness. And Azathoth shall laugh in Its sleep, without mouth, without mirth, as long as the Daemon Sultan's band shall play.

Thank you for coming to my talk. Expect no sequel.

(Stage and house lights go out. Pairs of hand rebound. The reverberation spreads. Other pairs emulate the motion until, on some unseeable, unheard signal, they cease. Dark splinters embedded in their vessels rise from their seats and leave for the outside world. Chaos spreads with entropy. Entropy spreads with time, and, occasionally, with ideas.)

MIGUEL FLIGUER & MIKE SLATER

MANIFOLD THOUGHTS
Patrick Freivald

Darren frowned at the swirl of shapes shifting and morphing across the trio of computer screens on his desk, chaotic and wild especially in comparison to the austere cleanliness of his office, where almost everything had a place and almost everything made sense.

Almost everything.

"Alice, check this out." He tapped the screen and got no response. "Alice?"

He hazarded a glance at the most promising graduate student of his career. Her mousy brown hair covered her eyes as she sat unmoving at the explosion of papers, textbooks, chargers, food wrappers, and hair ties she called a desk. Entropy personified. Her fingers tracing the equations in the book in front of her gave the only sign that she wasn't fast asleep.

"Alice!" He raised his voice, though he knew she'd heard him the first time.

With an exasperated sigh she slammed the book shut, causing a small avalanche of papers to fall the floor, which she swept under the desk with a foot before glaring at him through a curtain of hair. "I'm trying to study!"

"You're on the clock," he replied, turning back to his computer. "C'mere. I want you to take a look at this."

She stood and stretched, groaning theatrically in his peripheral vision, then shuffled over to look at the screens. On them, thousands of tiny, complicated shapes moved and twisted and changed form, almost at random, at least to the untrained eye. She leaned over his shoulder, a little too close, and he caught a sour whiff of body odor inadequately masked by something floral.

"What am I looking at, Doc?"

He suppressed a scowl. In sixteen months, no amount of insisting that she call him Darren budged her from the insipid nickname, and he suspected that she used it because she knew it grated on him.

He turned the question around. "What do you see?"

"SSDD, right? A very tiny region of spacetime. You've got ten to the six or so Calabi-Yau manifolds—"

"Two-dimensional renderings of three-dimensional cross-sections," he corrected.

She rolled her eyes. "Two-dimensional renderings of three-dimensional cross-sections of *computer simulations* of eleven-dimensional manifolds, if we're being technical. Anyway, you've got four-folds morphing on a braid, simulating, what? Proton scatter?"

He grunted, impressed. "Almost. Top quarks."

A gifted PhD candidate in the university's mathematics department, Alice Lavery had only taken a few physics courses as an undergraduate, and certainly no superstring theory. Her interest lay in the evolution of chaotic topology in theoretical systems, not descriptions of what might or might not be the real world, and she seemed to resent every minute of her time spent earning a paycheck working on his projects rather than on her own research. Obnoxious, flippant, vulgar, disorganized, and abrasive, with a nice face and trim body that could be pretty if she'd put in the slightest effort. If she weren't the smartest person he'd ever met he'd have fired her in her first week and said good riddance to bad rubbish.

"Neat." She glanced back at her desk, to her books currently un-studied. "Why do I care?"

"Just watch and tell me what you see."

She humored him, face deadpan, and said nothing for about a minute. Then, "There appears to be an emergent phenomenon in the evolution of the higher dimensions. It appears to be…throbbing."

"You could have chosen any other word."

She ignored his comment, as he knew she would. "What did you do to the program? I didn't include anything that would cause the macrostructure to evolve away from de Sitter symmetries."

"Neither did I, at least not on purpose. I just introduced a little chaos into the manifolds' shapes. I expected something nondeterministic. I expected the whole thing to crash, honestly. But got whatever this is instead."

"Okay. So why do I care?"

He sighed. "Because you're paid to. What can you tell me about plant intelligence?"

"Not really my area." Her brow scrunched in confusion, but her eyes didn't leave the screen, likely parsing the scene for the question's relevance. "I mean, I know some people who are dumber than your average plant."

"Some biologists argue that plants should be considered intelligent because they can sense and react to their environment and respond in both microscopic and macroscopic ways. They can adjust their morphology, their physiology, and even their phenotype in response to environmental factors, from too much or not enough water to attacks from parasites. Root ends can detect everything from gravity and nutrients to solid objects and turn away from a wall before they've even reached it. Plants don't have brains of course, but their parts communicate via electrochemical signals homologous to a nervous sys—"

"Like the distributed intelligence of an octopus, but way dumber."

He nodded. "Right. And without neurons."

She stood to her full height, no longer looming over his shoulder. "So they can't think, but they can sort of behave like they can think."

"I'm not sure we can say there's a diff—"

She jabbed the screen with her finger, distorting the image as the LCD display flexed. "Like these little bastards are doing right now. The Calabi-Yau manifolds are changing their behavior in response to a stimulus, similar to what a plant might do."

"Well—"

"If you think for one goddamned second that you're putting my name on a paper that says purely mathematical structures can think, you're not. I—"

He held up a hand. "Calm down. I'm not coauthoring you on anything you don't want your name on. But these aren't just mathematical structures. If supersymmetry is real—"

"And we don't have any actual, you know, *evidence* that it is, so—"

"Then we've got an extraordinary number of Calabi-Yau manifolds twisted up all around us, affecting…everything. Every force, every particle, every…everything, could be sensing and responding to its environment, at least as much as any given plant, and maybe much more so. And with enough computational power, I think we can find out what they're thinking."

"You want to know what spacetime geometry is thinking."

After a moment, he nodded. "Yeah, I guess you could say I do."

She watched the screen, and seconds stretched to minutes. He watched with her, letting her incredible mind process the ramifications at its own pace, and waited for her to take it all in. The most impatient woman he'd ever met could not be rushed.

"Jesus Christ, you're a fucking idiot." She whirled to her desk, swept up her book, yanked open the door, then stormed out of the office.

π

Ben reached across the table, deftly dodging the remains of Alice's burger and fries to grab her hand. "You okay, Sweetie?"

She didn't move, and her frown went nowhere, as if she couldn't hear him in the quiet din of the restaurant, nor feel his touch. He gave her hand another little shake, and she startled.

"What? Yeah." Her eyes fluttered and she picked up a French fry with her free hand, smeared it through the ketchup on her plate, and then just held it, staring off into space. "Just woolgathering."

"Exit interview stress?"

She waved the suggestion away with the fry, spattering the tablecloth with dots of red. "No, it's not that. Doc fucking nerd-sniped me with one of his ridiculous stupidities this afternoon and I'm having a hard time letting it go."

He smiled, drawing her beautiful brown eyes to his at last. "Let me guess, I'm not going to understand it if you try to explain it?"

"No, no, don't sell yourself short. Most of his bullshit is just trivial brute-force computations that don't really mean much, but today that bastard might have hit on something more interesting than trying to look up my skirt."

He chuckled, letting go of her hand to lean back into his seat. "That's pretty interesting to me."

"Yeah, but you're not a creepy skeeze-bucket."

"Skeeze-bucket? What is this, nineteen eighty-five?"

She ignored his question and spent the next several minutes talking about plants and spacetime and emergent phenomena, most of which he did, in fact, understand. Everything but the important parts.

"...So I think if we network them, the new quantum computers could run a full simulation and we could actually, like, talk to it. Or at least listen. See what it has to say." Finally, she ate the fry, and then the rest of them, with the gusto of a Labrador Retriever.

"You want to hear God's thoughts."

She smirked. "Bingo."

π

Alice arched her back against the chair, stretching to relieve the strain in her muscles. Darren had run millions of simulations on the quantum computers, tracking the eerily lifelike responses of the Calabi-Yau manifold networks, but if they had anything to say to the humans simulating them, they needed a translator. She hit 'Compile', and lines of gobbledygook streamed down the screen as the compiler got to work turning her program into machine code.

"How long?" Doc asked.

Between completing her PhD and starting her postdoc, it had taken her four months to write the translator, even with AI tools. It would take hours to compile. Her heart hammered at her ribs and her stomach roiled in anticipation.

"Patience, grasshopper. I'm meeting Ben for lunch." The thought of food made her want to throw up. "And then I'm meeting Rachel here to go over her thesis notes—she's having some trouble with Riemann Synergies. It should be ready by the time we're through, if not sooner."

He grinned at her, turning on a little of the smarmy charm she'd always found so off-putting. "Am I still a fucking idiot?"

"We're gonna find out." She grabbed her purse and headed for the door. "If it's done before I get back, don't you dare run it without me."

π

Almost two hours later, she stumbled straight into the office door when it failed to open. She tried the knob, muttering profanities under her breath, and it jiggled but didn't turn. Behind the frosted glass, the lights were on.

She knocked. "Doc?"

Nothing.

She tried again, harder. "Doc? You taking a nap in there?"

Putting her ear to the door, she heard a faint, intermittent drip. She crinkled her nose at the faint whiff of what had to be a dirty diaper from somewhere down the hall. Digging her key from her purse, she inserted it into the lock, turned it, and pushed inside to a charnel house.

Darren lay face-up on the floor, a ragged gash torn across his throat. Sticky

33

red blood pooled on the floor and his desk, including the smashed remains of his monitors and computer. Next to his right hand, also cut badly, he held a shard of bloody glass.

Alice screamed, and screamed, until her breath gave out, at times vaguely aware of the secretary, maintenance, other professors. At some point she remembered talking to a young policewoman in plain clothes who held her hand and asked her questions she immediately forgot.

When she finally got home, showered, and lay in bed listening to Ben breathe, she couldn't sleep. Behind her eyelids lurked Doc's body, roiling in the darkness, twisting and turning like a Calabi-Yau manifold responding to changes in its environment.

$$\pi$$

Nothing in Darren's notes indicated why he would kill himself. Alice pawed through every scrap of his now-spotless desk, with the permission of the department chair, and found neatly ordered notes in his tight, tidy handwriting about holes in manifolds and vibrational modes, including one that said, "Ask Alice about cascade transitions and topographic morphology." She wasn't even sure what that meant.

She frowned at it, and a shadow crossed her desk, drawing her gaze up to the source. The young detective who'd held her hand three days prior stood in the doorway, blocking some of the harsh fluorescent light from the hall.

"Miss Lavery? It's—"

"Detective…"

"Coussens."

"That's right." She stood and came around the desk to shake hands, cool and soft. "What can I do for you today?"

She frowned. "Nothing pleasant, I'm afraid. We're still trying to get a handle on what would motivate Doctor Simons to do what he did."

Alice gestured to the papers on Doc's desk. "Yeah, join the fucking club."

She took the pause as an opportunity to lean against the desk and might have blinked a little too long.

"You look tired," the cop said. "You holding up okay?"

Alice sighed. "As well as can be expected, given the circumstances. But you're right, I am tired, and I haven't slept very well in a couple of days, and I have a lot of work to do, so if you could get to the point, I'd appreciate it."

Coussens crossed one leg in front of the other and leaned against the doorframe. "Is there anything in Doctor Simons' professional life you can think of that might lead him to destroy his research and then...." She trailed off, as if not saying the words made anything better.

"And off himself? No. We were on the verge of a simulation of something he was really excited about, we'd been working on it for months and were waiting for the program to compile. It was literally going to be ready for an initial run at any minute."

"Was the project stressful?"

"No, no. If anything, it was a lot of fun. He was pumped to find out what it would reveal, and I still am."

"But he destroyed the computer."

"Nah, not really. His desktop in here was just a GUI, an interface to the Q-supes running the software. Maybe set me back a couple of weeks? Once I get back to it, anyway. Frustrating, but not fatal."

The officer visibly cringed at her choice of words. "Gooey? Q-supes?"

"GUI." She spelled it. "Graphic User Interface. And Q-supes are the quantum supercomputers in the Czech Republic. Any one of them is more powerful than pretty much all the computers on the planet put together, and there are four of them. They're the only things that have the horsepower to run our simulation, so the university rented time on them for us."

"This simulation is what the two of you were working on when he took his life?"

Alice nodded.

"And I assume this is something you can't easily explain?"

"Probably not, unless you know an alarming amount of higher-level geometry for a police detective."

She sighed. "What about his personal life?"

"How the fuck would I know?"

And then she frowned. "Did the two of you not get along?"

"Not really. He was my boss until I got my PhD, and then we were collaborating on a project."

"Did he ever make any romantic overtures?"

Alice snorted. "Not that it's any of your business, but he tried to get in my pants when I first started working for him. I told him to fuck off, and he fucked off, mostly, except for the occasional leer. Extremely unprofessional."

Her eyes widened. "Did you tell anyone about this? His wife? Doctor Mercer?"

"Why would I do that?" Doctor Mercer, their vaunted department head, leered at her at least as much as Doc ever had.

"It could have been a hostile work environment."

Alice chuckled. "Look, if anyone was hostile in our relationship, it was me. Not to speak ill of the dead, but I only put up with that douche because I had to. Like I said, we had research interests in common, but we weren't friends. You know how this boy's club shit goes down; I wasn't about to jeopardize my position by reporting him."

"All right." The officer took a business card from her pocket and held it out. "If you can think of anything you think might be relevant, no matter how small, call me."

"Okay." Alice took the proffered card and tossed it in the wastebasket the moment the detective disappeared from view.

In the sudden silence, Alice frowned down at the note. *Ask Alice about cascade transitions and topographic morphology.* Filing it away for another day, she booted up her computer and got to reconstructing the Q-supe interface.

The quantum computers could brute-force the shifting and changing eleven-dimensional manifolds, mapping how many holes they had and in how many dimensions, so that so-called strings could vibrate in complex modalities, each giving rise to a property of what humans would call a particle—charge, mass, spin, and so forth—but the complexity of even a microscopic volume of manifolds held too much information for a human mind to process, and of course no one could picture dimensions other than the familiar four of length, width, height, and time. That made actually seeing the results of the simulation impossible, even for a static situation where the manifolds themselves did not change, much less a dynamic process where manifolds reacted to stimuli like a plant might. The Q-supe interface translated that reaction to something at least closer to what a human mind could understand, sight and sound fit for general consumption.

Or so she hoped.

$$\pi$$

The eighty-bazillionth time her phone rang, she turned it off. At some point Ben showed up, worried, with a sandwich, water, and advice about coming home and showering she didn't take. Somewhere distant, hunger pangs told her to eat, but the sandwich lay untouched on the floor where she'd knocked it after screaming at Ben to get out and stop distracting her.

Thank God that had been before she'd finished the interface, before she'd turned it on.

Now her eyes didn't, wouldn't, couldn't leave the screen, and the sounds the manifolds made, though quiet, drowned out everything else—the white noise from the lights, the wind, the traffic in the distance, the flies buzzing around the rotting remains of the sandwich Ben had brought her however long ago. She could hear them but could no longer hear them in any way that mattered.

At least she understood why Doc had killed himself.

Too bad it didn't work.

The ideas that took root in her mind overwhelmed everything else—her desires, her wants, her basic physical needs. Somewhere in the back of her mind she understood that this would eventually kill her, but the terror of obliteration held nothing in light of the insatiable thirst of the nameless thing with which she had made contact. The tiniest break of concentration, and it would have her, and it would drag her screaming into itself, never living, never dying, consuming her pain and her grief for eternity.

Somehow, understanding the cascade transformations of the Calabi-Yau manifolds that made up the tiniest elements of spacetime had drawn its attention, let it know she was there. And it wanted her, to taste her as it had tasted and was tasting Doc, to tear her asunder to the very superstrings that made up her reality and drink her screams in an oubliette where time had no meaning. Death had not saved him, and it would not save her.

It took every shred of her will to keep it at bay, to push the squirming, probing tendrils of the entity's rapacious mind from the delicate thought-spaces that made her up and defined her being, and she had none left for anything else, not even to utter a warning, or to reach out and turn off the computer. She couldn't even allow herself gratitude that she'd driven Ben away.

When Doctor Mercer had come in to complain about the smell, he'd gotten a full dose of the message, streaming through his eyes and ears before he'd had a chance to react. The gurgling sound and thud told her something had happened to him, and when his bowels let go, the rancid burst of flatulence almost pulled her eyes from the screen. The blood pooling at her feet, warm at first and later cold and sticky, didn't garner so much as a glance. She couldn't afford it, couldn't afford one nanosecond of distraction. In the message, she could hear Mercer's desperate panting, feel his terror, and the relish with which he was continuously consumed.

A janitor joined them, and later still Detective Coussens. Unprepared and weak-minded, they succumbed instantly, and joined Mercer on the floor, a feast for the flies. As they joined it, as it ate, it grew louder, stronger, as if pulling from energies it never knew from the reality around it, and their agony became one continuous shriek in her mind.

Unable to move, unable to shift her concentration the slightest bit lest she be consumed, Alice prayed for a power outage, a lightning strike, a meteor—something, anything, to shut it off before she succumbed to thirst or starvation.

REAL NUMBERS
Liz Kaufman

It started as a joke.

A joke I made to myself, because even back then I didn't have anyone else to share it with.

I remember being surprised that the university's course page was so plain and lifeless compared to all the brightly colored material they'd mailed me weeks before. I resented being bored, and I was looking for anything that might make the process of selecting my one required humanities elective bearable. That's where the idea came from, you see: the boredom.

At the time, I thought the bright red acceptance package was a bit garish. Ugly, really. Not that I was one to find the beauty in things. It seemed to have the intended effect on my mother though. She waited for me while I opened it, standing in the doorway to my room. I usually would have told her to get the hell out, but I decided that she should get to see this. After all, this was the culmination of her dreams more than mine. She would finally get to be free of me, finally get me out of her house. It was all here—her hopeful future contained in bright red packaging.

For her benefit, I read aloud: "Dear Anthony, Congratulations! We are pleased to inform you that you have been accepted to…."

She had given a contained little whoop along with a tentative hug when I finished reading the letter, complete with scholarship offer. She always reminded me of videos I'd watched online of dogs rescued from animal fighting rings. The way they clung to the back of their cages, doing their best to not be seen, to keep their eyes down. Pathetic, just like my mother. I let her hug me for four seconds before lightly pushing her away and making my way back to my computer chair. She let me go easily. Sometimes I wondered if she enjoyed being rejected by me, if she got something out of it. I couldn't understand why she kept coming back for more. No matter; she had already disappeared, gently closing the door to my room before I had even settled at my desk.

In the days that followed, relief seemed to settle in my house, shared mutually between my mother, my father, and my two older siblings. The other members of my family did not bother to congratulate me on getting into my first-choice university. They had already learned their lesson long ago and opted to give me a wide berth.

Even though they all saw the grades I brought home, the consistent $A+$ average since age six, I think they were all worried that my application would be unsuccessful and that they would be stuck with me. I understood why—despite my academic excellence, people did not like me. It was as simple as that. And it wasn't just in person either. Even when I was chatting to people online, there was always a moment when the other person would recede, starting their slow retreat away from our conversation. Something I said, or the way I said it maybe. I never really understood it. Not until later.

I knew I looked a bit different than everyone, dressed a bit different too. I opted to keep my hair long and didn't take to shaving regularly when my beard started to come in at fifteen. I showered only when I had to. I didn't bother much with other upkeep. I just couldn't see the point. I wore some variation of a black, oversized shirt and black baggy jeans every day. I didn't care about looking nice or fitting in; the idea of it bored me to tears. I think that was what kept me the most separate from other people. Everyone cared so much about what other people thought, about making other people happy, about other people's feelings, and I just didn't care at all.

Besides, a not small part of me liked the distance that people kept. That included my family, who, other than my mother, mostly seemed to find ways to avoid me on the rare occasion that I came out of my room. It certainly caused conflict between them, with shouting matches between my parents about me typically a biweekly occasion. But that distraction was easily blocked out with my noise canceling headphones and very loud horrorcore music.

I didn't particularly enjoy making my parents miserable. No more than any other teenager, I suspect. But, as I already told you, I didn't particularly care about their feelings either. Especially after years of them subjecting me to child psychologist after child psychologist.

But neither my parents nor the psychologists seemed to realize that it was exceedingly easy for me to access any number of psychological assessments—complete with the associated scoring guides and diagnostic materials—online. I only had to memorize the answers to placate the clinicians. Just like at school, I excelled at this. My parents finally gave up trying to solve me at age ten.

I was honestly relieved when I started to feel them drift away from me and refocus their attention on my siblings, who seemed to require it like a flower needed sunlight. I prided myself on being more like the moss that grows between rocks, in the dirt. The intrusion of my family was an annoyance at best. I grew best in darkness and solitude.

But where was I? Right, the boredom. The humanities course page. My joke.

I didn't apply for an arts or humanities program. I was going into computer science. I had already started playing around with some programming languages in my last couple years of high school and was already fluent in at least the basics of Python, C++, Java, and—just for the fun of it—R. Not to mention, computer science was the ticket to the lifestyle I thought I wanted: minimum interaction with human beings, the ability to work from home, and a guaranteed well-paying career that would give me independence.

I did well enough in my English courses. It was easy when the teacher based the entire grade on multiple choice tests from *SparkNotes* for each assigned book. From all the available evidence, it seemed like she was a low functioning alcoholic who was waiting out her final years until retirement, but I didn't really care enough to look into it. Why bother when I was reaping the rewards of her carelessness? It's not that I didn't enjoy reading, but at the time I earnestly believed that these sorts of pursuits were pointless. That anything that took time away from getting my degree was pointless.

But the university required a humanities course. Something about making sure STEM graduates were well-rounded, making sure the first year was spent getting to experience different perspectives. As far as I was concerned, it was just another practice in pointlessness, something I had gotten used to over my last eighteen years of life. Pretty much my whole life up to then—90% of it anyway—fell into that category. What was one more dumb course?

After scrolling through the art course listings—black print against a white screen—for what felt like the hundredth time, my eyes started to feel like they were bleeding. On a whim, I hit *Control+F*, opening the small search box in the upper right corner of the screen.

"These idiots want me to take a humanities course, huh?" I remember saying out loud to myself in the quiet of my room.

Programming, I typed, and hit enter and laughed. Zero results on this page.

Computer. Again, no results.

Science yielded a somewhat intriguing English course about the sci-fi genre, but when I saw the course's reading list didn't include any Asimov, I rolled my eyes and moved on.

I tried a bunch of different science adjacent phrases, trying to see if I could find a course that was at least ideologically close to the other courses I would be taking. I didn't expect to find anything, and I knew my stupid joke was wasting time I didn't have. The deadline for course selection was a few hours away. If I didn't pick something by then, I would have to go in person to see what was left over, and I definitely wanted to avoid that. Besides, a small jolt of excitement went through me at the idea of being able to cheat my way out of this stupid policy.

It wasn't until I did a search for *Math* that I saw it.

Philosophy of Mathematics.

I laughed again, clicking out of the page search to take a closer look.

There were no philosophy courses at my high school. Religious studies was the recommended supplement. But I had seen enough memes to know the stereotypes about philosophy majors. They were people who went around after one class, pointing to random solid objects and asking people, "How do you know this is real?" They asked extremely stupid questions like, "How do you even know you're alive?"

I thought they were completely frivolous people. I had read some stuff online about the various philosophers—Socrates and his endless questions, Nietzsche and his syphilis. Enough to get the jokes. But thinking about thinking really seemed like such a ridiculous waste of time. I thought of the world as an incredibly simple place back then, you see. When you're in high school, you figure out the system and game it to get good grades. When you're an adult, you figure out the system and game it to get a job that requires the least amount of effort for the most amount of money, and then you use that money to buy shit you like. Everything else held very little interest to me.

But I always liked numbers. They made sense to me. Math made sense to me. Rules, order, logic. Hard science. These were the kind of things I could respect. What the hell could some stupid philosophy professor have to say about that?

I clicked on the course description, part of me curious and part of me ready to roll my eyes.

We welcome all levels and backgrounds to this year-long philosophy course. So it met the requirements and didn't require prerequisites. I remember thinking that probably meant it was easy and I needed to do well enough to make sure my grades stayed up so I could maintain my scholarship.

Examines the history of logic as it pertains to mathematical practice as well as problem solving and decision-making using mathematics. I remember thinking that sounded practical at least.

All readings available in the online course book. I knew this meant that there would be no textbook, meaning the money my parents would give me for textbooks for that course could be spent elsewhere. That was what clinched it if I'm being honest.

I hovered over the button that said *Register* at the bottom of the page for only a moment before I clicked it. I was pretty good at that, making big decisions at a moment's notice. Why waste time worrying about the consequences? At the time, I didn't realize how consequential that click would be.

π

Less than a week into my first semester, I was doing pretty well. Living away from home meant not having to engage with the inconveniences of my family. There was no one to bother me anymore. No mother telling me to clean my room or ask me stupid questions. No one to interrupt me.

My single-bed dorm room had filled up over my first few days of classes. Textbooks littered my desk and the floor, most of them still inside their plastic packaging. Most of my clothes were still in the suitcase they came in—my mother only got about halfway through unpacking them before she broke down into tears and then excused herself from the room. I didn't bother finishing the job when she didn't return. My desk already held the evidence of my usual caffeine habit, now unimpeded by my mother's nagging. A small mountain of takeout cups had formed, since coffee makers weren't allowed in dorm rooms. Apparently, they were a fire hazard.

It was either luck or my parents' intervention that saw me placed in a single room. I'm not sure if you can tell already, but a roommate would have been a disaster scenario. At least, until I made them so uncomfortable that they left. I was pretty good at that. The kids in the rooms surrounding mine had already learned to avoid me, to skip over my door when they were inviting people to go out and explore the campus. I already told you: that was the way I liked it.

I looked over my classes for the next day, figuring out what I would need to bring before settling into a night of drinking coffee and scrolling. It was only then that I saw the philosophy class in my schedule, first thing the next morning.

"Fuck," I uttered under my breath. I remember thinking about how I had been so careful to cultivate my schedule, choosing only afternoon classes so I could stay up as late as I wanted to the night before. I briefly considered skipping the class entirely, but curiosity got the best of me. I reluctantly set my alarm for the 10:00 a.m. class. There was something appealing about carrying out the action I still thought of as a joke to its natural conclusion.

Or maybe the numbers were already starting to affect my actions, even then.

π

I elbowed the door of the classroom open the next morning, careful not to spill my extra-large coffee, and looked around the mostly empty space. I quickly sought out a seat in the back row, as I had done in each classroom I entered that week.

It was in one of the older buildings associated with the university, a little bit off the main campus. The center of campus featured shiny, brand-new buildings that looked nothing like this. All of them bore the last names of wealthy donors, their photos proudly displayed inside like we used to display pictures of Jesus and the Virgin Mary at my house. The building the philosophy class took place in was named after some old university president, I think. Someone unimportant. It was probably too decrepit to tempt anyone to take out the checkbook for a rechristening.

I wasn't surprised that my only humanities course was taking place in this shithole. It was just another reminder that the world wasn't run by artists or philosophers or English majors typing out their long, pointless essays in the library. It was the tech giants, the scientists, the doctors, who all had sizable enough bank accounts to craft college campuses in their image. Poetry didn't make bank; industry did.

In addition to being in an older building—the desks marked with years of use, chairs of various heights and colors unevenly spread out around the room, mismatched and clearly gathered from the cast off of other buildings—the room was also quite a bit smaller than what I had gotten used to. It made sense. All of my other courses were entry level, feeding in a large number of first years who might drop out or flame out in the years to come. This course was technically a 300 level, despite the lack of prerequisites, and had clearly attracted fewer students. It turned out that most science majors looking to fulfill the humanities course requirement opted for some course about ancient Roman artists that was graded solely with online open book quizzes. Easy 100%, if you put in any effort. That course was probably taking place in one of the larger buildings on main campus, despite the subject matter. I guess rich people buy art too.

There were only about twenty other students in the class, I realized, as people finished shuffling in. I was pleased that everyone else managed to stay at least two seats away from me despite the size of the classroom. Either my reputation preceded me or my appearance continued to be effective at driving people away. Either way, I was satisfied.

The professor arrived moments later, pushing through the classroom door and greeting the students collectively with a quick nod. He looked like the stereotype of a philosophy professor—someone who spent his youth at Vietnam protests, smoking weed, lazing about until he had gotten a respectable job in his thirties. Someone who still thought he was pretty cool, but just looked old and worn out to everyone else. His silver hair was pulled back into a low ponytail, though it looked like its length was less than conspicuously hiding a bald spot on the back of his head. Clean-shaven, he wore a wrinkled, tan shirt tucked into gray chinos, which revealed a thin frame that matched his shorter height. He had a small, gold hoop earring piercing his left lobe and carried a brown leather backpack by his side to complete his look.

Yeah, to me he just looked like the definition of a loser. I disliked him immediately, which, to be fair, was my reaction to most people up to that point. I remember thinking that the only thing he was missing was a pair of Birkenstocks. He wore brown loafers instead.

The classroom started to settle down as the professor went over to a chalkboard—an honest to God chalkboard; Christ, how old was this classroom?—and wrote out his name.

What was his name? I can't remember now. I guess it wasn't important.

I had already started clicking around on my laptop, directing myself to my usual favorite online distractions, when his voice sounded out, louder than I thought it would be for such a small and unimpressive looking man. I do remember what he said though, because it *was* important.

"Have you ever wondered if numbers were real?"

My eyes shot up to the man at the front of the room, now looking at a captive audience of students seeming to range from first years to seniors. I remember almost letting out a laugh. The very thing I had seen repeated in meme after meme was actually happening. *Is this random thing real?* I considered opening my phone to start recording whatever this idiot was going to say next, but then realized I didn't have anyone to send it to. If I posted it online, I would likely be found out anyway. The classroom was too small not to notice where the recording was coming from. Besides, I knew I needed this course in order to stay in my program for the time being. So I just rolled my eyes instead.

A girl who looked like she spent the previous night doing all of her assigned readings before going to bed promptly at 8pm raised her hand slowly from the front row. The professor nodded at her.

"Well…I mean, they exist. We use them every day. We use numbers to count, but also to build things, to make sure that bridges stay upright and buildings don't collapse."

"True," the professor said, and I remember him looking pleased at this moment, like this type of response was what he was hoping for, before he continued with, "so if we accept that numbers exist, *where* precisely do they exist?"

I felt the furrow forming between my brow. What the hell was he talking about?

The girl shook her head, but he waited patiently. No one else raised their hands.

"I guess…," she stammered, clearly not prepared for this kind of scrutiny, "in our minds? When we think of them?"

"Are you asking me or are you telling me?" the professor replied, and I found that his tone was a bit sharper than his hippy exterior would have led me to expect.

"That's what I think…I think," she replied, bowing her head to try to end the interaction.

The professor clapped his hands together.

"But if numbers only exist in the human mind, then how is it that we can use them so successfully for prediction? Your own examples illustrate just how much we rely on the infallibility of numbers, of mathematics, in order to make sure bridges stay upright and buildings don't collapse, correct? But bridges and buildings and other structures exist in the physical world, outside of human consciousness, don't they? If we all died tomorrow due to some toxic poisonous gas being released into the atmosphere, if every human being in the universe ceased to exist, wouldn't you expect that our bridges and buildings would remain standing?"

Before the girl in the front row could squeak out a response, the professor started to pace, leaving her behind to address the larger classroom. I found myself suddenly disinterested in my laptop screen.

"But if numbers exist in the physical world, where exactly do they exist? Where do they originate from? Oil exists under the earth, diamonds in caves well below the surface, oxygen in the air. All of these things existed before human beings were conscious of them. Human beings discovered them. Did human beings discover numbers too?"

The professor went over to the chalkboard and wrote out the words *MATHEMATICAL REALISM / ANTI-REALISM* in large block letters. I already felt my mind spinning with confusion.

It was ridiculous. Mathematics is the rule that governs our universe. It underpins all of reality. It's more reliable than the scientific method, than any other form of prediction or study. It's only limited by the human inability to grasp it, to compute it, which is what computers are for.

It wasn't until I raised my head to see everyone, including the professor, looking at me that I realized that I'd said my thoughts out loud. I felt the unfamiliar feeling of embarrassment flood my system before the professor nodded vigorously in my direction.

"Yes, precisely, ah…what is your name?"

"Anthony."

"Well Anthony, in practice, we all treat mathematics in this way, or we at least rely on mathematicians and engineers and physicists who do. But what happens when we think about it a little bit? If math's ability outstrips human ability, doesn't that suggest an existence of mathematical objects and truths outside of human existence?"

I felt my mouth go dry, and my head nodding dumbly. The professor seemed satisfied with this display of idiocy and continued his lecture.

It was in that moment, as he continued on, that I first noticed it. My screen had gone black due to lack of activity and as I looked down to face it, I saw myself. But what I saw was *wrong*. I quickly moved my finger across the trackpad to return my screen to the browser window, feeling like I'd seen some sort of monster. I shook my head. I remember thinking that this was what I got for staying up until three in the morning, crushing energy drinks when the coffee ran out. I was overdoing it now that I didn't need to worry about anybody coming in to check on me.

I suddenly resolved to turn over a new leaf and started by opening a blank document and spending the next ninety minutes actually taking notes for the first time since I'd started classes.

π

I spent that night cleaning up my dorm room, hardened with a new resolve. I told myself that I was getting serious now, hitting my pace. I was, after all, finally an adult, living on my own. I couldn't keep up with the same childish games that I played to survive the stupidity and boredom of my home life. I wanted to make money, have a real career, and be successful. No more screwing around.

I told myself, as I filled a garbage bag with empty coffee cups, as I folded up and put away my clothing, as I wiped down the countertops that had already gotten sticky in the couple of weeks that I'd been living here, that I was doing it because I was finally growing up.

But that wasn't really the truth. At least not the whole truth.

I'd felt something in that philosophy class that I hadn't felt before. Surprised maybe? Impressed maybe? I had been doing math for years, even programming some algorithms in school. I understood a lot more about math than most people in my high school at least. But I had never, ever considered anything like the ideas the professor had talked about that day. It wasn't just mathematical realism, it was the way he spoke about logic, something I thought I understood. It was like the basis for my entire world was changing. Like the certainty I felt maybe wasn't so certain anymore.

Suddenly, having a clean and orderly room felt of vital importance. I couldn't explain why back then. I could now, if you wanted me to. I could tell you all about it. Stuff I did then without thinking, like making sure the posters I put up on the walls aligned with each other in rows of two. Like how I didn't feel safe until I refolded my clothing and repacked my drawers so they were filled with four rows of six socks, two rows of four shirts, and two rows of two pajamas. Like how I avoided my reflection as I went past the mirror fixed to my bedroom door.

I didn't even get it then, but I think, deep down, I knew.

Numbers are real. And they are watching us very, very closely.

π

After that night, and much to my own surprise, the changes stuck. I started showering not just once, but twice a day. I did my laundry four times a month, even if it meant I had to Google how to use detergent after the first failed attempt. I finally cracked my textbooks, committing to spending at least ten hours a week doing my readings.

Despite all of this, I seemed to be getting less and less sleep each night. I was averaging two hours per night—if I was lucky. Sometimes, it felt like I wasn't sleeping at all, just slipping in and out of distraction, losing time.

I felt tired, and the coffee still helped with that. But not sleeping didn't feel like I thought it would. In some ways, I had more energy, more clarity, than when I was sleeping for fifteen hours a day over the summer months at my parents' house. I was able to understand things better, to grasp concepts more quickly. I was clear. Clearer than I'd ever been. Maybe that's why no one else seemed to notice.

The biggest shock to me, and to my parents who visited over Thanksgiving weekend, was that other people started to talk to me. They would say hello to me in the hallways and even invite me out to things. Even more surprising was that I would sometimes go. I don't remember their names or faces now.

Not important.

They were not important.

This was a time before I really understood things, really grasped the nature of reality. I was still wasting time on things outside of the numbers, like other people who served no purpose. But every day I was learning more, refining my understanding.

It started with the reading list. The philosophy professor practically jumped out of his cable knit sweater with excitement when I asked if there were any readings or books he could recommend about mathematics and realism outside of the course listing. I had already completed the listed readings, both required and optional, by mid-November.

It took me some time to get through the new list, and the twelve new books stayed stacked on my desk for some time. I was still attending my other courses, so it took me much longer than it should have. More wasted time. Plus, some of these new books took a lot more effort to get through. No matter, Christmas break was spent in my dorm room finishing up the last book on the list, a dense text on Platonism and mathematics.

I had done fairly well on my exams in the rest of my courses. There was a dip from my high school grades, but my parents had read online that was to be expected, so they didn't make a fuss. They did make a fuss when I said I wouldn't be home for the holidays, at least initially. I think they wanted to show off their new and improved son to their friends. They gave up after I put my foot down. I wasn't that different from how I was before. Not yet, anyway.

In the end, I found myself interested, but ultimately unsatisfied, by each of the recommended texts from my professor. There were good ideas there, although there was also a lot of boring dithering about putting forth lists of conditions that might lead one to consider metaphysical existence of numbers. I was looking for books that asked the *next* questions in that line of inquiry. Questions like the professor had posed on the first day of class, and ones beyond that. Where were the numbers? What were numbers? What were they like? Could we see them? Touch them? What did they want from us?

These questions, forming in my head over the stretch of three weeks between my last exam and my first classes of the new term, were paired with my own growing realizations. For instance, the wrongness I felt in the world. Even then, I knew something was wrong when I saw it. It was a feeling that could hardly be explained by the scientific mindset I was used to. At least not initially. It started with me, with the feeling I got when I looked at myself in the mirror. I had never made much of an effort to look in mirrors before, but I was self-aware enough to know that I had been avoiding them for some time, maybe even since that first philosophy class when I caught my own reflection on the screen. It was because there was something *wrong* there.

I spent Christmas Eve looking at myself closely, forcing myself to even though I could feel an anxious panic gripping me as I did so. There was nothing there, at least on the outside, that was particularly out of alignment with what an average North American male looked like. In fact, the past few months of showering and regularly shaving, eating healthier, and going out more had led to an improvement in how I held myself and the amount of weight I carried around my midsection. But still, I could sense it. There was something wrong in my reflection. Something very, very wrong.

It was the same feeling I found myself encountering on my walks around campus. I started up the habit when I was trying to work through difficult problems in my computer science coursework. Now, struggling to define this wrongness, I found myself taking at least six walks a day. But instead of figuring out what the wrongness was, I started to see it everywhere else instead.

It was in the garbage cans, tied three to a post, that sat outside of the cafe by my dormitory. It was in the entrance to the small theater where the school's drama program performed their plays, seven steps up to the three working doors (one was perpetually out of order). It was even in the foyer of the business school, its large skylight sectioned into fifteen smaller sections of clear glass, obscured by the snowfall that finally came the day after Boxing Day.

Every day, I saw the wrongness in myself, and then I went outside and saw the wrongness in the world, and then I tried to square it with what I had learned. It felt hopeless at first. But it wasn't all bad. There were good things too. The philosophy course, two doors down from the double door entrance of the fourth building off the main campus. My dorm room, room 642, which provided a safe haven and had been the place of my rebirth into a better, more productive member of society.

It was also around this time that I started to realize that I was counting. Buildings. Windows. Bricks. Snowflakes. Everything. You might have already noticed. In some ways, it felt like something I had done my entire life, but was finally just taking notice of, like breathing. It also felt good to do. Right. There was a safety to it, an order to make explicit the numbers that lingered in each physical object on the earth. But it also felt like I was doing an important job. Like the objects around me were waiting to be counted, like a child waits for their name to be called out for attendance.

It was the second of January when my observations about the physical world, mathematical realism, and my counting finally collided into the answer I had been looking for. I was staring at the garbage cans, the ones outside of the cafe by my dormitory, bunched together in a group of three. The can closest to me was quite full, and someone had placed a single coffee cup on the rim rather than try to shove it into the near-overflowing opening. Almost without thinking, I slowly put my fresh cup of coffee down next to it. Changing it from one cup of coffee sitting on the garbage can to two.

I felt it immediately. The change. The knowledge of what I had done. I had made it better. And that was because some numbers...well, they were just better than others.

I walked around campus, testing out my theory with my eyes, leaving behind my full cup of coffee to serve a better purpose. It was undeniable, as I looked and looked, as I counted and confirmed the findings against my sense of the various objects I observed. The objects in twos, fours, and sixes were cleaner, better, and safer. Then there were the others: the nine steps down to the parking garage, the row of seven streetlights lining the main street that proceeded through campus. They were ugly objects, ones made dirty by their associations—or lack thereof, in the case of the single telephone booth I found at the corner which almost brought bile spilling out of my mouth and onto the street. I swallowed it back.

It was the even numbers, I slowly started to realize over that freezing week, that were safe. Odd numbers were, well, odd. It was right in the name. You're already starting to understand, aren't you?

Even numbers are good. They are safe. Pairs of things, fours (two pairs), even dozens, were all good numbers that corresponded to good things. And everyone knows about bad numbers. Thirteen for example. It is one of the worst, obviously. Nobody wants to get married on Friday the Thirteenth. You can look to any point in history to see odd numbers wrecking havoc. For example, the Civil War started in 1861. The Great Depression in 1929. World War II started on September 1, 1939, or 09/01/39—three odd numbers. September 11, 2001 is another triple odd number date. The list goes on and on.

How about in my life? Look at my family. I was the third child and fifth family member born. When I realized that, I finally understood why I hated what I saw in the mirror, why I never could get along with my siblings or my parents, why I could never stand to be around them. I was a mistake, wrong from the jump. And before you think you've solved it by adding three and five together to make eight—beautiful, round, soothing eight—you haven't. I tried it, but it's simply against the rules. Different levels, different categories, you see. After all, if that was true then there would be nothing wrong with me. Nothing that had to be fixed. And there was.

Yeah, I knew you would understand. That's why I'm telling you all of this.

Anyway, that was when I knew I had to remove myself from my family. I wrote them an email that night to tell them I was going to need to focus over the next semester in order to get my grades up and would not be able to see them for the rest of the term. It was a lie, but a necessary one to ensure our collective safety. Just like with Christmas, they didn't fight me much.

I also recognized that being a single man in a single room presented a problem. Ones were among the ugliest of the odd numbers. I now knew why being alone often felt so biting and bitter, despite my familiarity with solitude. Once I understood that, I devised a few plans in my mind to solve it. At first, I considered trying to enter into a friendship with one of my floormates. But that was unruly. I wouldn't be able to control how many other friends they had. What if it was only one other? Or five others? I would be odd again. No, that was much too risky. I decided, given the rules around the practice, that exclusive dating was the only possible escape from my oneness. I hated the idea of it, obviously, but it couldn't be avoided. The numbers didn't lie.

My attempts at dating did not go well. After making an online profile in January once classes had resumed, I went out on precisely four dates before I decided to stop. The women I met up with did not understand what I was trying to do at all. They didn't have an interest in the numbers, even in the limited amount I could share with them. One of them (the third one I dated, unsurprisingly) had the nerve to imply that I was misunderstanding realism, that she had taken the same course I was taking the year before. When I told her I wasn't going to take someone who wore three pins on one side of her denim jacket seriously, she stormed out of the restaurant. The odd numbers never cease in their attempts to destroy what is good.

When I finally let go of the dating endeavor, I realized my mistake. It wasn't as simple as undoing my third child/fifth family member status by pairing up with someone else. I had to find even symmetry within myself before I could seek it out in the world. That's when I realized that this would take more than the part-time hours I had been putting into this project. It would require absolute devotion. I resolved that I would only attend my philosophy course as well as one of my other courses. Two courses a week. That was good. That was safe. Even though I was already far beyond what was being explored in the coursework, I figured I owed it to my professor, what with all he had given me, to continue attending.

I started out my self-evaluation using the mirror in my dorm room. I was able to bear the wrongness I saw better now that I understood it and realized I could change it, just like I had with the coffee cup on the garbage cans.

What I saw wasn't all bad. I had two eyes, two nostrils, two lips (top and bottom). That was good; that was safe. However, I found that I ran into some trouble with my teeth and tongue. Could they be counted as two distinct entities, therefore being two, or was tongue one and teeth were…wait, how many teeth did I have?

I paused to count them as the philosophy professor watched me, his eyes darting to my tongue to catch its action.

Oh, that's right; I missed a part. After agonizing over my reflection, I had taken a trip over to the philosophy building to attend my professor's office hours. I figured he might be able to help me in my approach, and that it was time to talk to him about my plans for applied fieldwork in his course.

I had been telling him about my conundrum and sharing a bit more about the work I'd started in earnest over the winter holidays, when I found myself distracted by the task of teeth counting. It was really something I should have done before I arrived. I wanted to apologize for my unpreparedness, but it would have to wait until all teeth were accounted for.

Two, three, four, five…

My tongue moved swiftly across my upper back teeth.

"Anthony, I just think you're a really terrific student. Not that it matters in a situation like this, but what I mean is you have so much potential."

Twelve, thirteen, fourteen…

"First year can be hard, really. What I'm saying is, I'm glad you came to me, and I want to help you."

Twenty-five, twenty-six, twenty-seven—fuck, this was going to be close…

"Why don't we take a walk down to the student center? We can go together right—"

"Thirty-two! God, that was close. That was too close!" I jumped up and let out a small sigh of relief, running my fingers through my hair. It was getting long again. "Sorry, you were saying professor?" I said, turning my attention back to him.

I realized then that he must have startled backward at my exclamation of relief. He was against his desk, his left hand gripping the surface to steady him. The expression on his face was the exact opposite of my own. But how could that be? Shouldn't he be excited about my practical application of these concepts? I was breaking new ground here. Couldn't he help me? Didn't he say he wanted to help me?

It was then that I spotted it: one gold ring on his fourth finger, on the hand still gripping the desk as he stared at me. A single ring! Just there, by itself! I searched his other hand, and there was nothing there. No counterbalance at all. Just the one, sitting there all on its own. An odd number he chose to wear on his hand, willingly. He seemed to catch me looking at the ring and took another step back, placing his left hand in his pocket.

Up to that point, I really thought he could help me. He'd found a way to keep himself intact despite the proliferation of odd numbers occurring naturally throughout the human body. Fingers, toes, tongues, even genitalia. It didn't matter if you technically had ten fingers, ten toes, in total. I already told you: you can only add at the same level, within the same category. Pay attention. The fact remains that you have five left fingers and five right fingers. Odd numbers. Same with your toes. There was no escaping it. No getting around it.

But I was sure. I was sure that there must be a way of getting around it if the philosophy professor had done it, if he was happy and functioning with all the knowledge he possessed about this stuff. He had read all the books I had. He understood; he even said so on the first day of class. They were real, the numbers; they were real. And, if they were real, then how could they not be watching us? How could they not be keeping a close eye on everything that they created in their image?

But when I saw the ring, I knew. A true expert would never make such a stupid mistake. A single, odd numbered ring, without anything to make it even? It was insane. Why wear the ring at all? Why risk it? No, I accepted then that he didn't understand a thing about any of it. That he knew nothing at all about what I was talking about. And it made me angry.

He cowered, his hands raised over his face. I guess I said some of that stuff out loud. It was getting harder to tell, though I realized it had never been particularly easy for me to sort out what was happening in my head from what was happening outside of it. I understood why, of course, even then; even when I was still imperfect. That was my tongue's fault. The thing that made the sounds. A one. An odd number. If human speech was made with a bisected organ of the mouth, or something in four parts, then the professor wouldn't have felt the need to back out of the classroom, making sure to keep one eye on me while he made his way for the door. I looked down at his desk as the door opened and closed behind him. He hadn't even bothered to take his old backpack.

I opened it up, feeling the echo of the empty classroom as my odd-numbered tongue continued to speak on its own, narrating my actions and thoughts like it was a scene in some kind of bad movie. My even brain, which I knew was two hemispheres connected at the center (safe, but still subject to corruption), ordered it to stop. It tried to order my odd numbered fingers to stop too, as they rifled through the contents of the brown leather backpack. Up close, I could see how the leather was faded where it had come into contact with the professor's body and the forces of gravity over the years.

I remember thinking that I would have to buy him a new one at the end of the course, to thank him for what he had shown me. Even in my anger at his incompetence, at this lack of knowledge, I still felt grateful to him for setting me on this path. I wanted to say that so you could understand. I was never a threat to him. I was never going to hurt him, okay? I was going to buy him a brand new backpack. I even thought about placing my final essay in it when I gave it to him, a gift within a gift. A nice little surprise for him. I had already started working on it over the holidays.

It was then that I felt something cold, with grooves on its sides. My arm lifted from the bag, my nefarious odd fingers still working of their own accord, and

I saw that I was holding a rather impressive Swiss Army knife. Nothing at all like the small one my father had tried to give me for my seventh birthday, paired with some family story about how it belonged to his father or something.

I opened it, eager to count its various parts and make sure it was safe. Eight parts, including a corkscrew, a bottle opener, a knife, and a small saw. Eight was a good number, one of the best under ten, in my opinion. Certainly a good omen. I slipped the knife into my pocket, cursing my unfixed hands once again. Just for good luck, I rationalized. Besides, should a man who understands so little about reality really be carrying around a weapon?

I knew I would need all the luck I could get. I was going to be introducing the world to a new kind of numerical understanding, making sense of something that even my dear professor hadn't started to grapple with. People wouldn't have to live in a world made up of pain and discomfort anymore. I could help them. Well, I could help myself, but others were welcome to reap the benefits too.

If the pain, the discomfort, associated with the proliferation of odd numbers was the reason behind all the bad things in our world, then what would it mean to eliminate them? I decided that my work could no longer wait. People needed to hear this. My professor needed to hear this. Then he would get it. This was all a misunderstanding, a miscommunication. Of course the odd numbers would try to screw this up. They don't want to be found out, eliminated, removed from the world. But they wouldn't prevail, no matter how much of a foothold they had. I was determined to stop them, whatever it took. Even if it meant the first test subject of my theories would be myself.

$$\pi$$

I stopped going to class entirely after that. I had more important work to do. And zero is even, so attending no classes would be just as safe as attending two.

I worked days and nights on my essay, which was turning into more of a manifesto at this point. It included parts of my personal story, some more dense theory, as well as diagrams to illustrate my points. I'm sure you could find a copy of it if you search around the Internet. I realize now some of it might have been hard for the layperson to read, which is why I'm trying to tell this story as plainly as possible.

There was pounding on my dormitory door the morning after I completed my essay and first successful fieldwork trials. I thought I had been quiet, but I suppose the odd numbers were doing whatever they could to stop me now.

No matter. I was close. So close that the even numbers reached out to protect me from interruption. I could hear the discussion between the student life representative and a man who I guessed was a security guard outside of my door. Who had the authority to unlock it? They didn't know.

When the scene outside my door had quieted after it had finally been decided that they would go and call the police, I took my things and slipped out, taking the back stairs to make my way to the library. Even though it was already the end of April, it was freezing outside, raining and miserable. But I thanked the even numbers again for their quick thinking.

The cold slowed the bleeding.

I was so close now, so close to having it all typed out and finished. I just needed to make the finishing touches and hand it off. I could use the printer at the library, so the professor would have a paper copy he could review right away.

But raised voices saying something familiar—my name, maybe—rang out behind me and let me know that there wouldn't be time for that. No time, not when I was still adjusting to walking, hobbling forward in my shoes.

I nodded. That was okay. I had done enough. I had written enough. I took a left and ducked into an alleyway between two buildings, pulling out my laptop and connecting to the campus Wi-Fi. I shivered while I opened the email I already had loaded, in case of emergency. All university staff as well as several local and national news reporters were copied. Of course, my professor was the second on the list—a rightful place of respect and honor that he had more than earned.

I dragged over the document with two index fingers and attached it to the email, which simply read: *The odds may try to stop you, but some may join us. I am one myself and I wrote this, but please don't hold it against me. I made myself better, and they can too. All of them can now.*

Then, I sent it off, looking around to see if the voices following me had managed to find me. No. No, of course they couldn't. I was even now. I walked with the angels and other perfect beings.

I decided that I could still make my philosophy class, that I wasn't that far away. I had not attended since the day I had my unfortunate conversation with the professor, but this would be an excellent opportunity to explain what I meant, to show him that I was right. I had proof now.

I strolled over, noticing that I was finally getting used to my new gait, the grip of my newly even hands tightening over the straps of my backpack. It was such an easy fix. Anyone could do it. Soon, the procedure would be available to all and to anyone who needed it. They would see me, see the good fortune I had already had this morning, and would not be able to deny it. There was more work to do, of course. There would always be more work, but I knew it was important to spend some time relishing in my accomplishment.

I entered the classroom, struck again by its small size just like I had been on my first day there. It was already full and, to be fair, I was eighteen minutes late. The professor was at the front mid-lecture when he turned to me.

I went to apologize for my lateness before I remembered that I didn't have a tongue anymore.

I almost laughed at my mistake. I was still getting used to the changes.

Instead, I held up my hands as a way of apology and explanation. The professor dropped the chalk he was holding on the ground. For a moment, the only sound in the room was the echo of chalk breaking against the concrete floor. Then the screaming began.

I kept my eyes on the professor throughout the shouting and shoving of bodies that seemed to move in slow motion in front of me. It hurt a bit to smile, to contort my mouth in any specific expression, but I wanted him to see how happy he had made me, how much I was going to change the world, all because of him. I always hated being told to smile or cheer up. My family would always say things like that. But in that classroom, even though the pain almost made me pass out, I smiled as wide as I could.

Then a different kind of pain laced through me, starting at my side and radiating out. I broke eye contact with my professor, now one of the few people left in the room, and looked down. Little metal spikes seemed to be stuck to my side, attached to long strings. Three of them. Looking up, I saw the cop who was holding the gun where the string connected. He was yelling something.

"Drop it!"

As I fell to the ground, I realized that I was still clutching the professor's knife that I had borrowed a couple of months ago. As my body shook, I reflected on the fact that this was just further evidence of all the odd numbers that remained, both inside of my body and in the world, and that needed to be eliminated. I had thought that it was symbolic to use a tool that belonged to my professor to start the work that his thinking had led me to. But stealing was wrong. I never would have taken the knife if it weren't for my odd-numbered fingers working against me. Once the professor read my essay, he would understand. I was sure the police would too. Besides, the knife had already dropped to the ground as I collapsed. Of course, I would apologize for taking the knife, explain that now that my hands were corrected, four and four like they were meant to be, that they would never have to worry about me stealing again.

They would understand.

Or so I thought.

π

It seems my knife thievery was not as easily forgiven as I expected. That's fair. I'm an adult now, and I'm responsible when I mess up. But that's why I couldn't understand why they called my parents in, why I've been placed in this building with white walls and white uniforms. A place where I'm not allowed to wear shoes and I have to cut my food with the side of a plastic spork. That's a spoon and a fork combined into one truly useless utensil. in case you weren't familiar. Worse, these sporks had odd numbers of tines.

They tell me that it wasn't about stealing the knife. That I'm sick. That I need help. But I know the truth. Despite what my professor once said about infinity, I know there are more odd numbers in the world than all of the even numbers put together. And, more importantly, more odds who want to keep things the way they are: broken, declining, and getting worse every day.

I've written letters to politicians, to owners of Fortune 500 companies, to tech giants, to newspapers and reporters. To anyone who would listen. My story made the news, but they never printed my essay. The odd numbers never let it see the light of day. I mean, I can admit that it probably wasn't my best work. I did the final edits still adapting to typing with four fingers and recovering from blood loss. But I still couldn't believe they would just disregard it entirely.

I suppose I shouldn't be surprised. Do you ever watch these people on television? Count the buttons on their suits, count the number of words they say in their sentences on camera, and look into their eyes. Many of them are odd numbers...so many of them. Odd numbers that have no interest in changing. Odd numbers that want to see us all go down with the ship. I can't believe some of them used to be my heroes.

That's why I'm writing this to you. I've seen your potential. Be you even, or odd, you are someone who wants the world to improve, to recover from the freefall we seem to find ourselves in. I know you can feel it too—the way, year after year, things continue to get worse and worse. I know you want things to get better. I know you are willing to do whatever it takes to fix this world.

I wanted you to hear my story so you would understand. So you would see that these concepts really aren't hard at all. You don't need to be a math genius or a philosophy major to understand them. You don't even need to go to university.

You've already felt it in your own life, haven't you? The feeling of wrongness when you spot three dogs barking at each other in a park, the relief of two seats at a small table in a cafe afterwards. You knew, even before you started reading, that there's right and wrong in this world.

I understand if you're hesitant to take the measures I took, but you don't need to go that far right away. You can start small. First, remove one item from everything in your home that's odd numbered. Then, you can make sure that items stay clustered safely in groups of two, four, or eight on your kitchen counter. Start slow, then build up. If you're at a party at an odd numbered house, consider leaving or going across the street. If you find yourself walking with five friends, it's probably time to make a new friend or just go home.

Try it, even for a couple of weeks—two or four would be optimal—and see. See how things get better for you. See how your life changes for the better.

I know that mine has.

ERATOSTHENES' MAP

Damon Nomad

Aidan bolted upright in bed, screaming.

He felt a hand on his shoulder and heard Cassie's soft voice. "It's just a nightmare."

Cassie gently ran her hand through his hair as he lay back down. "Same thing?"

"Yeah." He took in a deep breath and exhaled slowly.

"Go back to sleep." She moved closer and rested her head on his chest. Aidan had seen his brother commit suicide a few months earlier. She had traveled with him to the States for his father's funeral. They stayed at his childhood home where his mother still lived. His brother was also there for the funeral. Cassie left the day after the service and hadn't experienced the horror two days later.

Early that morning, Aidan found his brother sitting alone in the family room. Phil had been depressed for years but never suicidal as far as Aidan knew. He saw the knife in Phil's hands just moments before he realized what was happening. Phil used his training as a medical doctor to produce a single fatal slash to his neck just as Aidan entered the room. The nightmares were a replay of that moment.

Aidan closed his eyes but knew that sleep would come slowly. There was a part of the story that he hadn't told Cassie about: what happened when he knelt next to Phil's body on the floor. He checked for a pulse and breathing. There was no sign of life. His brother's body suddenly went rigid and his eyes went wide open as he groaned, "I can't find the gate." More even than the suicide itself, this was what fueled Aidan's nightmares.

π

Early the next morning, Aidan studied the tired faces of a dozen graduate students in the small lecture hall. An English-language lecture in advanced mathematics. "We have spent the last several weeks laying the foundation for one of the most important conjectures in number theory. Part of a debate that has raged for centuries. Do prime numbers follow a predictable pattern? The accepted answer is that they do not, but there are curious deviations from the standard wisdom."

Aidan wrote a name on the whiteboard. *Bernhard Riemann.* Below that he wrote a short equation. "This is known as the Riemann Zeta function when it's extended to complex numbers in the standard form. We will explore this infinite series and then move on to Riemann's most famous conjecture. Riemann proposed that all nontrivial zeroes of the Zeta function are complex numbers with a real component of one-half. Proving this hypothesis would shed light on the mysteries of patterns involving prime numbers. Mathematicians have been after the proof for more than a hundred years." He turned and faced the large board as he started to scribble. "Let's dig into it."

π

Saturday morning, Cassie sat with her friend Monique in a café a few blocks from the grand bazaar. A spot halfway between their flats in a trendy middle-class neighborhood of Istanbul. She explained what was going on with Aidan.

"He's still having those nightmares?" Monique asked. "He should see a counselor to help him work through his grief. You know I think the world of Aidan."

Monique took a sip of her espresso. She set up a blind date for Cassie and Aidan nearly two years ago. Aidan had dark mysterious eyes, wavy thick jet-black hair, and a build like a distance runner. Aidan Diakos was a newly arrived thirty-six-year-old mathematics scholar from the United States. His parents had immigrated to the States from Greece. He would be in Istanbul for at least five years, and most importantly divorced six years ago.

Monique waved a hand at Cassie. "You have confessed your love for each other, *ma petite soeur.*" Cassie was thirty-two and nearly ten years younger than Monique. She thought of Cassie like a sister. They worked together at a private research institute dedicated to language studies. Her family moved to Paris when

Cassie was a young teenager. She was nearly as French as she was American.

Monique finished, "His happiness is your affair."

Cassie blushed as she tapped her index finger on her coffee cup. "It's more than grief." She paused a moment. Cassie had her own guilt because she had flown back early for a work commitment after the funeral. Even though she returned to be with Aidan as soon as she got the news. "There is some baggage and guilt from his mother. She is a good person and means well, but her religious zeal is clouding things for Aidan."

"How so?"

Cassie continued in French, "You cannot tell Aidan I told you. It's a private matter for him."

Monique nodded her agreement. "Of course, it will stay between me and you."

"You know that Aidan has Phil's ashes in an urn in the study in our flat. There is more to it than a remembrance. His mother told him that it is his duty to find a sacred resting place for his ashes. So that his soul can enter the gates of Heaven."

"A church?"

"No, something more than that. Somewhere in the Holy Land."

"Crazy!" Monique went quiet for a moment and lowered her voice. "Sorry, I'm in no position to judge people's faith. Does his mother have somewhere specific?"

"No. She has put the burden on Aidan to find a place and get the ashes there. I don't push him to talk about it. Honestly, I avoid bringing it up."

Cassie switched back to English. "This burden along with his workload is too much. He has his research and the courses he's teaching. Also, some project he is working on with Karl Reinhart."

"You said Reinhart was his dissertation professor in the States. You don't much like him, right?"

"I don't really know him. He came to the University about ten years ago. His wife was born in Istanbul. She died of cancer four or five years ago. I'm sure he was instrumental in the University offering Aidan this position. He's a dark and brooding person. Aidan says he has always been that way, but I have a bad sense of him." Cassie went quiet for a moment. "Aidan doesn't talk about their project. He said he would let me know if they make a breakthrough. Mathematicians can be superstitious."

Cassie finished her cappuccino. "I need to get back home. Thanks for listening, *ma soeur aînée.*"

π

Monday night, Aidan sat at the desk in his small office at the university, programming the computer with a series of equations he'd developed for his project with Reinhart. By preference, he avoided using a computer except for the word processor. This night provided a noteworthy exception. Computers were fantastic at rapid calculations for checking on convergence or divergence of functions. They were also good for graphical interpretation, manipulating parameters and visually studying the results. The human eye was the ultimate in pattern recognition.

At nearly ten o'clock, the building was deathly quiet. The only light came from his desk light, the computer monitor, and some light streaming in the window from the outside. A mix of moonlight and some street lamps. His building was away from the busy streets of the city and there were only muffled sounds of the buzz of Istanbul. His head ached from too much caffeine.

The mobile phone on the desk buzzed. "Hi, Cassie. Sorry I'm here so late. Just getting ready to leave."

"Are you okay?"

"Yeah, just tired. Ten minutes and I'm on my way home."

He laid his mobile on the desk and tabbed on the space key and studied the input file one last time. He used the mouse to tap on the execute button. The computer-generated a contour plot in less than five minutes. "Now we're getting somewhere." He printed out two copies on large paper, folded one up, and stuck it into his leather-bound journal. He powered down the computer, tossed the journal into his satchel, and headed out the door.

He headed through the dark alley to the isolated tram stop on the campus border. Dim light illuminated a small bench along a narrow stretch of a cobblestone street. It was inconvenient for cars or bikes; only the occasional tram used this road. He sat down and zipped up his jacket. A tall hedge row muffled most of the sound from the city street on the other side.

A rustling sound came from the darkness near the wall of an abandoned building next to the bench. Concerned about muggers, Aidan strained his eyes and saw some movement. A dark outline emerged, like someone in a long black coat with a large hood.

"I've only got twenty-three Euro," Aidan said.

A deep gravelly voice responded. "You should be strong of faith to search for a gate. If you have darkness inside, you will be drawn toward evil."

Aidan's pulse raced as he stood up and crept a few steps closer. He couldn't make out any more details, but the coat seemed to be full-length covering a tall thin person. "Who are you? What do you know about the gates?"

The dark figure loudly sucked in air before speaking, "Study the signs carefully if you approach. Look for the dove and the lamb. But the raven and leopard will disguise themselves if your soul is not pure. Seeing the true image of the gatekeeper is your last chance at the fiery gate. Your last opportunity to avoid giving over a soul to eternal damnation." The voice rumbled like distant thunder. "The fiery gate will consume any mortal who lingers in the chamber."

Aidan stumbled back a step with a gasp when light from a car's headlights briefly flashed across the face of the hooded figure. Mottled skin like a burn victim, an uneven rugged surface, and a pinkish-red color. Deep-set eyes like dark coals that showed no sign of life. Aidan turned his head at the sound of an approaching tram. When he looked back to the spot, the phantom was gone.

Aidan trembled as he stood in the tram for the short ride home. *Who was that? How did he know I was searching?* He muttered quietly, "Have I gone insane?"

π

Aidan saw the empty plate at the table in the small dining room as he came into the parlor. Cassie sat on the easy chair in the corner.

"I missed dinner, sorry." He laid his satchel on the floor.

"You didn't call." Her voice had an angry edge.

Aidan sat on the sofa near Cassie. "I'm sorry, Cass."

She shook her head. "Your special project again?"

"Yeah."

"Aidan, you can't keep going like this. You're exhausted and it's hurting our relationship." She pointed a finger at him. "Why did you take up this project with Reinhart? You have your own research and you are one of the top experts in number theory. He's an old has-been. Tell him you don't have time to help him!" Her face flushed with emotion as she went quiet.

Aidan stared at the floor. "I'm not helping him. It's the other way around."

"What? That doesn't make any sense."

Aidan sighed loudly then spoke in a near whisper. "Something for Phil." He went quiet.

Cassie sat up on the edge of the chair. "Aidan, you need to tell me. What's going on?" She realized the project with Reinhart had started a few weeks after they returned from the States. "Tell me everything."

"Okay."

She moved next to him on the sofa. "Are you hungry? I can warm up some dinner."

He shook his head. "I ate some junk out of the vending machine. Where should I start?"

Aidan explained that the church sect in the small village where his mother grew up was primarily Greek Orthodox. But some of their teachings were influenced by concepts from ancient Greek culture. Archaic and mystic ideas about Heaven and Hell. "These physical gates are hidden in the Holy Land. You can help a soul make the journey if you bring their remains to the gate."

Cassie squeezed his hand. "Two hidden gates, one for Heaven and one for Hell?"

"It's not really clear whether it's two gates or one serving two purposes. It could be one and the purity of the soul of the person transporting the remains triggers which spiritual gate opens. It's either that or two nearly identical gates, close to each other. Either way, the soul of the one carrying the remains helps them find the correct portal. According to this catechism."

"So, your soul's eternal destination depends on who transports you. Sounds like a medieval tale of honor. Why would someone intentionally send a soul on a journey to Hell?"

Aidan cringed. "Old world vengeful sense of justice. For example, the parents of a murdered child can send the killers to eternal damnation by bringing their remains to the gate."

"You believe any of this?"

"It was drilled into us as children. Honestly, I haven't thought about it for years." He paused a moment. "Until Phil's death." He went quiet.

"Because of what your mother asked you to do."

"It's more than that. Something happened the morning he died." He told Cassie about his brother's last words, when it seemed he was already dead.

She thought for a moment. "You're looking for a gate for his soul. Aidan that's...." She didn't finish the sentence.

"I know it sounds crazy, but I have to do something. Even if I don't really believe." He decided against telling her about his encounter with the dark specter. *She will think I'm crazy.*

"Okay, I understand why you feel obligated. How does Reinhart fit into this?"

ERATOSTHENES' MAP

Aidan grimaced, "He's kind of an expert in the intersection of mathematics, ancient philosophical beliefs, and religions. Kind of obsessed, to be honest. I thought he might have come across something about these gates."

"Sounds like the occult."

"It's a long and twisted history. It starts with the Pythagoreans, who trace back to ancient Greece but the roots of their beliefs survived into Medieval times. The underlying principle is that reality is governed by mathematics. Physical reality and spiritual reality." Aidan continued with more details of these beliefs and then he moved on to the famous Greek mathematician, Eratosthenes of Cyrene. "He did one of the first calculations of the circumference of the earth, developed an early method to search for prime numbers, and was an accomplished geographer. He became the head of the Great Library of Alexandria." He continued with his explanation.

Cassie slumped back on the sofa after Aidan finished explaining everything he had learned from Reinhart. "So, he showed you this map from a medieval French religious text. The map was supposedly first drawn by Eratosthenes. Some Aramaic scholar got his hands on the map centuries later and made annotations about the location of a gate to Heaven. That's what ended up in the medieval text. I don't get the part about prime numbers. That's where your work comes into this, right."

Aidan nodded in agreement, "Yeah. There is a long history of ancient religions and even some modern Christians who believe prime numbers are linked to the divine."

"Modern Christians, really?"

"It's fringe stuff, cherry-picking examples. The Holy Trinity—three is a prime number. Seven is a prime and the Bible says the Sabbath is the seventh day. You get the idea. Anyway, Reinhart says that the medieval text says that sacred numbers, meaning primes, can be used to locate the gate."

"How do you use prime numbers to find the gate?"

Aidan reached into his satchel and laid his most recent computer run and a copy of the map on the coffee table. "You see the ridgelines and canyons in these mountain ranges in the map. There is a certain way to graphically represent prime numbers, to try and find patterns. This is from the computer run I did tonight. You see how some of the lines kind of match up to these ridge lines and canyons on the map."

Cassie nodded her understanding. "I get it, you overlay the pattern on the map. But how does that point you to a gate?"

67

Aidan sighed loudly. "That's where some real guesswork comes into play. The map has hundreds of caves marked along the canyons and we are sure a hidden gate will be in one of the caves. We need to identify all of the canyons that match up to a prime number line from my plot. Then identify which of those canyons have a total number of caves that is also a prime number. I would need to go there and search each prime-numbered cave counting from the entrance of each of the prime canyons."

"You know what a gate looks like?"

"No, faith is supposed to help guide you. I know it sounds a bit preposterous."

"Yeah, it does. Keep going."

"The pattern of prime lines change depending on several parameters. I need to iterate more to get a better match to the map. We also don't know the actual location of the region. Just somewhere in the ancient Holy Land."

Cassie stared at the map of mountains, canyons, and caves. "Let's go to bed. Monique is an expert on Old French. Maybe she can find an electronic copy of this medieval text and see if there are any more clues to where this is." She kissed him on the cheek. "You won't be alone when you go looking. I'll be right beside you; I promise."

π

Weeks later, on a Friday, Aidan was busy cooking when Cassie opened the door of their flat. She laid her briefcase on the cupboard near the door and hung up her coat.

"You're home early," she said. "I thought you were meeting with Reinhart late this afternoon."

"He called and said he had to fly back to the States. His brother is very ill. Dinner will be ready in thirty minutes."

A few hours later, they were relaxing on the sofa and sipping wine. Cassie put her glass down on the coffee table next to the Atlas of Israel. "Have you been able to narrow down the location of the map based on what Monique found about Jericho?"

"We are getting close. Reinhart has been focused on that this past week. There are lot of low mountains near Jericho."

Cassie picked up her mobile phone as it vibrated. "It's Monique." She swiped her finger on the screen. "Just talking about you. Aidan is so grateful for everything you did."

Aidan could just barely make out Monique's voice through Cassie's phone. "Yeah, I'm calling about the map. It may not be what he thinks it is. I found more description in the medieval text."

"Hold on, let me put you on speaker," Cassie said, then pressed a button on her phone. Okay, what did you find?"

"Some commentary early in the text discusses the Aramaic notations on the bottom of the map. The medieval text says that the common interpretation is what Reinhart told Aidan. 'Bring ye souls to the glowing gate of Heaven.' It explains that the correct interpretation is 'bring ye souls to the *fiery* gate of Heaven.'"

Aidan gasped, "Fiery gate. How is that significant?" *The dark hooded figure used that phrase.*

Monique answered, "I showed a copy of the map to Hans Mueller."

Cassie nodded in agreement. "Yeah, he's the go-to person for Aramaic. What did he say."

"He confirmed that the correct interpretation is *fiery* gate of Heaven. He said this phrase has an ambiguous meaning in Aramaic. Heaven doesn't necessarily have the ordinary meaning. It could be a shrouded reference to the gates of Hell. There is no way to tell without more context. I looked further into the medieval text. There is a description of the oral history passed down about the map. It says that there were two Aramaic maps developed from Eratosthenes' map. They look very similar but they don't show the exact same portions of his original Greek map. One included the gate to Heaven and the other has the gate to Hell. Only one survived and there is no way to know which one this is."

Monique's voice cracked, "I know how important this is to you Aidan. Honestly, I don't believe in any of this. But I know I may be wrong in my agnostic views. None of us can know for sure. I don't think you should risk using this map to find a resting place for your brother's ashes."

Aidan stared at the phone. Cassie sighed, "Thanks, Monique. See you on Monday."

π

The passport officer looked through the window at the old man. Slicked back thin gray hair and dark eyes behind round black spectacles. "Remove your eyeglasses please." The officer studied the face for a few moments. Intense eyes surrounded by dark circles and a thin and heavily creased face. *Looks like a tormented soul.* The officer glanced at the picture in the passport, flipped to a page, and applied the stamp.

"Welcome to Jerusalem, Mr. Reinhart."

π

Saturday morning, Aidan found Cassie at the coffee table. "You're up early." Sunlight streamed through the window. The light struck her wavy brownish hair at just the right angle to create a halo effect around her delicate face. He always thought she could be on the cover of fashion magazines. "You look like an angel."

"In this old robe and slippers." She smiled with a nod but she had a serious tone. "Coffee is ready. I found something. I've been studying the areas you were focused on in the atlas. I think I found the location where the map fits outside of Jericho.

Aidan got his coffee and sat down next to Cassie. He studied the location that she had found. He traced his finger along the page of the atlas. "You found it. You don't look satisfied with your discovery."

She frowned with a sigh and tapped on the page of the Atlas. "This mountain in the middle is a religious site. I looked it up on my laptop."

Aidan read the name aloud. "Mount Quarantania. Never heard of it."

"It's called the Mount of Temptation. There's an ancient Greek Orthodox monastery carved into one side of the mountain. It's supposed to be the location where Satan tempted Jesus in the desert." She paused a moment. "I've never been strong in my faith, Aidan, but there are two ways to look at this place spiritually. A place of victory of Jesus over evil or a hiding lair for Satan."

She closed the Atlas. "Monique is right; we can't risk using this map to find a place for Phil's ashes. We need to know a lot more."

Aidan nodded in agreement. "You're right. I'm gonna stop running the prime number overlays. Maybe do some research for this other map, sometime later. I'm gonna take a break from all of this for a while. I'll tell Professor Reinhart when he gets back."

Cassie took a sip of coffee. "You know I've never much cared for him."

"Yeah, I know. He is a dark sort of character."

"I was suspicious when you told me he was helping you. Didn't seem like something he would do. Don't get angry at me but I did some digging. His wife's legal cause of death was assisted suicide."

"Cassie, what's the point of this?"

"Hear me out. Assisted suicide is a legal gray area in Turkey. One of my

70

friends at work is married to an attorney. She did some checking. There was a formal inquiry into her death, Reinhart is the one who helped her. There were no criminal charges and she was cremated. I'm not passing judgment on him." She frowned. "But I think he really wanted to find the gate for his wife's soul, not so much to help you. He knew you would have some useful techniques for prime numbers "

Aidan thought for a moment. "You could be right. I'll tell him I'm done searching for now."

π

Reinhart studied the GPS as the guide drove the rugged four-wheel drive. "Stop here." He laid out a copy of Eratosthenes' map and studied the low mountains and canyons ahead of them. "Set up the tents here."

A few hours later, Eiran had the camp ready for the eccentric old man. Ten thousand US dollars to drive him out into the desert and camp for three days at most. The man promised he wasn't stealing artifacts, but Eiran didn't much care given the big paycheck. The old guy would have to face those problems himself at the airport if that's what he was up to.

Reinhart sat at the table in the large cabin tent. He laid the clear plastic overlay from Aidan's most recent run on top of Eratosthenes' map. He circled a canyon entrance on the map and put Layla's urn into his backpack along with two flashlights, a walkie-talkie, and two large canteens of water.

He put on his hat and walked outside. He shouted to the guide lying in the smaller tent. "I'm ready to head out."

Eiran got out of the tent and walked over. Reinhart pointed to the canyon less than a quarter mile from their camp. He tapped on the spot circled on the map. "I'll contact you on the radio if I need help. If you haven't heard from me by four, come look for me."

Eiran nodded his understanding.

Reinhart pulled the backpack over his shoulders just as a small flock of white doves flew past. They headed straight towards the canyon that he had chosen. "A good omen."

Eiran watched the flock of black ravens headed toward the canyon. *Crazy old man.* He headed back to his tent to catch a nap.

Reinhart thought of his wife as he trudged toward the canyon. He promised he would find a sacred place for her ashes after her death. She was in a state of near panic about her soul because of their plans for her suicide. She had spent

71

her childhood in Turkey in a devout Christian family. Their minority status was one of the reasons her parents immigrated to the United States. He loved Layla deeply and believed in an eternal destination for the soul, even if it wasn't the same belief as hers. He knew he had a chance to find a place for her ashes when Aidan came to him asking for help. Aidan's skills with prime numbers would help him finally decipher Eratosthenes' map.

He was conflicted in his feelings. *I know you believed in the God of Abraham, Layla. I think there is a deeper eternal truth that flows from the divine power of mathematics.*

Less than an hour later he came to the fork where the canyon split into two smaller slot canyons. He put his backpack on the ground and got out a canteen. He took a long pull of the cool water. The one on the right was nearly a half mile long and the one to the left was only about five hundred yards. Both routes had a prime number of caves that he would search. He spotted some movement from the corner of his eye. A lone bright white young sheep. He muttered, "The Lamb of God." *Another sign from your God, Layla?*

The lamb scurried down the canyon to the left; there were only seven caves along that route. He would check three, five, and seven. There was no sign of the lamb once he got to the entrance of the slot canyon.

Thirty minutes later, he came to the third cave along the route. He took off his pack, took another long drink, and grabbed a flashlight before he put the pack back on. He didn't notice the Arabian Leopard sitting atop a large boulder near the entrance. Its eyes tracked him as he walked into the dark cave.

π

Nearly ten minutes later, Reinhart came to a spot in the cave with a small door-like opening to the right. He scanned the portal with his flashlight and saw something carved in the rock above the opening. He gasped with surprise and muttered, "It's real."

Barely visible were Greek letters worn by the passage of time. He knew it was the old Greek word for gate. He shuffled through the narrow passage which opened into a small natural alcove, roughly circular. Big enough for maybe thirty people standing close together. He scanned the chamber with his flashlight. *It's empty.* He had expected to find a space filled with urns or even skeletons covered in burial cloth.

He put the backpack on the ground, uncertain whether he wanted to leave Layla's urn lying alone in this lonely place. He felt a warm gentle breeze and heard the sound of swirling air. His eyes went wide with amazement as he watched a glowing column of mist rising up from the floor.

The mist grew in size and slowly transformed into a figure of an old man bathed in bright white light. The voice was like quiet thunder. "Do you know who I am?"

Reinhart gasped with shock and fell to his knees. He had not seriously expected to experience anything spiritual during this journey. He looked toward the ground. He knew what Layla would want him to say. *You are the Lord God and the ruler of Heaven and Earth.*

He looked up at the shimmering form in front of him. The manifestation looked like what most Christians would expect of God the Father. A belief influenced by medieval and Renaissance art. Reinhart knew that Christian artists had borrowed the image from ancient drawings of the Greek God Uranus. *A presence I would recognize and understand.* "You are the creator of infinities and the keeper of the gate." *I'll get you to a better Heaven, Layla.*

The voice rumbled, "Do you profess your faith?"

Reinhart stood up. "I believe in the eternal power of numbers that govern the earthly and spiritual realms."

"Do you bring a soul in need of an eternal home?"

Reinhart reached into his backpack and laid Layla's urn on the ground just in front of where he stood. "Yes. Layla." He closed his eyes. *I will see you in paradise my darling.*

He stumbled back a step when he opened his eyes. The supernatural figure's appearance was now that of a ghastly monster. Reinhart could hear his pulse pounding in his ears as he stared at the muscular dark gray-skinned creature. An upper body of a man, lower body of a hoofed animal, and large bat-like wings on its back. Yellowish eyes like a lizard and a long hooked nose.

It raised its arms and screeched. "Welcome home, Layla." It moved toward the urn as the room was consumed in fire.

Reinhart felt his skin blistering as he grabbed the urn and stumbled blindly toward the door.

π

Weeks later, Aidan stared at Reinhart as he lay inside the protective bubble of the severe burn unit. He had been transferred to Istanbul from Jerusalem days earlier. His face reminded Aidan of the dark creature he had encountered weeks ago. Reinhart was in an induced coma and would likely stay in that state for a month or more.

Reinhart's doctor told Aidan everything he had been told. An Israeli guide had called the police when he found Reinhart near death lying in a cave near Jericho. He was clutching a burial urn. A helicopter transported him to a Jerusalem hospital with a world-class burn and trauma center. The guide had been arrested, but the police determined there was no reason to suspect him. The authorities had no explanation for how Reinhart was attacked or who was responsible. His body was near an empty chamber with no evidence.

Aidan put on his hat as he walked toward the tram stop near the hospital. He was anxious to get home to Cassie on the cold and windy evening. He promised to tell her what he had learned from the visit. He sat on a bench along with a handful of others waiting for the tram.

He lazily watched people walking along the sidewalk on the opposite side of the street. He thought he saw something in a dark alley just as the tram arrived at the stop. Aidan jumped on the tram and found a spot. He glanced back at the dark alley and saw a figure in a long dark coat and hood lurking in the shadows. *I'll remember your warnings when I make my journey in search of the gate.*

THEY'LL SAY IT WAS THE COMMUNISTS

Sarah Lazarz

"This will be your station," said Mr. Elliot. I couldn't take my eyes off his hair. It sat unnaturally on his head, like a skunk flattened by a tractor. I nodded, looking around the room at the other computers like me, recruited from mathematics programs, actuarial departments, and financial institutions all over the country. At my station, a converted stenographer's desk, sat a slide rule, pencils, a stack of graph paper, and a compass, its sharp end stuck into a small cork. The desk next to mine inexplicably included an abacus.

"Your day begins promptly at nine in the morning," he continued. The shiny line at the edge of his hair caught the light of the office's fluorescent bulbs above. I stared, oblivious to the rest of his speech. I knew what I was here to do, what we were all here to do. Put a man on the Moon. All around me, people were calculating, figuring, *conjuring* our way to the stars. And I was part of it, much to my dad's chagrin.

"If you aren't applying the math, what's the use?" Dad's voice rang in my head. A professor of chemistry at Stanford and the father of a surgeon and an engineer, dear old Dad saw me, a lowly mathematician, as something of a disappointment. I'll admit, I'd do math for free; calculus, trig, even geometry. It came to me as easy as breathing, and everything about it was beautiful. Why screw that up with the ugly empiricism of physical science? The only thing that kept us from coming to blows about it was Mom, the philosopher. I had thought that working at Edwards Air Force Base would change his mind but throwing my lot in with the new space agency, NASA, was just another black mark for me. The southern part of California always brought out his pomposity.

Mr. Elliot's bizarre hair didn't move in the sudden icy, carrion-scented blast of air-conditioning that brought me back to my station while he droned on. I was in the middle of hoping the smell wasn't permanent when someone elbowed me in the ribs and I jumped. My station partner had arrived.

"So glad you could make it on time today, Alice," he glared at the tall, shapely woman. "Why don't you get Leslie here started, hmm?" I glanced at my watch. Ten minutes after nine.

Alice simpered, "Your coffee's on your desk, Mr. Elliot." As soon as he turned his back, she stuck her tongue out at him. I stifled a giggle.

"Hi, Leslie. I'm Alice Conroy, and yes, that's a toupee," she pointed to her hair and then in Mr. Elliot's general direction, now across the room. I grinned.

"Leslie Keyes. Nice to meet you." I took her offered hand and shook it, her tawny skin a golden contrast to my sallow freckles. I looked at our station. The square desktops pushed together to form a table where we would work face-to-face. The abacus caught my eye again, and I raised an eyebrow.

"Sometimes, the wisdom of the ancients is what you need," Alice said playfully, picking it up and rattling the beads at me. At a large glass board at the front of the room, a clutch of bespectacled men in shirtsleeves turned our way at the sound and just as quickly turned back to their clipboards, dismissing us.

"Are those all the engineers?" I asked.

"Yep, the men who couldn't do their jobs without us," she said. "See those clipboards? Full of our figures and solutions. Here, I'll get you started on today's functions."

Alice produced a manila file folder from her station and opened it. The papers inside contained several lines of equations.

"Our assignment for the morning." She scrutinized the numbers and held the paper out to me. "Looks like they're giving us something easy for your first day."

I took it from her and scoffed. Integral calculus. "Should I be offended?"

Her honey-brown eyes fixed on me. "Let's find out, shall we?" The friendly challenge in her voice was matched by the twinkle in her eye.

Just before our lunch break, Alice slid her paper over to me and held out her open hand for mine. I quickly scribbled one last number and gave it to her. By silent agreement, we began checking one another's work. I ignored the grumbling in my stomach as my eyes flew over the pages of her work, breathless. I knew it would be correct, just as I knew mine would be. But oh, how differently we arrived there.

I sat back in my chair and let out a low whistle. "Are you sure I need to be here? Because it looks like you don't need me at all." In addition to the solutions she'd calculated for the original problems, Alice had devised some of her own to play with while I worked on mine. Every single one of them was flawless.

"Come on," she shrugged, but her little smile was proud. "Let's get lunch before they close the cafeteria."

We waited in the cafeteria line with other civvies like us and a few uniformed airmen. As I picked up a tray, a clammy hand landed on my shoulder.

"You found your way to lunch, I see." Mr. Elliot's hand left a sweaty trail on my sleeve as he slid it down to my elbow. I stiffened, hoping he'd feel it, and let go. He pressed his fingers into my elbow before ending the contact. "And I see you've decided to grace us with your presence at lunch, too, Alice," his tone unctuous.

Alice's face wore the same syrupy smile it had that morning. I could tell now it was phony. "Well, with company like Leslie, it was hard to stay away," she said.

Irritation flickered across his face, and he nodded a curt goodbye to us. He took his tray and sat alone several tables away.

Alice led me to a table of chattering women, most of whom I had seen earlier at their stations, with their manila folders of equations. Everyone had a beige plastic cafeteria tray in front of them.

"Hoy, Alice! And you're…oh, they told me, don't tell me, I'm good with names," a redhead in a gingham dress called out. She patted the empty seat next to her and I sat down.

"Gloria, you'd forget your own name if it wasn't printed on your birth certificate," Alice joked and the other women laughed, including Gloria. "Leslie Keyes, everyone. Everyone, Leslie." Alice gestured at me, and I lifted my glass of iced tea in a friendly toast.

"Saw you got the Elliot treatment," the woman across from me said. She was a middle-aged brunette, her hair shot through with silver, with thick cat-eyed glasses on a chain.

"What Sylvia actually wants to know is, did he grope you yet?" Gloria asked around a bite of chicken salad sandwich. I glanced around the table. They all had similar looks of interest mingled with disgust on their faces.

I sipped my tea. I didn't know what to say, so I kept quiet. Alice piped up, "Don't go scaring her now." She looked at me apologetically. "But try not to be alone with him, if you get my drift." The others shifted in their seats. I nodded, her drift gotten.

We all ate in silence for a few minutes, and I tried not to picture what being alone with Mr. Elliot would be like. As I was imagining more of his oily sweat touching my skin, another woman joined the table. Her blank face wore a bland smile framed by washed-out blonde hair. She didn't look at anyone as she began mechanically chewing her food. Gloria, Sylvia, and Alice exchanged looks but didn't say anything.

Eventually, Gloria's irrepressible personality got the better of her and she held up her left hand up to her cheek, giggling girlishly and dancing a bit in her seat. "Isn't anyone going to say anything?" The glint off her little diamond chip ring wasn't going to impress Marilyn Monroe, but it got the rest of our table's attention. The washed-out-looking woman even turned slightly at Gloria's display.

"Oh-ho! Charlie's finally proposed, has he?" Sylvia said sardonically.

"Hush, let Gloria have her moment," Alice said. Gloria was wiggling her fingers now, her grin ecstatic. I knew I was supposed to be excited, but marriage talk always made my skin crawl. I put on the appropriate expression. Alice caught my eye and winked.

"You are looking at the future Mrs. Charles Emerson. Isn't it grand?" Gloria held her hand out, admired her ring, and sighed. The rest of our lunch conversation was devoted to Charles Emerson's various qualities. He sounded like a drip.

On the way back to our office, I hung back and Alice joined me in a slow walk. The silent, wan woman who had sat down with us walked ahead of us as far as the elevators and then took a right down a separate corridor. She walked almost aimlessly, as if she wasn't exactly sure where she was headed.

"Molly Sykes," Alice said, gesturing in the other woman's direction. "She used to be in our section."

"She seems...nice," I hesitated.

Alice grimaced. "Molly was at your station, actually. For just a few weeks." She didn't continue, but just shook her head.

"What?" I prompted.

Alice shook her head again. "She got a promotion. But Leslie, she wasn't always like that," Alice pointed with her thumb toward the other hallway. "Molly was pretty nice." She shrugged. "I mean, I guess she still is, but I don't think I've heard her say more than two words since her promotion to Alpha Section. She eats with us still, sometimes. But it's like she's not really there. You saw her."

I had nothing to compare it to, but Molly had seemed strange. "Maybe the work is harder? In this Alpha Section?" It sounded important, with a name like that.

"Maybe," Alice said, "but it's like she's, I don't know…sucked dry." She trailed off.

We were back at our stations, and Mr. Elliot was walking up and down the rows of desks, pausing every so often and leaning down to inspect a computer's work, his tongue flicking out lizard-like when he did. I was mesmerized by the track of a single oily bead of sweat inching down his forehead. When he passed us, I rifled through the papers on my desk for a set of equations to work on, lining up my pencils, and willing him to pass us by. Alice was more serious as well. The fun of our morning competition was now overshadowed by the appearance of Molly.

At the end of my first week, Alice sat on the edge of my desk, crossing her legs at the ankle. I pretended to still be working on a graph so that I could look down and admire the curve of her calves and thighs. She tapped a manicured nail on the corner of the desk.

"Have you been out and about yet? You said you moved here from Palo Alto. Don't you want to see the sights?"

I blinked up at her. "What are the sights of Lancaster, then?" The town was paltry, in my opinion, but it was where a lot of the single civilians lived. It was quieter than Edwards, but not by much. Flight patterns around the base went in every direction.

"There are a few cafes, some honkytonks, a couple of roadhouses." Alice paused to look me up and down. "But you seem like a cinema gal to me. Come on, we can get a bite, then go to a late showing of whatever's playing at the Bijou. What d'ya say?"

Pretty girls don't have to ask me twice, I thought. I gathered up my things and gave her my best Barbara Stanwyck. "I am at your mercy, ma'am." She hooked her arm through mine and led me to the bus stop.

$$\pi$$

"He gave it to me this morning," Gloria whispered at lunch a few weeks later, casting a furtive glance in Mr. Elliot's direction. He sat alone in the corner as usual.

"Gave you what?" I asked.

Sylvia set her fork down with a clank. "The problem? The promotion test?"

Alice turned to me. "To get into Alpha Section, you have to solve a supposedly unsolvable problem. Or problems. It depends."

"But if it's unsolvable, then how does anyone get the promotion?" I laughed.

Gloria smirked. "They just say it's unsolvable to scare people. I'm already halfway done. Charlie doesn't want me to work after the wedding, so this is my last chance to have a little fun and make some extra scratch." She finished with a shrug.

I suppressed an eye roll and Alice barely covered her grimace with a quick swipe of her napkin. A thought occurred to me. "Didn't Molly get that promotion?" Molly hadn't been in the cafeteria for at least a week. In fact, I couldn't remember the last time I'd seen her wan, ghostly figure.

Gloria straightened her shoulders. "I'm just going to work until the wedding. And besides, I can handle whatever they give me."

The current rumor about what Alpha Section did was that they worked on such theoretical equations that it drove the computers insane. I shuddered.

"Well, good luck," said Alice. "Not that you need it." We all toasted Gloria with our lunchtime iced tea.

π

Alice passed me her work from the morning. We'd fallen into an easy rhythm, checking one another's numbers and getting used to the patterns in each other's work. Somewhere along the way, we also started hiding messages for each other in our graphs and equations after Mr. Elliot reprimanded us for being too gossipy on the work floor. He did not understand that sometimes we needed to talk about the numbers. Our messages were clever ciphers or codes that we made a game of creating and breaking. Elliot never seemed to notice them, even when he stopped to check in on our work.

Buried in Alice's calculations today was a message couched in a simple Caesar shift cipher: "No Gloria again today." I raised an eyebrow at Alice. She shook her head and shrugged.

We left Gloria's seat empty at lunch anyway, just in case. "Do you think she's just eating in the officer's mess? I heard Alpha gets to eat in there." I repeated the gossip hopefully.

All I got was head shakes from Sylvia and Alice.

"I could have sworn I saw her yesterday," said Sylvia. "I followed her all the way to the elevators, but she disappeared." She stared down at her soup, forlorn. Gloria had been her station mate for nearly a year and a replacement hadn't been hired yet.

I felt eyes on me and looked over my shoulder. Mr. Elliot was at his usual table, staring in our direction. I could feel his greasy sweat from across the room. At his temple, the shine of his toupee glue glistened like a garden slug in the weak light from the window.

"Do you think Elliot looks different? Like he got a new toupee?" I asked. Alice twisted in her seat to look and I grabbed her arm. "Don't look now!"

Alice whispered hoarsely, "It moves." We all shared a shudder at that. "No, but really, it slides. I've seen it."

"It does seem to have a different, shall we say, sheen to it these days," Sylvia said.

Alice and I got a closer look at that sheen when we were getting ready to leave for the day.

"Ladies, before you clock out, I have some excellent news for the both of you," Mr. Elliot said, an oddly expectant look on his face. He laid two business-sized envelopes on Alice's desk. "As you may be aware, we usually only offer one promotion at a time to Alpha Section, but both of your work has been exemplary in recent weeks. The brass decided to give me the power to offer two promotions this time around."

Alice and I stared at the envelopes, then at each other, gaping. Mr. Elliot cleared his throat and shifted on his feet. "Well?"

"Are we allowed to work on it together?" I asked, knowing the answer. He snorted.

"If you are interested in the position, complete the enclosed problem and have it on my desk tomorrow morning. You are under no obligation, of course." His tone indicated otherwise.

I slipped my envelope into my purse and Alice stood with hers. "Good day, Mr. Elliot."

Once we were out of the building on our way to the bus stop, I finally broke our tense silence. "Alice, something about this feels off."

"Agreed. Let's not talk about this until we get to your place, though, okay?" According to our employee manual, Reds could be listening to us just about anywhere.

We sat in my apartment that night, eating hamburgers from the diner down the street and contemplating the problems Elliot had given us. I put on a Chet Baker record to cover our talking. You could never be too careful, I thought.

"These are challenging, but not what I'd call unsolvable," I said. Alice murmured in agreement. We worked for a few more minutes.

"Leslie," Alice said after turning over the record. "What do you think would happen if one of us didn't get the promotion to Alpha?" She stroked her chin in thought. I tilted my head at her.

"I guess that person would stay at our station." I said, catching her train of thought. "And be able to keep an eye on the other from the outside. Be a kind of backup." I smiled slyly. "Who wants to make a mistake?"

She slid into the chair across from me with an impish grin and twirled her pencil. "Ready when you are." She winked at me.

π

We presented ourselves to Mr. Elliot the next morning, sealed envelopes in hand. Mine contained a minor mistake and Alice's was perfect. It had taken us some time to determine where a mistake should be made, but in the end, we decided it should be something relatively minor, to make it seem like I'd rushed the work.

Alice handed him her envelope first. Elliot ran his fingers over the page lovingly and smiled up at her. "Just what I expected, Miss Conroy. Really delicious solution you came up with." He licked his lips and smacked them like he'd just eaten Thanksgiving dinner.

When Elliot took my envelope, he opened it gingerly and held it by one corner, scanning my work briefly, and then dropped it like it had grown fangs and bit him. "I have to say, I'm a little disappointed in you, Miss Keyes. And I hate to break up your little partnership since you work together so well. But it looks like Alice will be moving on without you."

I did my best to look unhappy about it and let out a dejected sigh. Elliot pressed his lips together in a tight line and showed me the door.

"You can work with Sylvia since you are both without partners. Good day, Miss Keyes," he said, closing the door in my face.

I didn't see Alice for three days after that, not even on the Lancaster bus. Sylvia and I worked together efficiently, but it wasn't the same as with Alice. There were no hidden jokes or messages, no fun little ciphers to kill time. I missed her little finger snaps when she was stumped. I missed the way a tendril of crinkly hair would always escape her French twist by the end of the day.

Finally, on the bus home, I saw her. She wore the same clothes as the day we had both visited Mr. Elliot's office, her hair escaping its twist in more than one place, her makeup gone. I elbowed my way back to her and sat in the seat next to her.

"Alice, are you alright?" I whispered nervously, clutching at her arm. "Where have you been?"

She turned blankly toward me. "Leslie? Oh, hello. I'm fine." Her tone was robotic. I shook her shoulder when she began to turn away from me to look back out the bus window.

"Alice!" I hissed. The man in front of us turned sharply, and I smiled apologetically, lowering my voice. "Alice, have you been home at all?"

"Home," Alice said with no inflection. It was unnerving.

"Yes, home. It's been three days," I said, a bloom of panic in my chest. The bus stopped at my corner and I hurried us down the steps and toward my apartment, too afraid to let Alice return to hers. I led her by the hand after she stopped to inspect the display in front of the hardware store and tried to pick flowers from the window box outside the hair salon.

I busied myself in the kitchen making tea while Alice sat on the sofa, staring straight ahead at nothing. After setting the cup in front of her, I went over to the record player and started another Chet Baker LP, hoping it would bring Alice around.

"I think you should stay here tonight. You don't seem like yourself," I said, touching Alice's wrist.

She turned to me again, like she had on the bus, all slow and mechanical. Puppet-like. "Leslie. Leslie, Leslie…." Her voice sing-songed and faded into the music, but she picked up the tea and drank some. I studied her profile as she drank, her golden skin now gone ashen, her eyes leached of warmth. I knew if I tried to talk again my voice would shake, so I bit my lip, the sharp pain grounding me. Alice put the teacup down. I waited for her to say something, but she was staring at the blank wall again.

"Can I get you anything, Alice?" I asked after a while.

With a lifeless smile, she answered, "Paper and pencil."

Alice scribbled in the notebook I gave her while I made myself eat and gathered clothes for her to change into. I couldn't make heads or tails out of most of her chicken scratch when I caught a glimpse of it. I led her to the bathroom and gave her the clothes when she paused in her scribbling.

"Get cleaned up, and I'll make up the sofa for you, okay? You can tell me all about it in the morning. How does that sound?"

"Leslie," she said, as if seeing me for the first time. "Thank you."

I woke up the next morning to an empty apartment and a pile of Alice's clothes on a chair. On the sofa was the notebook I had given her, every page filled with her distinctive numbers and script.

Except that none of it made sense. It was a confused jumble of half-finished equations, doodles, and fractions. None of it contained Alice's delicate touch, and none of it led anywhere. I sank onto the sofa, breathing in Alice from the sheets, and turning the pages of the notebook. I hoped Alice had gone back to Edwards because then at least I'd know where she was, but the longer I looked at the weird pages of the notebook, the less sure I was she would be safe there. Maybe the rumor about Alpha driving computers insane was true.

$$\pi$$

"A quarter past nine, Miss Keyes," Mr. Elliot towered over me when I finally made it into work, tapping his wristwatch and tutting at my lateness. I hastily shoved the notebook into a drawer and scraped my chair across the tile floor, scooting closer to the desk.

"Sorry, Mr. Elliot," I said in a breathless rush. "Won't happen again."

He shook his head and tutted disapprovingly. "See that it doesn't."

Sylvia gave me a quizzical look. "What's wrong with you?"

I waited for Mr. Elliot to go into his office before I answered. "I saw Alice on the bus. She was at my place last night—"

"How is she? Is she okay?"

"No, I don't think she is." I kept my eyes on Elliot's door while I spoke. "She hardly talked and she…well, she just wasn't herself."

A trio of male engineers passed by, one's jacket brushing Alice's abacus on my desk. I leaned forward and hissed, "She's just like Molly."

Before either of us could say anything else, Elliot was back with the day's assignments. I worked slower than usual, my mind on the notebook burning a hole in my desk drawer. When Sylvia tapped me on the shoulder, I jerked, surprised to find that it was lunchtime already.

"You coming, Leslie?" Concern clouded her face. She gestured with her head toward the cafeteria. "Come on. Some conversation might help."

I slumped down, rubbing the back of my neck. "I'll be there in a bit, Syl. My numbers are bad today. I'm just going to fix this and then I'll be down." She hesitated a second, then left. I felt guilty leaving her on her own, but I wanted to look at Alice's notebook undisturbed.

π

My hunger got the better of me after about twenty fruitless minutes and I decided I couldn't think anymore without food in my belly. My footsteps echoed in the barren hallway, reverberating forbiddingly.

When I neared the elevators where we'd seen Molly all those weeks ago, I heard the swish of an elevator's doors. I rounded the corner in the opposite direction of the lunchroom, curious.

Someone's heels tapped an uneven staccato, and I glimpsed the distinctive floral pattern of the skirt I'd loaned Alice disappear around the corner.

"Alice!" I caught myself just in time to keep my shout from carrying all the way to Catalina.

"Alice!" I hissed again, picking up my pace and scurrying around the corner. The empty corridor stretched for what looked like the length of the building. It was painted the same drab beige-green as the rest of the place, but the doors were all shut and none had windows.

Most of the offices where we computers worked were open bullpens and the engineers and managers, like Mr. Elliot, had offices off short hallways attached, their doors nearly always open and a window taking up about a third of it. I tiptoed past several doors, the silence pressing down on me. Not a phone ringing, not a stapler or Teletype machine, none of the regular sounds of any office. About halfway down, a shimmer of bluish light leaked from around the edges of a barely open door.

I crept as close as I could and tried to peer through the slim opening. A noxious miasma of decay kept me from being able to look too long, but I made out the backs of several women sitting at desks. I had to pull away because the stench made my eyes water, and I heard a wet squelching sound from behind the door. My stomach somersaulted over my intestines, and I hurried away before I started heaving right there.

I fled down two flights of stairs and locked myself in a bathroom stall, a paper towel drenched in cold water pressed to the back of my neck. Repeated scrubbing with the harsh industrial soap from the dispenser did nothing to remove the smell of rot from my nostrils. There was no way I could work now. I had to get Alice's notebook and go home. The backs of the women I glimpsed could have belonged to anyone, but one of them had to be Alice. It just had to be.

I was able to leave early at the mere mention of ladies' issues to Mr. Elliot. His toupee listed slightly to the right, and he swept a hand over his forehead when he waved me off, blanching. With Alice's notebook on my lap, I leaned back into the cushion of my sofa and pulled the sheet she'd slept on up to my face. Traces of her perfume still lingered, and I breathed deeply to cleanse my sinuses of the reek from the office. I twirled a pencil in my fingers and tapped my foot to the beat of the record I put on. This time, I was hoping Chet and his band would jog my memory and shed light on what was in the notebook.

For a time, I let the notes drift around me, finding the tune between them. If only I could be as cool as Chet's jazz, I thought. My jangly nerves finally quieted, but no memories came flooding back.

The notebook was open to a page in the middle. Some numbers had been traced over and over so many times that the paper was nearly torn; I traced the eraser end of my pencil lightly over them, trying to decode the mess they were a part of. Lazily, I went over each number several times, then turned the page and ran my finger over the impressions Alice's pencil had made. Equations, numbers, and symbols all running together.

The scratching of the needle prompted me to turn the record over. I closed Alice's notebook and hugged it to my chest as I lay down on the sofa. Drifting off to sleep, I pictured the pages. Messy and jumbled, but still obviously some kind of problem being worked out. I fell asleep with the image of Alice scribbling in the notebook, head bent close to it, her hair framing her face.

$$\pi$$

My neck was cricked the next morning from sleeping on the sofa, and I massaged it while pouring some coffee. There was no way I could go back to work today, but I had no better idea of what to do with the notebook this morning than I had the night before.

Walking to the drugstore to use the pay phone helped clear my head a bit. I left a message with the switchboard that I was still sick, then bought some blank notebooks and pencils and took them back to my apartment. To relax, I decided to rework the promotion test problems from Elliot.

I found my original mistake and snorted ruefully to the empty room. It felt good to do the work correctly, to lose myself in the functions and graphs. Setting it next to Alice's notebook on the table when I was done, I flipped her notebook open to a random page. My eyes flicked back and forth from one to the other. At first, all I saw was the contrast between the neatness of mine and the messiness of hers.

Reaching for my coffee, I stopped, my hand blocking out part of Alice's page. What was still visible was a graph like what I had just drawn. Untidy, but the same. Coffee forgotten, I started to see parts of what she'd done. It was the promotion test problem, disjointed and rearranged. I flipped pages, looking for another function, my eyes skipping from line to line, parts of what she had done starting to come together.

In between the broken parts of her solution emerged something else, now that I knew I was looking at components. Our cipher. The same word encoded over and over: *mistake, mistake, mistake.* Questions tumbled one over another in my mind. None of them had a straightforward answer, but one thing was certain. I had to get into Alpha Section.

π

The next day, I knocked on Mr. Elliot's open office door. He didn't look up from what he was reading. I cleared my throat.

"Yes, Leslie? Feeling better?" he said, still not looking up. A small desk fan blew his rank body odor around the office.

I put on my best contrite act. "Mr. Elliot, would you reconsider me for Alpha? I know it's not usually done, but, well, I'd truly appreciate it." I handed over an envelope with my new solution to the test problem.

He looked at it dubiously, hesitating to touch it, and raised an eyebrow at me. He took it and opened it with clear reluctance. As he read, still not saying anything, he seemed to relax. I clasped my hands behind my back and waited.

"Well, Miss Keyes," he said finally, "this is utterly delightful."

My math has never been called "delightful" and in his mouth, it sounded grim, accompanied as it was by Elliot licking his lips. I could have sworn he was drooling a bit, too. I suppressed a tremor of revulsion. He stood up quickly from behind his desk, the sudden jerking motion making his toupee slip. With a sickening undulation, the hairpiece righted itself, leaving behind a yellowish slick at his temple.

I swallowed down my rising gorge. "Is it delightful enough for Alpha?" I didn't even recognize the treacly simper as my voice.

"Oh, absolutely, Leslie, no doubt in my book." He stroked the paper on his desk again. "And as it happens, a seat opened up this morning. I'll have to make a few arrangements, but I think you can start after lunch!"

He offered his hand and I shook it, waiting to wipe the clamminess on my skirt until I was out of his office.

π

I followed Sylvia down to the cafeteria at lunchtime, scanning the room for Alice. "They found her last night," Sylvia whispered, eyes darting around the cafeteria. "Exsanguinated, they say."

"Who? Who did they find?" I had only been half listening to her after I sat down. I was trying to figure out a way to tell her about my meeting with Elliot.

"Molly Sykes," she said. "Her landlady was around to collect rent. Hadn't seen her in weeks, so she let herself into the apartment. Poor old thing passed out right after she called the police."

I finished chewing my bite of chipped beef on toast. "Have you heard from Gloria at all?"

"No," Sylvia said, knitting her brows. "And Charlie called me last night asking, too. Do you think we should tell the MPs or something?"

Before I could answer, Mr. Elliot stopped by our table.

"Alpha Section awaits, Miss Keyes!" He tipped an imaginary hat and ambled away.

"Syl, I've been trying to figure out a way to tell you all morning," I stammered at Sylvia's surprised face.

She shivered and shook her head. "Just stay safe."

π

"Come, sit, we don't want to waste a moment."

Mr. Elliot held the door open for me; the same one I had tried to peek into before. The room was windowless. Arranged in rows were study carrels, like in a library. In one corner was a tall stool. Mr. Elliot ushered me to one of the carrels and I sat. The desk was a lot like my station in the bullpen: paper, pencils, everything lined up neat as a pin.

"The others will be in shortly. If you open that folder, you can begin."

I opened the folder and took out the page of functions, none of which appeared to be anything different from what I had been working on before. As I worked through them, the shuffling of many feet passed behind me. I tried to lean back to see who was walking there, but before I could make anything out, they had all slipped into chairs. I could see the women's shoes on either side of me and recognized Gloria's red pumps to my right.

"Now, ladies, if you please," Mr. Elliot's voice came from the corner, and I raised my head slightly. He sat on the stool and I could only see his toupee over the tops of the carrels. Almost as one, the women's pencils began scratching on their paper. I was tempted again to try and look at who was sitting on my left, but I kept working, biding my time. The light from the overhead fixtures flickered and was replaced by a weak yellow glow.

The strange light made it hard to see, so I bent closer to my work. I got lost in the math for a little while, the familiarity of it giving me a chance to collect my thoughts. I hadn't counted on being here so quickly and didn't exactly have a plan. What plan I did have amounted to "gather information." I sighed, smoothing a fresh sheet of paper down, kicking myself for not paying closer attention to the section of the employee manual about counterintelligence.

From the wall behind me, I felt the rush of the air conditioning hit my sweaty back, but instead of the barely detectable scent of coolant that usually came with it, it was that noxious smell that had driven me off before. Shifting in my seat, I tried to get out of the vent's direct path. I shifted again, thinking the sound my seat made was weird, but it didn't stop when I stopped moving. The wet, popping squelch accompanied a fresh wave of the fetid smell. I waved my hand in front of my face to try and fan it away.

Squaring my shoulders, I tried to focus on the paper in front of me again and began the next solution. Something moved just out of the corner of my eye and disappeared over the top of the divider between my carrel and Gloria's when I quickly turned my head. I started to think I'd imagined it when I saw movement again, but this time I kept my head down. Slowing my breath, I kept at the problem on the paper as much as I could, but my pencil kept slipping in my sweaty fingers.

I felt a cold drip on my shoulder and whatever it was oozed a short trail down my arm before I jumped up and swiped at it in disgust. The back of my hand made contact with cold slime, sinking into the spongy flesh of a blue-flecked tentacle just before it retreated over the divider.

Taking one step back, I could see Gloria now, her pencil moving across a piece of paper, her head drooped down over her work. Attached to her temples were two more tentacles, the blue spots on them pulsating. I sucked in a horrified breath and scrambled back to my seat, screwing my eyes shut.

Sitting perfectly still, I tried to make sense of it. Not Communists. Not even industrial espionage. I was afraid if I tried to run for the door, one of those tentacles would manage to catch me and squeeze me like a boa constrictor, so I sat there stock still. I looked down at the desk, at the problem I had been working on before. That thing had made its approach while I had been working on it. I needed to get a better look at it, I decided, so I started on the function again.

It didn't take long before I heard a slithering coming over the divider. I worked methodically, moving nothing but my pencil. I chanced a flick of my eyes to the right and saw the tip of it nearly at my elbow. The more I worked, the closer it got.

A cold ooze hit my shoulder again and the shock made me skip closing a parenthesis before continuing. At my mistake, the tip of the tentacle reared back as if I had burned it. I froze. So did it. I fixed my mistake and worked on the problem some more, letting the tentacle get closer. I stopped writing and chanced an actual look at the thing. It was inches from me, suspended over the divider and dripping its slime onto the corner of my desk. Pockmarked with pustules, each one spewing more of the greasy slime, the tentacle was the size of a tree branch at its widest, tapering to the width of my hand. It swayed and I caught a glimpse of the underside, segmented and shiny.

Gradually, I started again, breathing shakily. But this time I purposely made a basic arithmetic error. The tentacle recoiled even further and faster than before but didn't retreat over the divider. I worked more, making several more mistakes until the monstrous thing was out of sight.

Mistakes, mistakes, mistakes. Alice's message. I stifled the yelp in my throat, gulping down huge breaths of the fetid, disgusting air of the office. My heart beat jackrabbit fast and my page swam in front of my eyes. After a minute, I peeked over the other divider of my carrel, toward the far corner of the room where I had last seen Mr. Elliot.

The ruins of a body sat on the stool, split in two down the middle from scalp to belly. A mass of slime and flesh spread out from it and tentacles reached toward all the computers in their carrels, over the dividers. There was no sign of a toupee, but it had to be Elliot. Each bluish appendage pulsed like the throat of a reptile swallowing its prey whole. The center of the creature's mass increased and emanated more of the carrion stench with every pulse.

Panicking, I scrabbled over to Gloria and grabbed one tentacle that was attached to—sucking—her temple. I yanked it off her and the other tentacle let go simultaneously, the jagged, tooth-filled orifice at the end of it gaping and dripping. Gloria's body slumped against me, revealing a ragged bloody opening where the tentacle had been attached, with bits of gray matter stuck to the skin. I let the thing go, and it reeled back toward Elliot's body.

Mistakes. What had I done to Gloria? Her head lolled back and her empty eyes stared up. Dead. I let her down quietly and bit back a sob. Guttural, muffled moaning came from the slimy, writhing mass in the corner. I raced to the next carrel. I didn't know the woman sitting there, but she had the same pale and sucked-dry appearance Molly Sykes had when I first saw her.

I resisted the urge to rip the tentacles off her. Over the far row of carrels, the tips of several tentacles rose as if tasting the atmosphere, glowing a bilious green. Puckered sphincters on each tentacle leaked mucus as they went. I crouched down next to the woman and carefully pulled the pencil from her fingers. Without it, her arm went still, and she laid her hand on the desk. I scribbled "3 + 3 = 11" on the paper, then I erased some of what she'd written and replaced it with random numerals and letters. The woman didn't react. The tentacles at her temples stopped pulsating, though. I put the pencil back in her hand and tried tracing over what I'd written. The tentacles let go of her, hovering inches away.

I had to get them to make their own mistakes somehow. More searching green and blue tentacle tips slid closer, creeping along the tops of the dividers like so many snakes. I hurried in the opposite direction, realizing almost too late that I was going toward the source of the tentacles. I stopped and half-crawled under the nearest desk, coming face to face with the familiar floral print of my skirt.

I scooted out and looked up at Alice. Her hair was mostly loose, the winding, crinkly tendrils haloing her head. I had to stop myself from seizing the tentacles suckered to her temples. I clenched my jaw tightly in thought. Somehow, I had to get her and the others to make their own mistakes. I sat there for an eternity, powerless.

My eyes streamed and I choked up—and not just from the putrid stench. Crying about mistakes. The only time I ever cried about making mistakes was when I was learning to do algebra and my sister would start counting loudly backward from one hundred to distract my train of thought. Every time she did it, I would make some basic errors and cry in frustration. It made her cackle with glee that she had gotten me to cry without ever laying a hand on me.

I got as close to Alice's ear as I could, the slime and the stench of the tentacle there turning my stomach to acid, and started to whisper in her ear, "One hundred, ninety-nine, ninety-eight, ninety-seven…."

I continued, watching her write. By the time I got to the seventies, she made her first mistake. I kept going, reversing the count at forty, then going backward again. I glanced at her paper, now full of mistakes. At last, the pulsing and sucking of the tentacles stopped and they retreated. I pushed the paper away and took the pencil from her fingers.

"Alice, Alice, can you hear me?" I shook her shoulder, my voice gone hoarse. Her head wobbled, and she clutched my arm briefly. A trickle of blood inched down from her temple to her cheek and I swiped at it, my eyes searching hers for any sign of recognition. From the other side of the divider came a wet slither and Alice's eyes widened.

Haltingly, she turned to face me, her mouth a rictus of fear and her fingers sinking into my arm.

"Alice, can you talk?" She worked her mouth and squeezed her eyes shut before shaking her head. I put my hand over hers and squeezed. "You were right, Alice. Mistakes." Her eyes lit up in understanding, then she tilted her head. I smiled. "I'm going to try and feed it more mistakes. Get under the desk."

She nodded and watched me crawl to the woman at the next desk. I had to maneuver around three slick tentacles as thick as my arm to get to her ear. It took me several minutes of whispering numbers to her for her to start making mistakes. The greasy slime pooled under my hand where I rested it on her desk. I kept going even after the last tentacle let go of her. Alice watched from under her desk, new understanding dawning on her face.

By the time I was two desks away, Alice had crabwalked out of her hiding place and was bent close to another woman's ear, lips moving slowly, finally able to force herself to speak. I was at the end of Alice's row of carrels and I glanced down to where she was, whispering to another woman. There were four women between us—not counting Gloria's corpse—slumped in their chairs, eyes blinking and hands twitching. I did some quick math, now that I had gotten a better look at the room, and calculated that there were probably fifty women left with that thing sucking the life out of them. The quivering mass in the corner expelled a stream of yellow, clotted material and expanded to encompass several more feet.

I watched Alice at the next woman's desk, her movements surer now. She whispered in the woman's ear and I noticed the tentacle's pulse as the woman's mistakes started. Instead of a blue-green glow that traveled back to the main mass of Elliot's ruined body, a red streak appeared instead. When it reached the mass in the corner, the whole rubbery mound bubbled and shook, then resumed its pulsing as the rest of the women's work fed it.

Crawling as fast as I could, I joined Alice at the other end of the row, my idea becoming clearer when I got there, seeing another red streak fly and another tentacle release.

"Leslie!" She threw her arms around me in an awkward hug, a kiss landing on my ear. "I knew you'd figure it out!"

"*You* fig—" I began, then shook my head. "Never mind."

I hugged her back, my mind racing. Quickly, I explained what we needed to do, gesturing at the women we'd already freed. All of them were now out of their chairs, making their way toward us on all fours, avoiding the dripping tentacles that still searched the room. Once they were all close enough, I repeated my plan.

"If we stand up—"

"We can't make that much noise, that thing will—"

I held up my hand, stopping their protests. "If we don't do this, none of us have a chance. Come on." A shuddering groan from the corner shook the room, silencing any more discussion.

Alice and I joined hands and stood up, the others following. With a nod, we started our backward count. The rest of the women joined in. After we reached the eighties, our chants overlapped one another.

At our increasing volume, every tentacle that wasn't feeding from a computer turned our way, searching us out. The woman next to me swayed on her feet but kept chanting numbers through clenched teeth. I grabbed her hand and her eyes flew open, terror replaced by relief when she saw me. We both nodded encouragingly and chanted louder.

Red streaks started flowing up more of the tentacles and I nodded at them to Alice. Her chanting got louder, too. More and more red streaked toward the writhing creature, the tentacles in my line of sight stiffening with each new mistake. The stench filling the room compounded, a cloud of sickening green rising from all the tentacles, the slimy ooze evaporating. Every woman must have been making mistakes, mistakes of every conceivable kind in their arithmetic, calculus, trigonometry, and differential equations. Computers who never made mistakes, who were always precise, abruptly starved the creature of its sustenance at precisely the same moment.

All at once, an explosion of gray-green filled the room, coating every surface with spongy fleshy flecks and dripping yellow pus. I continued chanting through it, Alice's chant right along with me and her hand still holding mine. The woman beside me let go of my hand and I wiped my face with the back of it. I looked around the room. Women were half-sprawled out of their chairs. Some were coming around, eyes slits in the gooey mess that covered everyone. One by one, we all stopped chanting and stared at the corner.

I picked up a slide rule and moved toward it. Alice briefly pulled my wrist, but I shook her off. I had to make sure it was dead. Inching closer, my feet slipped in more of the muck and spongy bits on the floor. No trace remained of Elliot, or his skin, or whatever the creature had been masquerading as. I nudged a mound of quivering jelly with a toe and it lost its shape, pooling out into the rest of the glop. Looking back over my shoulder at Alice, I shot her a weak smile.

She came over to me after helping one woman up from her chair. "Well, what's your plan now?" she asked.

I put my hands on my hips, but before I could answer, the door burst open. Men in Military Police uniforms skidded into the room, their boots no match for the slime. A few of them blanched at the smell. A sergeant who remained in the doorway radioed for reinforcements.

π

Several hours later, we were dismissed. No one asked about the smell, the tentacle parts, the spongy flesh, or Elliot. It didn't matter that we all told the same basic story. They concluded that some kind of Soviet device had been deployed in Alpha Section to thwart the work being done there. At any mention of the creature or what we thought it had been doing, the men exchanged looks. Looks we were all familiar with. Looks that said they were done listening to a bunch of neurotic women.

A pair of MPs dropped Alice and me off at my apartment in a Jeep after we'd signed papers promising never to divulge what we thought we'd seen. We took turns in my shower getting cleaned up and finally settled on my sofa, wrapped up in blankets, with Chet playing on the record player.

"Hysteria, that's what they called it," she said finally, taking a sip of the tea I had made after our showers. I didn't answer right away. The men in gray flannel suits who had questioned me said similar things. "Maybe it was the Commies," she muttered.

I blew out an irritated sigh. "It doesn't matter what it was—space aliens, the Creature from the Black Lagoon, the mob, they'll still say it was the Communists. It's the only way they can try to make sense of it." I could tell by her face that Alice agreed with me. It didn't matter; those men would tell their own version of it.

"It was feeding off us, wasn't it?" Alice said, looking into her cup of tea.

I shuddered, remembering the way the tentacles squirmed and sucked when they were attached to Alice's head. I couldn't imagine what that had felt like.

Alice continued, as if reading my thoughts. "It felt like…oh, I can't describe, Les. Every problem, formula, and function I'd ever seen, swirling around in my brain, and I couldn't focus on anything else. It got harder and harder to think, to do the math. The longer I was in that office, the worse it got." She paused, getting quieter. "Until I barely knew who I was. Everything slipping away. I was losing everything that was me. I was losing it all." She looked at me, her eyes shimmering with emotion. I gathered her up into my arms, ignoring the tea that spilled onto the sofa and blanket.

I kissed the top of her head, inhaling the scent of my shampoo—and under it, Alice. Just Alice. Her arms wound around me and we sat in one another's embrace until our breathing was in sync.

"You found your way back to me. You left me that message, in the notebook."

She pulled away from me a short distance and looked me in the eye. Her gaze was steady, and her tears stopped. I took in a sharp breath to speak, my words dissolving at the press of Alice's lips on mine. In that moment, I forgot it all: math, Elliot, tentacles, NASA, and let Alice kiss me.

SARAH LAZARZ

TRAINS PASSING

Martin Zeigler

A voice, confident but prerecorded, booms over the speakers, welcoming everyone aboard VFAR.

Jean Albers, nestled in her window seat, feels welcome indeed. Very welcome aboard the *Very Fast Automated Railway*.

Three months ago, while searching online for the perfect summer vacation, she happened across VFAR's website. She clicked on the *Very Fast* button. She clicked on the *Automated*. And before she knew it, she clicked on the *Railway* to place her reservation.

If only she could have invited along one or two of her best students. She is certain they would have felt as welcome as she.

A momentary lurch, and the train pulls out of the station. "Get set for the ride of a lifetime," the voice continues. "A superfast, automated journey along three thousand miles of perfectly straight track, with not one curve or crossing to slow us down!"

Already Jean can feel the train pick up speed. In no time, it will reach the astounding velocity of 400 miles per hour and hold steady all the rest of the way.

Well, most of the way, she concedes. Obviously, the train will need to slow down as it nears the end of the line. But that's a long way off, and besides, she has no interest in the end of the line or in the luxurious hotel awaiting her there. The end of the line is merely a place to spend the night before catching the morning train back.

The morning train with an even faster speed of 440 miles per hour.

Impressive numbers indeed, 400 and 440. But it was not the *Very Fast* that sold Jean on this trip. It was the *Automated.* The speeds can be 20 and 22 for all she cares, as long as they remain perfectly constant.

Jean prefers perfection. Those perfect straight tracks. Those perfect, uniform speeds. That perfect travel story she hopes to tell her most perfect students.

Although seated by the window, she resists turning to it and looking out. She already knows what's outside, having perused VFAR's homepage with its breathtaking images and breathless prose. "Come," the wording urged. "Hurtle with us at eye-opening speed through miles upon miles of deep green forest. Past endless stretches of glistening, golden sands and white-capped waters. Through enduring distances of colossal mountain ranges and vast, colorful canyons."

The view, along with the jaw-dropping velocities, might be just the thing to captivate the average VFAR rider, but not Jean Albers. She has seen pictures of a forest, a beach, and a mountain, and therefore has seen them all. True, she does have a reason for sitting next to the window, but it has nothing to do with casting her eyes on wood, sand, or rock.

So she turns away from the window and takes in the rest of the car. Except for the seat next to her, every place is taken. She figures the other dozen or so cars are nearly full as well.

Seeing these people around her, seated in neat rows and columns, reminds her of a classroom, albeit a very narrow one. She would very much like to stand before this class right now and expound on her reason for embarking on this trip, but she suspects these students would continue staring out their windows at the passing wood, sand, and rock, oblivious to her every word.

She focuses instead on the monitor suspended from the ceiling. A digital map shows two tracks running side by side. The dot on the southbound track represents a train well on its way. The other train, represented by the dot on the northbound track, has recently left the station, as she well knows, since this is the train she's riding and feeling very welcome aboard at this very moment.

A number adjoined to each dot confirms both trains are now tooling along at their maximum velocities. And as if that isn't encouraging enough, a third number floating between the dots assures Ms. Albers that her adventure will begin within the hour.

"Excuse me, is this seat taken?"

Jean turns to the woman standing in the aisle and nearly recoils at the sight of her unusual appearance. Jean feels a rush of self-consciousness for reacting like this, and yet here she is, frantically casting her eyes elsewhere, on the arm of the empty seat, on the backrest, on anything other than the woman's face.

Jean knows this is nothing new. Her mind shoots back to those students of hers who were teased relentlessly over their looks or their physiques or the way they dressed. She recalls how she seated them in the back of the classroom and seldom called on them, how she behaved like their tormentors more than she cared to admit.

And now, facing this stranger who has asked a simple question, Jean finds herself staring at the woman's shirt collar, unable to utter a single syllable.

"Silly me," the woman says, filling the uneasy pause. "Of course, the seat's taken. I reserved it. I just couldn't figure out what else to ask."

The woman slips into her seat and adjusts its recline position, all the while staring at the forward bulkhead directly in front of her. "I suppose we can't do any better than this," she says. "First pair of seats in the first car, at the very front of the train. Any farther forward, and we'd have to wake the engineer."

"Except," Jean declares, "there is no engineer to wake on a train that's—"

"On a train that's fully automated," the woman says, completing the thought.

Jean feels every bit the fool, thinking the woman needed correcting, when obviously she was trying to be witty, perhaps as a defensive mechanism to mask her insecurities.

"Sorry," Jean says, glancing over. "Nothing worse than explaining a joke to the person telling it."

"That makes one silly me and one silly you," the woman says with a smile. "We're even."

Jean glimpses the smile and immediately seeks something else to look at.

"My name's Sam," the woman says, extending her hand.

Jean balks at the hand's scaling and redness as if they might be contagious. Then, taking a deep breath, she grips the hand all the heartier and offers her best smile. "Pleased to meet you, Sam."

"It's short for Samantha."

"Then Samantha it is. I'm Jean."

"Hello, Jean. And Sam's fine. I'm used to it. Most people see me as a Sam anyway."

Jean gives a brief nod and would like to leave things like this, with the introductions out of the way and no more to be said. It then occurs to her she will have to spend nearly eight hours in the company of this woman, and it would be rude not to say at least something every once in a while. So she tests the waters with, "Is this your first trip on a train, Sam? You know, because of not knowing what to ask?"

"Yes, as a matter of fact. And I live close by, believe it or not. Close by the VFAR station, I mean, which isn't all that close to us anymore. You'd think I would've taken this trip long before now. I've had plenty of opportunity. But I suppose I just wanted to wait until the time was right. It's a big decision."

Jean nods ever so slightly, unsure why a train trip would qualify as a big decision. "It is a bit pricey," she ventures.

"It was a freebie," Sam says.

"Oh, a special offer? It's good you waited."

"I suppose that's how some would see it. But what about you?"

The conversation has turned into one of sitting back in seats, facing forward, and glancing now and then in the other's direction. Jean prefers it this way, and she imagines Samantha feels the same.

"I wasn't so lucky," Jean says. "I had to pay full price."

"No, what I mean is: is this your first trip as well?"

"Why, yes, it is."

"Back when I was a child," Sam says, "there was a game our neighbors played with me called 'two words.' Someone asked you a question, and you had to answer it in exactly that many words; no more. So, Jean, if you had to summarize your reason for being here in just two words, what would they be?"

"Two words...that's it?"

"I'm afraid so."

For Jean, the implication is clear. If a pair of words is all that's required, then any two words will basically put an end to further discussion. But to simply pick two words out of thin air and call it good smacks of a shoddy trick a lazy student might pull to finish an assignment. The least Jean can do is give this some thought, take up the challenge of boiling down her trip's singular purpose into a brace of relevant words.

Finally, she says to Sam, "Okay. I think I have it. How about *trains passing?*"

"Ah," Sam says. "That's interesting. Like ships passing? Ships passing in the night?"

Jean already somehow expected that two words wouldn't be sufficient, that there would follow the inevitable questions, extending the two words into the full-blown conversation they were supposed to prevent. But that's all right, she decides. She was hoping to open up to someone about the whys and wherefores of her journey anyway. It might as well be to this poor unfortunate thing sitting next to her.

Jean shrugs. "No, nothing as mysterious as all that, I'm afraid. In truth, you'll probably think my reason ranks as another silly me."

"Well, then, silly me right back, because I'd really like to know."

Jean flashes Sam a smile. "It has to do with living a story problem."

"Story problem? From algebra, you mean?"

"Yes. I'd like to think I'm an excellent math teacher, you see, and—"

"And I bet your students just can't wait to find out how old Mary is if she's eight years older than Bill and in six years will be twice as old as Bill will be," Sam says with a chuckle.

"Mary's ten," Jean says. "And Bill is two."

"Let's see…say, you're right. What do you know? I just made that up on the spot."

Jean wonders if Sam actually worked this out or is simply agreeing. She has witnessed this behavior before, this desperate desire to be on an equal level.

Jean says, "You obviously remember those kinds of problems very well. Story problems. Or word problems, if you prefer."

"Oh, I definitely remember the word problems from back then," Sam says. "In algebra, first of all. Then history. Then home economics and phys ed. Eating lunch in the cafeteria. Riding the bus to and from school."

Jean, about to admit she doesn't understand, realizes she fully understands, having overheard those sorts of words being flung at others out in the hallway while in her office between classes.

"But enough of my fond high school memories," Sam says, waving them aside, "I want to hear all about how one lives a story problem."

"You sure, Sam?"

"Oh, absolutely. Hit me, as they say."

Fully in her element now, safely tucked under her blanket of expertise, Jean twists in her seat to face the woman she has up to now pretty much rejected. As long as she treats Sam as an entire classroom and darts her eyes about as if from student to student, the going will be much easier.

She begins by pointing to the same monitor she looked at earlier. "See those dots?" she says.

Sam glances at the monitor, then over at Jean. "Yes, I do. Two dots."

"Well," Jean says, "the one on the right is our train, heading up north. The dot on the left, on the other track, is the train coming down *from* the north. Do you see them?"

"Yes, Jean. I still see them."

"Those numbers next to the dots tell us how fast the trains are traveling. Can you tell me what they say?"

"Really?" Sam says. "You want me to read them aloud?"

"If you will, please."

"Okay," Sam sighs. "Our train is traveling at four hundred miles an hour. The other train's going four hundred forty miles an hour."

"Very good, class. I mean, Sam. And do you see that number between the dots?"

"Yes, I do see that number. Would you like me to read it so the rest of the car can hear?"

"Oh, Sam," Jean says. "I am so sorry. I do get carried away at times, especially when it comes to imparting knowledge."

"I apologize, too, for being short with you. I don't know what got into me." She utters a nervous laugh. "First train ride jitters, I guess."

Jean responds with an understanding smile and says, "Anyway, that number between the dots—and, no, I won't make you read it to me—gives the current distance between the two trains. But it isn't quite where I want it yet. Once it gets to one thousand two hundred sixty miles, *that's* when the story problem begins."

"The one you'll live."

"Yes, that's right. Would you like to hear it?"

"I'd like nothing better."

Closing her eyes, visualizing the problem in her head exactly as she had formulated it months ago, Jean lays it all out. "Two trains, traveling toward each other on parallel tracks, are one thousand two hundred sixty miles apart. Their speeds are four hundred miles per hour and four hundred forty miles per hour. How much time will elapse before the trains begin to pass?"

"I've certainly familiar with four hundred and four hundred forty by now," Sam says. "But where did you get one thousand two hundred sixty?"

"Teachers do their homework, too, Sam. I studied the VFAR website long before placing a reservation. I learned the range of distances involved. Any distance between the trains can be used, but I chose a distance that makes the problem work out nicely."

"Meaning twelve hundred and sixty miles."

"Exactly."

"So once our trains get that far from each other, the answer to your problem will tell us how long it'll take before the southbound VFAR comes by."

"A very good way to put it, Sam. And I'll be right here by this window when it does come by."

"And that's why you took this train on this particular day?"

"Well, Sam. It could have been any day. The answer would still be the same."

"Then why take the train at all?"

"Simple. To witness, firsthand, a textbook problem reflecting reality."

"Reality?"

Recognizing the look of confusion on the part of her student, a look Jean is blissfully familiar with—a confusion begging for clarification—Jean explains, "Think about it, Sam. These kinds of problems, what are called time-rate-distance problems, rarely represent real life at all."

"No?"

"No. To take a simple example, they'll have Joe driving along at sixty miles per hour and then ask you how far he will travel in one hour. The expected answer, of course, is sixty miles. But since when has anyone driven down the highway at a steady, never-changing speed of sixty miles an hour for an entire hour? Forget the hour. Try it for five minutes. You can't do it. At some point you'll let up on the gas or press down, if only slightly, which will change your speed and ultimately your distance. Joe's kind of driving usually only happens in the world of textbooks."

Jean pauses for effect, hardly noticing the woman next to her raising a finger to exclaim, "Aha! But with VFAR you *do* keep a constant speed, because the trains are fully automated."

Expecting a question and hearing none, Jean continues on. "But with VFAR, Sam, no one's foot is on the gas, so to speak, because the trains are fully automated. And do you know what this means? It means their speeds remain constant."

"I believe that's what I said, Jean."

"Yes, but do you see what I'm saying, Sam?"

"Yes, I believe I do."

"Are you sure? This is important."

"Yes, I definitely see. Your story problem actually works, because the speeds never vary."

Jean exhales a sigh of success. With a little patience, she has finally gotten through to her student. "That's right. Now you may ask: how, then, will I live this problem? Well, Sam, I'll tell you. Right now the timer on my cellphone is set to the answer to the problem. Once the distance on that overhead monitor reads one thousand two hundred sixty, I'll activate the timer. Immediately, it will begin its countdown. And the instant the countdown hits zero will be the instant the southbound train comes barreling past my window. That's why I chose a window seat. Not to watch the trees and the tides whiz by, the way everyone else is doing, but to watch the engine of the other train fly past my window. At exactly zero seconds. Exactly."

Before Sam can respond, Jean says, "Will that engine pass by when the timer's at three seconds, Sam?"

"Uh, no. Zero seconds."

"Will it pass by at two seconds?"

"No, it won't."

"How about one?"

"Jean, will you please stop?"

Jean understands the exasperation in Sam's tone but maintains this sort of drilling is necessary. "When will the train pass, then, Sam? Take your time."

"Zero seconds, Jean. I already said that. When the timer on your cellphone hits zero seconds, that's when the other train will pass."

Jean squeezes her fists in academic triumph. "Absolutely correct. And so I hope you can see that what we have here is a perfect example of a real-world problem."

Sam looks up, if only briefly. "Do you mean that, Jean? A real-world problem? Do you even know what a real-world problem is?"

"Of course. I recognized it as one right off. That's why I'm here. To see it in action. Who says life doesn't have a purpose?"

Sam, completely still for a moment, slowly raises her hand.

"Yes, Sam. Question?"

With a resigned look on her face, Sam drops her hand in her lap. "Never mind."

$$\pi$$

Jean settles back in her seat and faces the bulkhead, feeling that burst of satisfaction she has often experienced after getting a concept across. She senses the wheels beneath her gliding smoothly and swiftly along the silver rails, obediently maintaining a constant velocity.

"Jean, it's about there."

Jean snaps out of her reverie and turns to Sam, follows her pointing finger to the monitor. The two dots are approaching the magical 1,260.

"Oh, my, Sam. Thank you so much. What a shame it would be to go all this way and miss this moment."

"I figure, since I'm here, I might as well live your story problem right along with you."

Jean takes out her cell and brings up the countdown app, already preset to the proper time. She hovers her finger over the start button.

"Now," Sam says, matter of factly.

The distance on the monitor hits 1,260 just as Jean initiates the countdown.

"You're a lifesaver, Sam."

"I wouldn't go that far."

"I would."

Sam shrugs. "Anyway, we both have an hour and a half. Not too long a wait when you think about it."

"What did you just say?"

"It's not too long a wait. In the scheme of things."

"No, before that."

"Oh," Sam says. "An hour and a half. That's how long we'll need to wait."

"My God, you solved the problem! I didn't think you—" Jean stops midsentence, realizing this was often how she treated her troubled students, with minimal expectations. "I mean, how did you do it?"

"I just figured each train travels its own distance in the amount of time it takes until they pass. The total of those distances is twelve hundred sixty, so you solve for time by dividing that by eight-forty, the sum of the speeds, and you get one and a half hours."

"Well, I'm proud of you. You did it. You really did it."

Sam taps a finger to her own forehead. "That's because I'm really, really smart."

Jean smiles, uncertain whether to smile. "Yes. Yes, you are."

"That's how my father always introduced me, you see. My sister is absolutely gorgeous and no slouch intellectually. But when company came over, it was always, 'I'd like you to meet my beautiful daughter Angela. And over here is Sam, the brains of the family.'"

Listening to this, Jean comes to realize that for the past few minutes, she's been able to look at this woman without any thought as to her appearance. Now, conscious once again of Sam's—how best to put it? Imperfections?—Jean feels she ought to say something. She can't just sit here and remain silent. But what should she say? That looks don't matter? That Samantha is beautiful in her own way? That even homeliness disappears if you stare at it long enough or treat it like a classroom?

Jean reaches over and lays a hand on Sam's shoulder. "Sam, I'm not exactly a swimsuit model myself."

There, the words are out, in all their dishonest truthfulness. No, Jean has never modeled. Yes, she's been to her local swimming pool in a bathing suit many times.

Sam nods cordially. She's obviously heard everything that can possibly be said, including the silences. She pats Jean's hand, indicating it's all right to remove it from her shoulder, and says, "Maybe not, Jean, but you're a teacher. You face your students, and they face you. My job interviews never went that well. I'd face the person behind the desk, and they'd face their fingernails. Eventually, my father, using his influence, was able to land the brains of the family a position at a small startup company."

"That's good. Isn't it?" Jean says, withdrawing her hand.

"It was perfect, Jean. I worked in perfect solitude, and no one had a problem with me whatsoever. Even in the early stages, during the design phase, when I was up in front giving presentations, it was me in the shadows and my presentations in the light."

Jean decides to let her keep talking.

"I designed everything. The timing algorithms, the security procedures, the innumerable failsafe systems. These things functioned so well, in fact, that during the testing phase, I usually just sat alone in the quiet control room and stared at the error-free screens. And the screens didn't mind one bit. I've always had a good rapport with bright screens and blinking lights."

"That must have been encouraging in a way," Jean says.

Sam smiles politely. "For my job, yes. But after work, there was still that annoying thing called life. My dad had died unexpectedly, you see, and I inherited the huge, empty family home, along with all its reflective surfaces. After a year or two of that, I finally decided it was time."

"To move to a smaller place?"

"To take this trip."

On the one hand, Jean can't help but wonder, again, why Sam has waited so long to take this trip. On the other hand, this next hour and a half—or, more precisely, eighty-eight minutes and forty-two seconds—constitute the sole reason for

Jean taking this trip, and she wishes she could just settle quietly back in her seat. Settle back and pretend she wasn't let go during her very first year of teaching. Settle back and picture a handful of the world's sharpest students peering over her shoulder at her timer as it ticks away those problem-solving minutes.

Still, hearing out Sam's reason shouldn't take too much more time, if it's handled properly.

"Sam, can you tell me what made you decide to take the plunge?" Then, with a wink, Jean adds, "In two words?"

"Ah, yes, the game my neighbors played whenever I had a story to tell. Well, let's see. *Busman's holiday?*"

"Goodness," Jean says, catching on. "VFAR is the company you work for! You finally decided to ride the thing you helped create."

"Yes. Although I had to make a few adjustments before boarding."

"I think we all do that when we travel."

"Not like these."

"Oh?"

Sam points to the monitor. "Take those dots," she says.

Jean sees the dot coming down from the top. The dot heading up from the bottom. The number between the dots, so much less than it was before. And the speeds, just as unwavering and breakneck as they've been for some time.

It's the monitor pretty much as it's always looked, and Jean has no idea what Sam is referring to. "I'm afraid I'm missing it," she says.

"Right there. See? Looks like the other train didn't slow down one iota, which means the transition was perfect. Who says life doesn't have a purpose?"

"I still don't see—"

Sam says, "It's really quite simple, class. It's called a switch. Train A, which is our train, and Train B, which is coming down from the north, are no longer on different tracks."

Jean squints at the screen to bring it into tighter focus. The graphics are quite clear once you know what to look for.

So, too, is the number on her cellphone, diminishing its way steadily toward zero.

She tries to look over at Sam but can't.

She tries to find the words but can't.

She turns to look out her window. The world rushes by at such an astonishing speed, she hardly recognizes it, though she's certain she's seen it before.

She grips the armrest of her seat much too tightly, and Sam lays her possibly diseased hand atop Jean's. "Please don't give up living our problem," Sam says. "Yes, it's now more of a 'trains meeting' than a 'trains passing,' but the answer's still the same."

ASYMMETRICAL DREAMS

Josh Snider

Professor Sam Collin sat at his desk, fiddling with two new lamps that just arrived that morning. They were supposed to be identical, but minute differences made them two individual lamps that might have appeared the same to a less-observant eye. A small chip in the brown paint of one held his attention for the last hour as he mixed and remixed paint to match. He dabbed on the most recent attempt, finding the colors to be spot on.

"Perfect," Sam whispered to himself, smiling at his handy work.

The grandfather clock rang out three times, indicating time for his web seminar.

"Hell." He snatched the laptop from next to him.

An empty thud echoed through the room as he set the computer down a little too hard. Sam looked around as the computer booted up. Four bookcases lined the entry wall to his office, spaced perfectly even from each other and their opposing walls.

The computer booted up, displaying his log in screen. The background was covered in what appeared to be a random display of numbers that, when examined closely, revealed themselves to be evenly distributed and mirrored from one side to the other.

He quickly typed in the password and opened the video chat where he was set to present.

The camera loaded, showing an image of himself staring back. A small red dot on the left side of his forehead caught his attention.

"Crap." Sam leaned towards the camera, prodding the red spot.

The dark bump refused to budge, not yet ready to be popped. Sam dropped his hands in defeat, the one unevenly placed bump on his face now seared into his overattentive mind's eye. The webcam image staring back made it almost impossible to forget.

He sighed and clicked to enter the virtual room. The wheel spun around for what felt like forever before loading a larger picture of his face. No other cameras loaded. A blinking zero flashed at the bottom of the frame, indicating the number of participants.

After five minutes of staring at the unchanging digit, he began to inspect the number itself. The pixels appeared mirrored side to side, but something was off. He considered the plant where his computer had been manufactured.

How often do they calibrate the manufacturing machines?

He thought of the thousands of computers that were probably made before calibration, the minute changes in position that would mean some pixels wouldn't be quite exactly the same as the others.

Another five minutes of examining the zero and he gave up, ending the digital room.

A screen popped up displaying the name of his lecture:

The Symmetry of Numbers.

No one seems to care anymore. They're just happy to live in asymmetry and chaos.

He slammed the laptop closed and pushed himself back from the desk. The chair rolled easily across the hardwood floor and hit the wall behind him with a crunch.

Sam cringed, sitting still for a moment before risking a look. A small hole in the drywall glared back at him, irregular and crumbling.

Sam gave a defeated sigh and gently stood from his chair. He looked again at the hole. The darkness felt like it glared back and mocked him. He shivered and walked away before hyper focus could take hold.

The hall of his home was shadowed as the sun set outside, sending rays of orange light through the door on the front window. The right side of the hall was taken up by stairs, leaving the left feeling unbalanced and awkward to decorate.

He had settled on nothing more than a simple table with a bowl for his keys as the lone decoration there.

He peered down the hall, debating how to spend his newly free afternoon. Whoever designed the house decided the kitchen should take up nearly two thirds of the first floor. The only separate places were his office, the dining room across the entry way, and the thin restroom under the stairs.

Upstairs was split into two rooms, one on either half of the house. Sam spent the majority of his time up there, finding a relative peace in the mirrored sides. Even if he used the spare bedroom for storage rather than sleeping.

After the disappointment of another failed lecture, Sam decided a nap was the only thing he had the energy for.

Sam made it to the third step before a knock at the door forced him to whirl around in surprise. He stumbled and fell down the few steps to the landing. His tailbone radiated pain out into his hips and back as he tried to stand.

"Ow." Sam rubbed his low back and stepped to the door.

"Hello?" He called out, loud enough for anyone on the other side to hear.

Silence.

"Odd...."

He peered side to side to check the porch for anyone hiding beside the door. Seeing nothing, he dared to crack open the door.

Cool air flowed in from the autumn evening and sent a chill up his spine. He shivered in delight, breathing in the scent of fall before opening the door wider to check for visitors.

"Hello?" He called again.

A gentle breeze blew through the yard, sending multicolored leaves scattering across his lawn. Sam inspected both sides of the street, discovering no prankster out in the evening.

Sam looked down to find two packages placed perfectly on either side of his tan welcome mat. Both were the size of a textbook, wrapped in brown paper with a single, perfectly centered, piece of tape.

Annoyance bubbled in him. *Just another prankster, making fun of my OCD.*

He crouched down and snatched one of the packages, pulling it to his chest. Sam reached for the other one but found it missing. His brow furrowed as he tapped on the porch where the package had once sat.

Something above his hand shifted. The package now floated still in the air at the same height as the original he clutched to his chest.

"What...?" He reached out and poked the floating package.

The one in his grasp shifted slightly to the side as he pressed the other in the air.

A small pang of fear was quickly replaced by excitement and curiosity at the strange set of packages.

He stood, watching the second one rise parallel to his motions. It took some maneuvering to get the pair into his home before he could close the door. He went to enter his office and found the opposite book floated away from him into the dining room opposite his office.

"Huh." He walked back towards the center hallway of the house.

The package floated back towards him as well. Sam slowly backed away, carrying the package to his desk and gently setting it on the edge. Across the entry way, its double floated perfectly still in the air. He turned the package to face him lengthwise, gaze flicking to the mirror image as it spun around to face the far wall.

Sam lifted the far edge of the package, standing it on end and watching as the movement was mimicked.

What in the world are you two?

Sam picked up the package again and considered for a moment. Across the house from him, the dining room had an entirely separate set of furniture from his office. A china cabinet filled with the rarer books in his collection rather than pointless dishware. A small table and two chairs in the middle of the room, where empty space would be in his office. He gently tossed the package toward the approximate location of the chair.

Sam's eyes went wide as the package he just held bounced off of nothing, its copy hitting the chair noisily and falling to settle against the leg. The near package rested the same, against open air. His heart quickened at the results of his experiment. Sam couldn't wait any longer and snatched the package back up, excitement rising as he moved between the desk and chair to examine it.

He pulled the chair under him, watching the mirror copy float silently again in the dining room. Apprehension stayed his hand as he reached for the tape holding the paper closed.

What the hell am I doing? Sam shook his head, trying to clear his thoughts. He looked at the package in front of him, then its counterpart across the house.

Sam reached again for the tape. *It's just a dream, packages can't float.*

His fingernail caught the edge of the tape and tugged gently at it. It peeled back from the brown paper, lifting the corner with it. Sam glanced at the twin package. The flap on it also lifted.

A nervous excitement fluttered in his stomach. He pulled more at the paper, opening it fully to find a book looking back at him. The cover was ink black and devoid of text, almost like a black hole in the universe situated nicely on his desk. He tossed the paper away into the waste basket.

Another quick glance into the dining room. The paper was crumpled and sat as if it rested against the side of a trash can. Sam's heart hammered in his chest the further he investigated the strange occurrence happening in his home. His mouth dried as he considered the implications of this discovery.

Leaving the book on his desk, Sam got up and walked into the dining room. He examined the second book and waved a shaking hand underneath it. Nothing but empty space.

"How in the world…?" He tried to push the book down.

It didn't budge under the light push. Sam pressed down harder, lifting himself off the ground as he did so. A low groan escaped his desk from the office as if he had sat on the corner of it.

Sam released the book and backed up from it.

Truly perfect mirror images, but both are limited by what touches only one.

Sam gingerly picked up the second book and carried it towards the center of the house. As he crossed into the entryway, so did what he thought of as the first book. He held out the second one, slowly moving them closer together. Fear rose in his chest as the pair neared each other. Images of the books exploding violently raced through his mind. Sam gently pressed the tops of the books together. Nothing happened, save for meeting the resistance of the opposite book. He blew out a sigh of relief and chuckled at his own baseless fears. Sam grabbed the first book and walked back to his desk, letting the mirror float back across to the dining room.

He reached out and gently lifted the jet black cover. Yellowed pages inside felt uncomfortable on his fingers. They were too smooth, too perfect to have been crafted by man. Sam ran his fingers across the pages, finding them to feel like the same material as paper he was used to, though it was the texture of buffed marble.

The anxiety in his chest fell as he leafed through the floating book. The world around him stayed the same. No one came banging on his door for their possessed set of books back.

They are strange. It would be a shame if I didn't at least look through them.

He opened it past the first few pages. A language he couldn't recognize filled the first few pages, entirely alien compared to any written language he knew of. Strange symbols and lines went in all directions, even interconnecting on separate lines. The text continued for a few pages before diagrams and unusual shapes started filling entire pages. The shapes started as ordinary squares and circles. As he continued to turn the pages, they merged into each other, forming more complex diagrams that became harder to recognize. Every picture had been clearly hand drawn, the pages pressed inward where the pen would have scrawled them. Even so, he could find no flaw in the calligraphy.

The lines were exactly straight, the ink filling each indent perfectly aligned and the same width as every other one on the page.

Sam felt a strange tingle in the back of his mind the further he looked, like something being dragged across the nape of his neck. As much as he had fought against his own mind, the incessant need for perfection and order, he had never achieved such a level of symmetry as this book's author had.

Sam admired the lines on the first page with diagrams. The tickle in the back of his mind grew with each moment he looked at the pictures. Sam suddenly remembered the twin of this book still sat on his desk. He looked up to see it was open, a page hanging partially open as he held its duplicate up.

He dropped the page and jogged back to the first book. The contents were exactly the same: a language he couldn't place and perfect drawings.

The tickle came back as he compared the original book to what he saw in its partner. Slowly it turned into a growing pressure like someone stood behind him with their head pressed to the back of his, actively pushing into him.

Sam closed his eyes and held onto the desk for support. The pressure receded immediately, leaving him off balance and shaky.

"What the hell was that?" He rubbed his eyes.

Sam closed the book before opening his eyes again. The tome sat quietly in front of him, unimposing beyond the cover so dark it seemed to drink the light in around it.

His mind felt fuzzy the longer he looked at even the cover.

"Okay, I hate this dream." Sam rubbed his eyes again.

He left the book on his desk and gave the floating one a final glance before going up to his bedroom. A dull throbbing ache grew behind his eyes as he entered the dark room. He kicked off his house shoes, sending them scattering across the fluffed carpet. A small voice in the back of his mind screamed about such haphazard housekeeping but was drowned out by the growing pain.

Sam shook his head again before sitting on the bed. It felt like his brain was liquefying and sloshed inside his skull with each movement. He snatched open the bedside drawer and removed a bottle of painkillers. The rattle it gave seemed to vibrate to his core.

"Fuck." Even the whispered curse was too loud and grated on his ears.

Sam's vision shifted and flowed before he fell backward onto the bed.

π

Sam woke to the sound of birds chirping outside his window. He sat up and gazed lazily around his spartan room.

A king-sized bed was centered in the room, flanked by two dark brown bedside tables with matching lamps and an empty glass on each. White dressers sat on either side of the door. Only one held his clothes, though; the other remained empty in the hopes of a future partner.

Sam rubbed his eyes before standing. The night before felt distant, like a faraway thought from years long past.

"I really need to get this under control." He meandered to the bathroom. "Dreams about duplicate books?"

His disheveled reflection stared back at him. Brown hair stuck out in all directions and dark stubble prickled his face. Tired blue eyes gazed back, their whites reddened with exhaustion. A red dot with a white center poked from under his hair, just below the hairline.

Sam hummed at the sight and leaned in towards the mirror. He pressed a finger on either side, squeezing it. A light sting started where he squeezed and seemed to migrate to the other side of his forehead. The white dot in the center disappeared back under the skin as he squeezed.

"Damn. Not quite yet." He looked at the angry red skin around where he pressed.

Sam shrugged and turned on the faucet to wash his face. He closed his eyes and splashed the warm water up. As soon as his hands contacted his face, creating a more complete dark, images of his dreams from the night before flashed forward.

Strange shapes he had never seen before floated across his eyes. Ever-shifting cubes filled his mental vision before transforming into spheres, the Platonic solids, and figures for which he had no name. The ground beneath his bare feet shifted like it was alive. A landscape of mirror images and morphing reflections greeted his gaze he fell into the dream world that cascaded over his waking mind. Shadowed figures moved across the land without a single limb changing position. Sam felt himself turn to face the side of a cube that reflected his own face back. His reflection transformed into pure shapes before reforming into a nightmarish creature of symmetry. Teeth molded together, his eyes shifted towards each other and changed to yellow as they merged into a singular smooth globe.

Sam gasped, inhaling the water in his hands. He collapsed on the counter in a coughing fit. Warm steam filled his lungs as he breathed in before coughing again.

Sam let himself fall to the floor to escape the onslaught of water and steam. His shirt was soaked through, face dripping with spittle.

"What *was* all of that?" He glanced around the bathroom carefully.

The images from his dreams had burned themselves into his mind. The countertop felt wrong as he gazed over it. The shapes in the sky seemed to overlay themselves on top of it and reveal minute changes in the surface that created an uneven surface.

Sam rubbed his eyes again, the images fading as he did so.

"Okay, maybe this has gotten out of hand."

He stood slowly, peering from squinted eyelids to ensure the shapes didn't return before fully looking. Only the white of the bathroom counter and walls met his gaze. In the mirror he could see how much of a mess he made.

Sam took a deep breath and thought about what had transpired the night before.

"A failure of a lecture, then the books, and whatever those dreams were." *But the books had to be a dream too, so when did I actually go to bed?* He grabbed a towel and wiped off his face.

The soft cloth scratched against the stubble on his face. Sam ignored the towel rack, tossing the damp towel on the floor and wandering from his room. The hallway felt surreal as he entered it. Nothing was visibly different, but the feeling of it was…off, somehow.

Sam looked at the walls and pictures, finding them to be the same as always. So were the offset stairs. He glanced to the window behind him, finding nothing off about it either.

What is wrong with me? He stepped to the stairs and his hand hit the railing.

Sam looked down at the railing. He'd lived in the same house for fifteen years now, and hadn't run into the railing since the early days of his tenancy.

He grabbed the railing. "Why do you feel closer?"

Sam carefully made his way downstairs and turned around. Again, nothing looked any different, but felt wrong.

He rubbed the side of his head. "Must've been a hell of a headache."

The rest of the house felt normal as he maneuvered through his morning routine. Passing through the entry way and turning to pass the stairs. Sam stumbled into the kitchen, shoulder bumping into the doorframe.

I swear that doorframe was further over.

Sam shook his head and focused on getting some caffeine. The scent of coffee filled his home as the coffee pot burbled to a stop.

Sam poured a cup and took a deep sip before sighing audibly. The last of the fuzziness in his mind cleared at the taste. He glanced at the calendar on the fridge.

"Saturday. A good day to stay home and relax." He smiled at the freedom the day offered.

Sam slowly made his way to the office, sipping more from his cup as he walked. The stairs seemed back in their normal and expected position as he passed without running into anything.

He froze in the doorway. The black book sat on his desk still, a void in his home. Sam glared at it over the edge of his cup.

Either I'm not awake yet, or you actually exist. He lowered the cup and glanced into the dining room. The book's double floated in the dim light, looking even more like a hole in reality than the first one, a floating void in the dining room.

Sam took a deep breath in before slowly padding towards the book. "I should call someone about you...."

He pondered the idea for a moment. "But if I do, then I'll lose the opportunity for discovery."

He thought of the empty lecture from the day before. How every lecture was slowly gaining less and less popularity. Math was simply a dying interest, especially when it came to obscure specialties like his study of symmetry. He found it beautiful, the connection between math and art, but so very few saw what he did.

"One more look."

Sam sat at the desk again, carefully setting his coffee down. He scooted the chair over enough to see both books in one glance. He relaxed his shoulders and opened the book to approximately where he had left off. The synchronized flipping of pages echoed from its double across the house as it mirrored the movements of what Sam had begun thinking of as the "original" book.

The shapes appeared the same as before, perfectly symmetrical or exact mirror replicas of each other. The precise nature of the drawing made him uncomfortable, while sating some primal desire in the back of his mind.

He turned the page again. On this page the shapes were different. They took on an almost organic quality. Random offshoots looked more like limbs than simple shapes.

Sam leaned forward, fascinated by the unusual figures. He turned the page again, this time finding the shapes looked not only organic but nearly alive. They were interconnected, almost in the same fashion an artist would outline a drawing of a dog. Rectangles in place of limbs and circles where joints would be.

The itch in the back of his mind began again, though it was overshadowed by his intrigue in the book.

Each turn of the page was echoed by the sound of moving paper in the dining room. He glanced up every so often, watching as the second book mimicked the one in front of him.

Another turned page and he froze. A drawing of a dog. An extremely detailed and gory picture of what he would have guessed to be a picture of an autopsy. The drawing felt more like a captured image of a real animal than one made with any writing utensil.

The animal was splayed open, flesh pinned to whatever ground it would have been on before the drawing. The organs inside worried Sam. The heart was duplicated from left to right. Two complete hearts. The lungs were perfectly symmetrical in size and shape, even in the way they spilled from the body. The stomach was its own oddity, with two exits into two sets of intestines that spiraled around each other like a helix of DNA before rejoining and merging into a singular rectum.

Sam felt his stomach flip at the sight, while his mind was fully focused on the intricacies of the creature. Nausea lost the fight to wonder as he continued to examine and search for any flaw from one side to the other, finding none.

The next page was heavier than the last, like it had been soaked. The paper still made the same near ripping sound as he pulled it up, the page flipping heavily down. It was covered in another autopsy style drawing. This one was of a human.

Dark red lines had been scrawled across it. Circles and asymmetrical notes covered the torn open body. Flesh had been flayed from every limb, pinned open. Half of the limbs were opened down to the bone, while the others stopped at muscle.

While the language was unrecognizable, it became clear to Sam that these were criticisms of the human form. Circling every inconsistency and disproportionate piece in the body.

Nausea fought to the surface again the more he looked at it.

"What the hell is this?" He whispered, carefully drawing over the heavily inked page with his right index finger.

"Ow!" He jerked the finger away.

Something on the page cut him. A thin red line from fingertip to the pad of his finger. Bright red blood trickled out.

He looked from the finger back to the page. Nothing on the page *could* have cut him at first glance. Looking closer revealed the center of the drawing was ever so slightly raised, as if folded to keep the center-line clear, done so perfectly it was near razor sharp.

Sam shot up from the desk. "What the hell *is* this book?"

He made his way to the downstairs bathroom. The medicine cabinet opened with a light squeak that twinged his head, warning him of a worsening headache.

Sam winced as he pulled a bandage out, his left forefinger stinging now. He checked it, finding the same cut on it as his right finger.

His brow furrowed. "How did that happen?"

He compared the two fingers, finding them to have the same length cut, at the same depth. Even the small trickle of blood followed the fingerprints in the same fashion.

Wait. He looked closer at his fingertips. The fingerprint was an exact duplicate now.

"That's…not possible." Much to his annoyance, he'd never heard of anyone with identical fingerprints on the left and right hand. Certainly his own were never symmetrical before.

A dull thud seemed to come from everywhere at once. He jumped, looking around for the source but finding everything in its rightful place.

He stepped from the bathroom and checked the hall to find everything the same as before, though something again felt wrong. The hair on his neck stood on end. Gooseflesh crawled up his limbs as he peered for any signs of change.

He walked to the office again. Sam felt anxiety rise in his chest as he passed the front door, the place where he allowed this grotesque book into his home with its impossible partner.

He turned around, checking on the book in the dining room.

Sam felt his heart skip a beat as he turned. The dining room was gone. In its place was his office, with the duplicate book on the corner of the desk.

He whirled around again, finding the original office still there.

Sam looked between the rooms, locked in a loop of disbelief before falling with his back against the front door.

The stairs were now in the center of the hallway, with two paths around them. The hall table had a partner across from it on the wall.

The morning sunlight felt wrong as well, pouring through the window in impossible replicated patterns.

He looked back and forth between the two sides of the hallway. Anxiety gave way to fear as his head whipped side to side. Nausea forced bile into his throat. His knees shook as they fought to hold his weight.

"What the fuck is going on?" His voice was little more than a terrified whisper.

Sam gave one last look at the book, then the other. Something in him longed to read further, but the twinge in the back of his head grew worse with each look at the tomes. He swallowed and settled on the idea of getting outside.

His hand swung through empty air where it normally would have hit the door handle.

"No." He swiped again without looking.

Nothing.

Sam turned to face the door. Both sides of it had hinges connected to the frame. No handle to be found, just a door mirrored down the middle and unable to be opened. Fear gave way to an animalistic anger as he found himself trapped.

"No." He banged on the door.

The world outside felt impossibly far away, forever just out of reach.

"Okay, window it is." He stormed into the office.

Sam slammed the cursed book closed and picked it up. Across from him in the duplicate office, its mirror raised as well. He lifted the book high above his head and threw it at the window.

The glass shattered in an uncomfortably beautiful display as it broke perfectly from side to side. Large shards flew out onto the porch and scattered in mimicked directions.

Sam smiled at the breeze that blew into his home. He walked to the window and stepped out, careful not to catch himself on the sharp bits of glass left in the frame.

He took a deep breath in through his nose, feeling the headache ease as he did so.

The scent of cooling coffee hit his sinuses. Sam opened his eyes.

He was standing in his office. Sam looked down. Bits of broken glass lay all around him on the carpet. A horrified glance up revealed his fears come true.

The window was shattered, but lead to his office again. The outside world was gone, replaced by another mirror image of his home.

"Fuck!" He shouted in desperation.

He leaned in through the window, finding nothing beyond his office and a copy of the book lying on the ground.

He looked back, seeing yet a third copy of the book behind him on the ground. A quick glance confirmed what would be a fourth book in the fourth iteration of his office, like four mirrored rooms all interconnected. Perfectly symmetrical in their mirrored edges.

"How many of you bastards are there?" He stood and kicked the book hard.

It bounced off the desk and flopped open. The page it landed on showed a humanoid figure. Once again, it was an autopsy drawing. The creature had no hair, its skin a light gray color. It had a singular yellow eye in the middle of its face, with two small holes where the nose would be. The mouth was little more than a partially open slit revealing four square teeth, two on the top and two on the bottom. He recognized it as the creature his reflection became in his dreams.

As he stared at the figure, it became clearer that this was a being of perfect symmetry. Few details, almost like it was designed to be easy to mirror from side to side.

A series of four in-time thuds from the kitchen startled Sam into action. He sprinted for the stairs, dashing up them to hide.

He burst into the bedroom and slammed the door behind him. In the split second he could see the mirrored door across the hall, he would swear a copy of himself was doing the same thing.

Sam huffed, fear coursing through his veins.

I'm going insane. That's it; I'm insane.

He started to laugh, unsure of what else to do. The house creaked and groaned around him.

Sam looked to the bedroom window, seeing only a mirror of it on the other side of the glass. Whatever duplicated his office was now continuing with the rest of his home.

"I'm gonna die here." An insane smile pulled at his lips. "Alone and crazy."

Something shifted in the mirrored room's corner.

Sam froze, breath caught in his throat. His gaze locked on the duplicate room through the window. Across the bed, in the farthest corner of the room, stood a gray figure. It stared off into that mirror room, gaze averted from the window into his currently occupied one.

It moved again, skin throbbing in the low light of the bedside lamp.

Sam stood still, watching as the creature turned toward where the door would be in the mirror room. It was the creature from the book. Its singular yellow eye watched without emotion before it took a step forward.

It's moving away from me.

Mild relief flooded his veins. The creature continued to walk forward before disappearing from the view of the window.

Sam relaxed, letting his head hang down.

"Okay, I'm okay." He whispered to himself.

Sam opened his eyes again and saw two gray feet pointed at his own. He looked up into the uncaring yellow orb in front of him.

It reached out both arms at once, grabbing his wrists gently before lifting Sam's arms out straight and examining them. The creature laid a finger on each wrist and dragged them inward towards Sam's chest. The one on his left arm reached the shoulder just a fraction before the right. The beast hummed thoughtfully. The hands lifted from Sam's arms, moving to his chest. The fingers on the left side thrummed each time his heart beat, while those on the right stayed still. A growl came from low in its throat before the mouth opened.

The voice that came from it was disgustingly even and perfect in its tone.

"Asymmetrical."

CRITICAL MASS
Rivka Crowbourne

Everyone has at least seen a fire; everyone can visualize an explosion. When the Earth's most powerful minds were corralled at Los Alamos to kindle a dark star in the desert, they all knew roughly what they were hoping and dreading to see. White light; black flame. But breaking matter into energy was only half the equation.

Easterly, the horizontal greyness yielded slowly to a dead yellow gloom like the buzz of an old fluorescent. Reluctant day metastasized across the Badlands; a few bleak snowflakes hung in the gibbet of the bitter air. Harsh chemical smoke escaped from a number of Dr. Valmont's facial orifices as he flicked the red end of his cigarette from the walkway into the vast brown carrionscape below.

"Seriously, Valmont, who smokes anymore?"

He turned laconically to face his colleague, Dr. Calloway, a tall, slim American woman with a face just a trifle too shrewd to be pretty. Not that his oft-broken nose left him much room to critique the physiognomies of others. "Old British professors marooned in the colonies," he said.

Calloway ambled over and leaned against the railing, the mist of her own breath faintly visible. The sun rose swiftly; far off, at the edge of vision, one could just make out the glint of Devil's Lake.

"Where do you even get those things?" she asked.

"Oh, I found an old cigarette machine in one of the sub-basements. I may have…eased open the glass."

"Bloody hoodlum. But for pity's sake, they must have expired years ago!"

"Back around the time I was boxing my way to a bachelor's degree, by my calculations. Still, better than nothing, you know."

"Oh gee, did you box at Oxford? You've never mentioned that in the past few hours."

A new voice, earnest and deep: "My friends."

They both turned to greet Dr. Ilibizaga, a man big enough to be a linebacker, but so meditatively quiet that he never seemed to take up any space.

"Our guest is waking up," he said gravely.

"Shake a leg, Valmont!"

The three physicists hastened down the stairs to the elevator. Each occupant peered impatiently into the retinal scanner and punched in a personal code. The small, cold box plummeted through forsaken tectonic depths, and each of them was scanned and coded again before the heavy steel door hissed open.

Beyond the door was a corridor. Chilly, white, and sterile, it stretched like an old dead maggot from the elevator to the distant door of their lab. Along the way were other doors, none of them bearing words or names, identified by esoteric symbols comprehensible only to the researchers working on each individual project—and, presumably, to the shade-veiled intellects overseeing the cryptic laboratories of Surtex Industries.

At the end of the hall was another nondescriptly impregnable door. The marking on this one was simple:

$$m = \frac{e}{c^2}.$$

Here they plied their impossible trade, straining the nascent science of numinometrics, battering the inner walls of the outer limits.

The bright, antiseptic chamber of stainless steel, lit with gelid LEDs, housed hundreds of millions—perhaps billions—of dollars in gen-after-next technology. Desks and tables lined the walls, leaving the central space uncluttered; large, fibrous arrays of probes and sensors, quivering like nine-foot-long spider legs, clustered around the translucent circular column in the middle of the room.

"We're positive it can't get out?" Calloway asked.

Ilibizaga nodded, Zen-calm. "Nor can it see us."

The figure within the column, designated L1, began to stir, muttering. Valmont drew his flask and gulped some bourbon. Ilibizaga quintuple-checked the recording equipment. Calloway held her breath.

The figure sat up.

Inside the column, the air was warm and the light soft. The encircling wall, opaque, was a soothing mauve. Pure oxygen circulated the enclosure. None of these atmospherics palliated L1's yellow glare.

The "L" stood for lycomorph. Of course they couldn't just use the word that everyone knew, Valmont reflected mordantly; the powers that be wanted a bit of neologistic jargon, to reduce the thing.

"*Kto ty?*" Broken glass, that voice. "*Chto ty khochesh?*" The fists clenched, knuckles crunching like dead leaves. "*Ya tebya ub'yu.*" Slowly, L1 rose.

"Here we go," Calloway said, and tapped a button.

Inside the column, the light became a hard, flashing red. The floor began to rattle erratically. The temperature spiked, ammonia came through the ventilation, and a grinding, deafening klaxon blared.

Both sides wanted them. They were strong, they were fast, they could bite through metal; they viewed conventional weapons with malevolent mirth. Their brutal temperament, though not without its administrative challenges, was perfect for shock troops, as long as one kept them pointed at the enemy. Even an idiot could see their military value—but Surtex Industries did not employ idiots. If their math was right—and they had every reason to believe it was—the lycomorphs contained something far more valuable.

It was happening. L1's body contorted horribly—began to rock and split. The drab, tidy uniform shredded at the seams, abruptly overflowing with fur. Muscles like bridge cables bulged and coiled; nails lengthened, ripping out from flesh, curving into claws. L1's mouth stretched like a hideous nightmare mask, giving freakish birth to jaws that snapped and slavered and finally issued the bone-shaking howl of accursed antediluvian myth. The scientists cowered and slapped their hands over their ears.

Huge, deformed, bipedal, it loomed in the epileptic light. A stomp crushed the cot. A flurry of slashes covered the wall in curves and loops, claw-scrawled geometrics, a lunatic roadmap to Hell. When these scratches on the transtitanium nanocage repaired themselves, the creature went *truly* berserk.

"Dear God," Valmont whispered.

They'd all seen footage—dozens of hours of it. And the longer the rampage continued, the clearer it became that the containment would hold. And furthermore, the slightest hint of breach would bring a team sprinting in with photon tasers and gravitonic hypermesh deployers. None of that, however, addressed the primordial fear of beholding a thing both subhuman and supernatural, a thing not meant by Heaven, a thing that *must not be*.

An undeniable underpinning of the universe: an object cannot change its mass. Its weight, certainly; that was easy: stand on a denser planet and you weigh more, a lighter one and you weigh less. But mass, the amount of matter an object was composed of—by definition, the only way to alter that was to physically add or remove matter. $A = A$. QED.

And yet, the damned werewolves.

As expected, the numinometers lit up like pinball machines. Lycomorphosis added around 100 kilograms to the body mass, which converted to 8.99×10^{18} Joules—nearly 2,150 megatons of TNT equivalent, which in turn equaled around 45 Soviet Tsar Bomba hydrogen bombs. The question now was twofold: where did the energy come from, and how could it be harnessed?

At last, L1's terrifying rage subsided. The column's interior was now painted with clumps of blood and fur from the monster smashing itself against the cage over and over again; both wall and wolf were already healing. Slowly, crookedly, the abomination folded and cracked itself back into human form. L1 dropped to the floor, cross-legged, and closed his eyes.

Preliminary data sheets slid into the printer tray. Calloway picked them up and straightened them with visibly shaking hands. "Come on, let's get some air."

They headed back up to the walkway. Valmont lit a cigarette, drank from his flask, then let the smoke sigh out of his alveoli. Wordlessly, his friends extended supplicating hands—Calloway for a smoke, Ilibizaga for a drink.

After a smallish sip, the big Kenyan perused the data while the others leaned and puffed. The ringing in their ears from the bedlam downstairs was eerily absorbed by the monumental silence, a sea on which drifted the crinkle of paper and the groaning of the frigid wind.

Then: "It is not possible!"

Calloway glanced up. "Whattaya got, Thomas?"

"The energy, it comes through a quantum tunnel."

"Okay? That corroborates our best hypothesis."

"But look." He brandished the papers with uncharacteristic violence. They looked.

A long pause.

Halting, unwilling, Calloway said, "If this is right...."

She trailed off, and Valmont finished: "The tunnel's length is infinite. It's at

126

right angles to the whole of existence. The whole of reality."

"So…" she gestured aimlessly. "What does that mean?"

"We must stop our research," Ilibizaga said grimly. "At once."

"Now hang on a moment," Valmont spluttered.

"Edward, no. This is not the Manhattan Project. What is at stake is not a city, nor an island, but everlasting damnation for every human soul."

"You don't know that! We don't know *anything* yet. It could be a portal to bloody Rivendell for the evidence we've got. Besides, if the Sinos aren't already working on this same technology, they soon will be."

"Then Sinorussia will have its own choice to make. I hope they are wiser than we."

"Guys." Calloway held up her hands. "Take a breath. We're all good guys here."

"All right, listen," Valmont said, moderating his tone. "Every once in a great while, we suss out something important. You can hit harder and lift more if you've got a tool. If you put a seed in the ground, it turns into food. Fuse some nuclei and you can blow things up. It's all very impressive to the other primates, I'm sure, but ask the universe if it's intimidated. The Sun's been fusing atoms all along. The planet's been growing food all along. Tools? The cosmos has electromagnetism, I doubt it's flabbergasted by the pulley."

"What's your point, Valmont?"

"My point is: this is different. We're not learning to harness a natural process. We're transcending the natural order altogether. This is us getting a leg up on the universe for the first time since time began."

Ilibizaga said quietly, "I do not think of the universe as my enemy."

"Yet you assume that a tunnel leads to Beelzebub when it could just as well lead to Buddha. Perhaps it is better to seek truth, whatever the price."

Ilibizaga shook his head but couldn't muster any further argument.

"Agreed," said Calloway. "Also, I'm crazy curious now."

Together, they returned to the lab and found L1 in two pieces.

No one spoke. The lycomorph lay steaming, partially transformed. The wolven hands were red. The human face, several feet away, was fixed in a final yowl of misery and pain. One of the feet still twitched.

"We did this." Calloway's face was pale as the whites of her eyes, the pupils like coals in snow. "How could we do this?"

"We had no choice," Valmont muttered.

"We did," Ilibizaga said. "We do."

The computer dinged: 0800 hours, time for their daily status update to HQ. When Surtex learned what had happened, they would send a collection team for another specimen.

"They'll just get someone else if we quit," said Valmont.

Calloway, almost inaudibly: "I don't want to quit."

The wall clock, beyond the twisted headless body, clicked to 8:01. The computer dinged again.

LOST AND FOUND

Joe Stout

No twenty-five-year-old male is fond of the word "lost," much less admitting it applies to him.

I was uncertain of my location, and the condition had created an unhealthy panic within me. Instead of staying in place and waiting to be rescued, I ventured further and further, in the desperate hope of recognizing a landmark that would allow me to find my way home.

The sun had begun its descent as I leaped from stone to stone across a wide, shallow stream. I shouldn't have done this; I hadn't crossed a wide, shallow stream while getting lost, and had no reason to suspect that such a stream had sprung into existence in a place I had previously traversed. As I leapt from the last stone to the shore, I lost my footing and landed in the water with a splash. Soaked, I looked up to find a pair of blue eyes staring back at me.

If I hadn't already been in the creek, I would have fallen in when I saw her. She was a pale, Nordic beauty with long blonde hair. She wore a flannel shirt with blue jeans and boots, looking almost like a hunter.

"Hello," I said, getting to my feet.

Her eyes went wide, and she turned and ran into the woods.

"Hey!" I sprinted after her. Shy, scared, or whatever she was, she was the only human I had seen for hours, and my best chance of getting home.

We crashed through the woods, my lungs on fire from the exertion, but my quarry didn't seem to be tired at all. She splashed across another creek, then we ran up a long, steep hill. Toward the top, I lost sight of the blonde locks flying behind her when I stopped to rest, putting my hands on my knees and wheezing, wondering where my youthful energy had gone, and suspecting it had been left in the cold waters of the creek.

Once able to move, I kept climbing the hill, hoping to figure out where the young woman went. A camp, if I was lucky, or perhaps a rural store.

It was neither. Standing at the top of the hill, I found myself looking down at an old Victorian-style house in the middle of the woods. The trees had grown in around it, making the fading white paint almost blend with the forest's colors. Beyond the house, I could see a small clearing where a garden had been planted. Barking came from a low building at the edge of the clearing.

"Dogs," I muttered. "Why dogs?"

Walking down the hill, I climbed onto the porch and knocked on the front door. After waiting about a minute with no answer, I knocked again.

A few seconds later, it swung open to reveal a white-haired woman with a large shotgun in her hands. It was probably a normal-sized gun, but the woman's diminutive stature and my current predicament made it seem plenty big to me.

"Can I help you?" she asked pleasantly. She reminded me of Granny in those old Tweety Bird cartoons, cordial and pleasant, but with the potential to be dangerous as hell.

"Yes ma'am, my name is Tim Porter, and I think I'm lost. I saw a girl and chased her through the woods, but she was too fast to catch up to. Luckily, I saw your house, and wondered if you could help me."

A smile crept across her face. "A student," she whispered. "Goodness me, I haven't had a new student in years." Stashing the gun behind the door, she grabbed my arm. "Come in, please, come in. My name is Ms. Watford, and I am a teacher of mathematics. The girl you saw was probably my servant, Irene. She is a shy soul. You probably startled her, the poor thing, but I'm glad you've found your way here."

She led me into a parlor that looked as though it hadn't been changed since the house was built. The walls were covered in fading wallpaper adorned with baskets of blue and purple flowers. The horsehair couch I sat on was uncomfortable, to say the least, and I had to firmly plant my feet on the floor to keep from sliding off. "Can I get you something to drink? Coffee? Tea? Something stronger?"

"Coffee will be fine," I said. She pulled on a bell cord, and a few moments later, the girl I'd seen in the woods appeared.

She'd changed into a blue gingham dress and pulled her hair back into a ponytail. "Yes, Ms. Watford?" she asked, barely glancing at me.

"Please bring Timothy and myself some coffee, then make up the guest room. He will be staying with us tonight."

"Oh?" I was surprised, then looked out the window at the growing darkness.

"Of course," Ms. Watford said with a smile. "It's hard enough getting off the mountain in daylight, and almost impossible in the dark." She turned back to Irene. "Roast for dinner tonight?"

"It *is* Thursday, Ms. Watford," the girl confirmed. "Dinner will be ready in an hour."

"Wonderful!" The old woman turned back to me. "It will be so nice to have company! Irene is lovely, but her appreciation of mathematics is unfortunately lacking."

I thought back to my last math class, as a junior in high school, and being proud of the C I managed to escape with. If math was Ms. Watford's idea of stimulating conversation, it could be a long evening.

"So, Timothy, why don't you tell me about yourself?" she said as Irene left the room.

π

Ms. Watford dominated the dinner conversation with math talk. Something called "Belphegor's Prime" was her main talking point, a one followed by thirteen zeroes, three sixes, thirteen more zeroes, and a final one:

$$1000000000000066600000000000001.$$

I nodded along politely, pretending to be interested. Although I had taken a few college math classes, it was hardly the stuff of stimulating conversation. But Ms. Watford didn't seem to agree, droning on about the history of Belphegor's Prime.

Irene came in and out of the dining room, bringing food and refilling our cups. It was a welcome distraction. She really was pretty, even if I couldn't get her to look me in the eye. Finally, after a dessert of bread pudding, Ms. Watford bid me goodnight and Irene showed me to my room.

"Is she always this boring?" I asked as she swung open my door.

A soft smile appeared on her lips, and she opened her mouth to say something. Then she seemed to remember who she was talking to and looked away. "I have chores to do. Goodnight."

"No! Wait!" I called behind her, to no avail.

Lying on the bed, I stared up at the ceiling, thinking about the strange reality I had wandered into. Not only was I lost, but now I was in a strange Victorian world with a retired math teacher and her young servant. In all my years exploring these woods and mountains, I'd never come across this place, or even seen it on a map. It had to be an old logging camp or something.

My bed was an old four-poster with drapes over the top. An old wooden armoire was next to it, and a cedar chest was at the foot. All of the furniture looked like it had been here since the home was built; even the bedsheets and curtains had faded with age.

π

The tree outside scratched at my window, but I ignored it. After a moment, the scratching got louder, and I realized it was someone tapping.

Irene crouched on the roof outside the window, looking around like she expected someone to catch her. I opened the window, and she dove inside, pulling it closed behind her.

"What are you doing?"

She locked the door, then turned back to me. "You're in danger."

"What?" I sat on the bed. "What are you talking about?"

"My name isn't Irene. I'll start with that."

"It isn't?" She shook her head, her blonde hair dancing on her shoulders. "Then why does Ms. Watford call you Irene?"

"So people don't realize who I really am. Not that anyone would remember after six years."

"Six years?" I asked.

She nodded. "My real name is Abigail Spahn."

My eyes widened in recognition. "I remember you! You were the Forestry student who went missing. The whole college was talking about it."

Abigail nodded, tears welling in her eyes. "I went for a hike and got lost. After two days, I found this place. Ms. Watford seemed nice at first, but after I failed her test, I became her prisoner. 'Remedial math,' she called it. Three more tests, then I flunked. Permanently. Now I'm her slave, even if she calls me her servant."

I sat there for a minute in shock. She sat down on the bed next to me, and I put my arm around her. "I'm sorry."

She sniffed. "It's okay. That's the first chance I've had to tell someone what happened."

"I guess not many people come this way."

Her head shook again. "You're the first person I've seen besides her."

"What about an escape?"

She took my hand and led me to the window. Even in the half-moon, I could see the figure of a dog in the garden below. "There's twelve of them." Raising her nightgown, I saw a modern tracking device on her ankle. "She always knows where I am. The creek where you saw me is the boundary. If I go further, she'll send the dogs to hunt me down and tear me apart."

I gulped. Dogs weren't infallible, but on unfriendly land with a skilled tracker to guide them, they were formidable.

Leading me back to the bed, she put her hand on my chest. "I'm ashamed to say this, but I almost want you to fail the test. I'm tired of being alone here, tired of listening to her ramble on about math like it's the greatest thing in the world. It'd just be nice to have someone else to talk to."

I nodded. "I can understand that."

She laid her head on my shoulder. "I know we just met, and I just unloaded a lot on you, but I want something."

"Okay."

"This could be the only night you're here, and, well...."

I put my finger under her chin and lifted it before pressing my lips softly against hers. She threw her arms around my neck, pushing me back onto the bed before lifting her nightgown off and reaching for the button of my jeans.

$$\pi$$

I woke once more in the night, and Abigail was no longer lying next to me. Had it been a dream? No. My pants were on the floor, and my member was still sensitive from her enthusiastic participation.

But why? Why would she come in here to warn me? Was it a mind game, a greater conspiracy between her and Ms. Watford? Or had it been sincere, a real need for human connection after years of being isolated here?

I didn't know, but I spent what felt like hours thinking about it before I drifted back to sleep, the uncomfortable mattress making me toss and turn as my brain refused to stop contemplating Abigail's actions. Sleep finally came after I made a decision: if Ms. Watford was going to make me her student, I would be an impossible one.

π

A knock on the door woke me the next morning, and I opened the door to see Abigail standing there, this time in a green gingham dress.

"Good morning," she said, bowing her head. I could see the slight grin that played across her lips. "Breakfast will be served in half an hour."

"You could look at me," I whispered. The grin got bigger.

"If I look at you, Timothy, breakfast will not be served for an hour, and that would make Ms. Watford angry." I stepped into the hallway and wrapped her in an embrace, kissing the top of her head.

"Then I suppose I will get ready for breakfast," I whispered.

Twenty-five minutes later, I was dressed and sitting in the dining room when Ms. Watford entered. She was dressed much like Abigail, but instead of gingham her dress had a pattern of cows.

"Good morning, Timothy," she said as I stood. "I trust you slept well?"

"Very well, thank you," I pulled out her chair, and earned an approving nod.

"Such good manners, young man. I shall be sad to see you go."

"Ah," I said, sitting back down. "How long will it take to get to town?"

She looked at me, a sly grin crossing her face. "That depends entirely on your mathematical prowess. You see, I cannot allow you to leave until you have proven you are a competent mathematician. It is a simple test, one that you can surely pass with no difficulties."

"Really," I said, as Abigail entered the room carrying two plates. "It sounds an awful lot like kidnapping."

"That's such a dirty word," Ms. Watford said as Abigail put a plate in front of her, then one in front of me. "Here I am, trying to ensure you have been well educated, and you go and use a word like that."

"I would apologize, but the word is accurate." I took a bite of my eggs. "These are delicious. Local?"

"Yes," Ms. Watford said. "Irene gathers them from the coop every morning."

"Irene looks awfully familiar," I pressed my luck, taking a bite of bacon. "I think she went to my college. As I recall, she went by Abigail then."

Ms. Watford pressed her lips together in a tight line. "She prefers Irene now." Her hand came out of her lap holding a handgun, a chrome-plated Glock 19. Probably the only modern instrument in the house. "And I must insist, Timothy, on being allowed to test you. There is no reason to be ugly."

"And if I refuse?"

"You can try to make it out of here, but it's twenty miles to civilization. Twenty miles of being hounded, if you get my drift."

On cue, the dogs started barking, making me jump. I sighed, looked at the gun, then at Ms. Watford. "Fine. I'll take your test. But when I pass it, I'm taking Abigail with me."

Watford laughed. "You think I'm going to let her go?" She held up the gun. "I'm the one with the power here. I am your teacher, and you are my student."

I looked over at Abigail and saw a tear rolling down her face. She looked at me, and I saw a glimmer of steel flash in her eye, followed by a barely perceptible nod. "Fine," I said. "We'll do it your way."

"Good boy." She put another bite of eggs in her mouth. "Too much salt, Irene."

"Yes, ma'am," she said, returning to the kitchen.

π

The classroom was at the front of the house opposite the parlor. A single student desk, an old wood and metal contraption, sat in the center of the room. At the front were a teacher's desk and a large chalk blackboard. "Ms. Watford" was written on the blackboard in flowing script.

I took a seat at the desk and waited. A few minutes later, Ms. Watford entered.

"Good morning, class," she said, looking at me.

"Good morning, *teacher*," I muttered. She opened her mouth to protest but decided not to press the issue. Walking to her desk, she took the pistol from her pocket and placed it in clear view.

"I am here because mathematics is the most important subject I can teach you," she said. "My life has been dedicated to enlightening students with knowledge that, if applied correctly, can change the world. Today, several years after a failure of a student, I have another chance."

"If you're talking about Abigail, you can use her name," I said.

"Backtalk will result in discipline," she said, picking up a flexible rod from the corner.

"Is that how Abigail got the scars on her back?"

The rod whipped through the air, passing an inch from my head and slamming into the desk. "I don't know what you and Irene did while I was sleeping, and I don't care. But you will address her by her proper name, and you will not disrespect me in my classroom!"

"Let's just get on with this test," I said, leaning back in my seat. "I've got things to do, you know."

She glared at me for a moment, then smiled. "Very well. Let's begin. What is the only even prime number?"

"Two." I replied, drawing a one in the air to indicate my score. Outside, the dogs had stopped barking.

"That is correct," she said. Going to the board, she wrote a series of numbers:

$$1\ 1\ 2\ 3\ 5\ 8\ 13\ 21\ 34\ 55\ 89.$$

"Identify the numbers you see here."

"They're Ms. Watford's numbers," I said, and the rod whistled through the air again, striking the side of my head.

"I have had enough of your insolence," she said. "If you insist on continuing, it will become quite painful for you."

I felt a trickle of blood on my cheek. "Give me a turn with that and I'll show you a thing or two."

It whistled through the air again, but this time I was ready for it. Grabbing it, I yanked it out of her hand and snapped it in two, then four pieces.

"Oops."

She glared at me. "Detention, Timothy." Stepping into the hallway, she returned with another rod. "I keep a supply. You have no idea how many I went through with Irene."

I smiled at her. "You have no idea how many you'll need for me."

She raised the rod again but stopped herself before swinging. "The numbers, Timothy."

"Fibonacci. The golden ratio." I said,

"Very good." Picking up an eraser, she wiped the numbers from the board.

"Not really. I'm starting to wonder if you really care about math. This stuff is middle school at best."

The eraser hit me above my ear, bouncing into a corner of the room. Ms. Watford approached, bending over and putting both hands on my desk.

"Never. Question. My. Love. For. Math."

I leaned toward her. "It's just like everything else in your life. You can love it, but it will never love you back."

The rod broke over my head, and she stomped off to the hall to get a new one. When she came back, she stood in the door, glaring at me.

"You think what I've shown you is middle school? Very well." Going to the blackboard, she picked up the chalk and wrote:

$$x^8.$$

"In the sixteenth century, Robert Recorde, who also invented the equals sign, suggested a name for this notation. What was it?"

I laughed. "Beats the hell out of me. Don't you remember?"

Three quick swings, and another rod was broken. As she stomped to the hall for another, I smiled through the pain. "Maybe you should bring a few. Save you some walking!"

She stopped for a moment, then continued her walk, slamming the door behind her.

$$\pi$$

By the time the lunch break came, my face and hands were covered in blood. Returning to my room, I washed my hands using the pitcher and porcelain bowl that had been laid out. Taking a washcloth, I wiped the blood from my face before looking in the mirror.

I looked like hell. Blood matted my hair, pressing it against my scalp. An errant swing had left a bruise across my jawline that was an ugly shade of purple and green. Holding up my hands, I saw they were swollen from repeated blows, the knuckles bloodied from deflecting the swinging rod. I didn't look like a math student, I looked like a prizefighter.

But I was winning. She'd managed to get six questions in, and I'd answered four correctly.

Lunch was soup, beans, and cornbread, served by Abigail. When she sat the bowl in front of Ms. Watford, I saw a small smile appear on her face. I ate quickly, ready to return to the classroom and continue our battle.

$$\pi$$

Ms. Watford sank hard into her chair. "Goodness, I'm not sure that soup agreed with me." A loud fart echoed in the room, and her eyes went wide. "Excuse me!" She said, her face going red. "Now, your next question.... What is Legendre's Constant?"

I knew this—she had mentioned it at supper last night—but before I could answer, she fell forward in her chair, head landing on her desk with a nasty crack.

Abigail appeared in the doorway. "That took longer than I thought," she said, studying Ms. Watford. "The dogs went much faster."

"The dogs?" I asked, raising an eyebrow.

"Surely you noticed they haven't been barking today. I tested the poison on them."

"You poisoned her?" I yelled, but I hadn't meant to. The shock and confusion came rushing out my mouth before I could stop them. A tear appeared in her eye.

"I thought you'd be happy," she said. "No more math, no more beatings."

I exhaled, then stood and walked to her. "I'm sorry. I was just surprised."

"I want out. I knew if you got out, it'd be years before I got another chance." Tears were rolling down her face. "I'm not a killer, but I had to do something."

"I know," I leaned down and kissed her. "It had to be done." I turned to look at the body. "Guess I better go dig a grave."

π

When I came inside, a feast was on the table. Fried chicken, greens, macaroni and cheese, biscuits, green beans, potatoes and gravy, and more. On the sideboard, a pecan pie and a massive cake waited.

"Holy cow," I said, looking at the food. "This looks delicious."

Abigail smiled. "It seemed the least I could do. While you were out burying Ms. Watford, I was thinking."

"Oh," I smiled, wrapping her in my arms. "And what were you thinking, my dear?"

She looked away for a moment, like she was gathering courage, then back at me. "I was thinking we don't need to leave right away, do we?"

My only response was to kiss her.

A STRANGE THING HAPPENED AT THE COFFEE SHOP

Brian Knight

Carina scrolled through her social media feed while nursing a large pumpkin spice latte. She had ten minutes of break left before her final three hours at work, including the five o'clock rush. Her two goals in this short calm before the rush overwhelmed her were to make her drink last the entire break, and not let the social media shitshow wind her up.

She sipped, sighed, rolled her eyes at some nonsense about the Trump-Biden election posted by an old school friend that she had mostly ignored since graduation.

Sip, scroll, a smile as she stopped to watch a video of a celebrity playing with her cat.

The low hum of conversation—barely audible in her quiet corner furthest from the social center of the café, the small tables and plush chairs where groups tended to settle—fell silent. In its absence, Carina heard a man's low laughter and the unusually loud rasp of his pencil flying across paper, pressed near to the snapping point.

She hadn't noticed the man earlier; had no idea how long he had been there, if he had come alone, what, if anything, he'd ordered. She should have remembered, since she'd been the one making the drinks before James sent her out for her break.

She turned to see if James was aware of the situation, whatever the situation was, and found him staring at the digital reader board high up on the wall above the drive through window.

A full color panel displaying seasonal pumpkin spice drinks seemed to be pulsing, brightening, dimming, flickering. The header—"It's Pumpkin Spice season!"—began dropping letters, replacing them with odd characters, what looked to Carina's uneducated eye like mathematical equations. The foam on top of a picture of the pumpkin spice latte, began to swirl and darken, then opened, sucking in air the way an open drain sucks in water. Napkins fluttered, then flew like strange butterflies into the whirling eye of the vortex. A stack of paper cups joined them a moment later.

"Stop that man!" A voice shouted from the open door. A new woman burst through just as the strange laughing man rose and bolted across the café, past the newly-silenced clutch of customers, past the bar, where a malfunctioning espresso machine blasted steam in James's face.

James screamed, the weirdness of the transforming reader board fleeing his mind in favor of the exquisite pain of what promised to be second or third-degree burns.

Carina's phone slipped from her hand, struck the table, and the screen turned black.

A large red numeral 5 seemed to burn itself through the flat black of the screen.

"*Five!*" A voice blasted from her phone's speaker as the strange man stopped beside her to face the closed storeroom door a few feet away. The voice was feminine, thunderous, terrible, as if her cell phone's digital assistant had become an angry goddess. "*You have performed an unsupported operation!*"

The 5 on her phone screen became a 4.

"*Four!*" A woman rose from the group in the common area, screeching, and began to claw at her eyes. Her friends watched, expressionless at first, then their mouths opened in impossibly wide screams, and they began to tear at their own faces with fingernails that were too long to be real. "*Logic error! Incorrect conditional expression in if statement!*"

The red 4 oozed up through the screen like blood and became a 3.

"*Three! Introduction of unknowable dynamic…,*" a moment of indecipherable static, then "*quantum syntax!*"

Carina reached for her phone, then froze. Her reaching hand seemed too wide, too flat, the fingers paper thin. It fluttered in the breeze created by the air-sucking vortex on the reader board, and before she could pull it back, tore off at the wrist and flew away to join the napkins and paper cups. There was no blood, but there was pain. She opened her mouth to voice that pain, but no scream came out, only the rustling of paper in a strong wind.

A sound like a sonic boom—like a giant hand clapping—drowned out the screams of pain and hysteria.

She could still hear the strange low tittering of the scribbling man. He turned toward the new woman, standing by the front entrance, and smiled. A long tongue flicked from between a large gap in his upper front teeth and licked his eyes. They blinked, the lids closing vertically, like a lizard.

"Stop that man!"

A command from the only person who seemed unchanged by the weirdness, the failure of reality. She passed the group of women who now stood, seeming to watch the proceedings with white blanks where their faces had been only moments before. They were no longer women, but a chain of life-sized paper dolls, holding hands like the doll chains Carina used to make when she was little.

The woman ignored James as he reached out to her with a supplicating groan, the skin of his face hanging and dripping from his head like melted wax.

The black hole latte on the reader board sucked in bottles of flavored syrup, a canister of coffee beans, a stack of paper cups from the counter, the hat from James's melting head.

The desperation on the pursuing woman's face broke Carina's paralysis. She leapt up and flailed her too long, too thin arms toward the giggling man.

He brushed her aside as if she were leaves in a hard breeze and took his final few steps toward the closed door marked Employees Only.

At least it *should* have been marked Employees Only.

Symbols and numbers flashed and changed across the door's flat black surface as if slashed into it by some unseen instrument.

"*Two! Permission error! You do not have permission to access the base....*" The voice was now booming not just from her phone but from the café's sound system. A large blood red 2 appeared on the door beneath the evolving string of numbers and symbols, then faded.

The frantic woman dashed past Carina, and she felt herself swept up bodily in a powerful wake like a paper doll tossed in a storm.

The man stopped before the door, clutching his notebook tightly to his chest with one hand. The other hand moved in sharp, short motions, a single extended finger seeming to direct the new lines of characters that sizzled and sparked across the surface of the door.

"*One!* Unsafe operation," more static, then, "*quarantine and removal of corrupted string....*"

The café's speakers squawked with feedback, then blew out.

A moment later he reached the door, grasped the knob, and turned it.

The door did not open. The man did not step through.

The long lines of arcane code flashed, then burned out. The man flattened, became two dimensional, flickered like a dying lightbulb, crackled like static on a television tuned to dead air, and winked out of existence.

The pursuing woman stopped, her quarry having escaped a mere moment before she reached him.

She turned to Carina, who seemed to be coming apart like dandelion fluff in the air.

"I am so sorry," she said, and faded like an apparition to nothingness.

Carina's world ended in one final, colossal sonic boom.

π

Amber sat near the open door of the employee break room, nibbling the corner of a granola bar that tasted like ass and chasing each bite with a sip of iced tea. The room was barely more than a closet with a tiny desk and wooden chair that reminded her of her old grade school desks. The splintery old seat was a relic of the '70s. This was the '90s, and all the customer tables and seats were made of faux wood laminate and molded plastic.

The break room door should have been closed. The claustrophobic chaos of the small space clashed with the open tidiness of the seating and display areas, but Denice had asked her to keep a lookout for new customers while she made out with the new guy in the storeroom. The storeroom door *was* closed, but a thump against the break room wall would get Denice back out and behind her register before a new customer could step up to order.

Well, if she didn't have to button or tuck anything in first.

A faint sound of screaming came from outside, barely audible until the customer entrance swung open. The man who stepped inside was the clear cause of the ruckus outside. He was not screaming, but talking aloud to himself, tracing invisible figures in the air with an extended and crooked index finger. Amber thought she could see the outline of the traced figures lingering in the air, but decided it was only her imagination.

She thumped the wall above the break table with a closed fist. Waited for an acknowledging return thump, and when it didn't come gave another, harder thump.

The strange man weaved his way through the the scatter of customers and seats, pausing for a moment at each in turn, then continued toward the bar.

Amber gave the wall a final, frustrated thump and rose to take the order herself. He may have been an obvious weirdo, but weirdos were a good twenty-five or thirty percent of their customer base. Once he had his caffeine fix, he would probably be on his way without making too much of a scene, she could continue her break, and Denice could continue dry humping the new guy.

She had to hurry to slip behind the register. He moved with real purpose as he continued tracing in the air and mumbling.

"Thanks for coming in. What—" *can I start for you,* she meant to finish, but he continued past her as if she was just a part of the background. His eyes were fixed on the closed storeroom door, his right index finger continuing to trace while his left hand clutched a tattered notebook to his chest.

A spinning circle of characters—no, not a circle: a spiral—rose to the door's surface, glowing like molten metal, spitting sparks like a Fourth of July sparkler.

Amber opened her mouth to speak again. She meant to say, *what the hell is that?* She meant to say, *you can't go in there.*

What she did say was...

"*Three! Parallax error! Your position is flawed. This string will not support your incursion.*" Amber marveled at the voice booming out of her mouth, not her voice, but the voice of God in some old Bible Epic—at least if God happened to be a woman. The words were nonsense, they meant nothing to her, but the voice that wasn't hers declared them with real authority.

The stranger paused and turned his head to regard her. His wide eyes rippled like still water disturbed by drops of rain. His smile was a child's drawing of a leering boogeyman grin. His voice was static.

"I will fix my error in the next iteration." The fingers of his right hand continued their sinuous twiddling, weaving their glowing lines, quickening the spiral. "Not even a god gets it right the first time."

Now no more than a passenger in her own body, Amber could only bear witness as she stepped out from behind the counter.

"*Two! Your error is systematic. No correction is possible while you remain a part of the equation.*" She pointed at him. The intelligence that had taken control of her mouth now seemed to be running the rest of her as well. "*You are not a god.*"

His grin flipped, did not change, but flipped upside down to become a grimace. He snapped the long fingers of his right hand, and the bright, sparking spiral of characters flashed brightly. A sonic boom crashed down over the world, shattering the windows, the glass displays, driving the witnesses in the café to the floor with the crunch of bones and tearing of flesh.

The broken people did not die. They screamed.

"Not yet." He turned away from Amber and opened the door.

She expected to see Denise and the new guy, confused, surprised, maybe even broken and screaming on the floor. There was nothing beyond the rectangle of the open door. Not the storeroom, not her coworkers, not even darkness.

Just nothing.

The man took a step toward that nothing.

"*One!*" She stepped after him. "*A fatal error has occurred. Unsafe operation!*"

He stepped through the open door as her fingers brushed his back.

Then he was gone. The nothing beyond the open door was gone, and in its place was a storeroom that looked like it had gone through a blender. The shattered remains of two humans lay at the threshold, screaming up at Amber.

The controlling presence was also gone. Her body was her own again.

She had no time to explore any options this returned control afforded her.

Her final moment of sentience seemed to stretch on in frozen eternity.

$$\pi$$

Kenny could have made it through the intersection before yellow turned red, but he'd have had to jump on the gas a little to get through. Maybe more than a little, and if he didn't make it, the intersection cameras would have got him for sure. When he was younger there were no such things. If the cops didn't catch you red-handed, you were pretty much home free, but the Clarkston PD started installing the cameras in 2009, and now three years later almost all the controlled intersections had them. It just wasn't worth taking the chance. When you drove for a living, your CDL was your livelihood.

Kenny wondered if 2012 America was the future George Orwell had been trying to warn the world about in *1984*. Not that Kenny had ever read *1984*, or even watched the movie; he only knew about it, and its author, because the political hacks loved to hold Orwell up when bitching about how the *other side* was destroying America.

The car behind him honked, and Kenny restrained the urge to raise a one-fingered salute out his window. The *How's My Driving* sticker on the back bumper with the company phone number stayed his middle finger most of the time.

A STRANGE THING HAPPENED AT THE COFFEE SHOP

The car, one of those sporty new things Kenny was seeing all over the place, blasted its horn one last time before turning into the center passing lane and gunning it into the intersection, ignoring the red light and crossing paths with a much less sporty '60s pickup, a rust and primer shit-box that could plow its way through a few dozen sporty little cars without even denting what appeared to be a very expensive custom diamond plate steel bumper.

The collision was jarring, a bang that undoubtedly drew every eye within a three or four block radius. The car, a little more U-shaped than it had been moments before, bounced from the center passing lane into opposing traffic, balancing for a moment on its driver's side tires, almost tipping, then falling with a crash back on all four wheels. Another car crossing from the left stopped inches short of caving in the driver's door, and pedestrians on both sides of the road snapped pictures with cell phones before calling for help.

The old man driving the pickup climbed down carefully from his cab and made his slow way to the wreckage.

Well, Kenny thought, *I know what I'm doing for the next hour or so.*

A flash of light to Kenny's right drew his eyes to the parking lot of a mini mall with a hair salon, an accountant, a cell phone shop, and a chain coffee shop.

Kenny didn't know what had caused the flash, but he could see what was now drawing everyone's attention away from the drama unfolding in the intersection of 3rd and Bridge Street.

The man was very tall, very thin, oddly shaped somehow, like a cartoon caricature. A hunched and grinning boogeyman clutching an old notebook in one over large hand and a pencil in the other.

"*Halt!*" The voice of authority, a voice perfectly pitched, perfectly projected to demand compliance. The voice of an angry goddess.

Everyone halted, even the wrecked car's driver, who had emerged from the corpse of his expensive toy screaming and charging at the pickup's elderly driver with raised fists.

Even the cartoon caricature halted, but only for a second. Then he turned his grinning full moon of a face toward a teenage girl standing at the crosswalk who had been, moments before, staring at the accident with everyone else. Now she faced the strange man, upraised arm and pointing finger seeming to freeze him in place.

"*Six!*" she said, and her voice seemed to come from everywhere, from the air itself, drowning everything else out. "*Numerical algorithm error.*"

She took a step toward the man but was somehow several feet further away from him than before. The sidewalk between them stretched like gray taffy. She took another step, and another. Giant steps, aggressive steps. She covered most of the distance between them in a moment, startling him back. She darted forward again, her hands reaching, and he sidestepped.

She missed him by inches.

"Five! Boundary and dimensional conditions deteriorating."

The grin on his cartoon moon of a face was a sneer now. He bolted for the coffee shop, seemed to melt his way through the glass doors instead of opening them.

He disappeared, and the girl followed him inside, opening the door to enter.

The two men from the wreck stood side by side in the crosswalk, peering intently into the glass storefront. The inside was lost to darkness, as if the windows were painted black.

From inside, as though from the bottom of a deep pit, the girl's voice sounded one last time.

"Four! Cascading faults…environment overload. Three! Dimensional collapse…."

The first policeman had arrived at the accident but ignored the smashed vehicle draining its vital fluids onto the pavement. He stared at the blackened coffee shop façade, then the contracting horizon.

The world around Kenny was flattening into something not quite two dimensional, but not exactly three. The mini mall became a false front, a flattened set piece, an inadequate placeholder for the building that had stood there. The horizon became a flattened backdrop, the Blue Mountains to the south of Clarkston stood like a painted landscape against a paper sky.

The world darkened and flattened as Kenny and the rest of the bystanders waited for what was coming, then it slammed shut on them like a closing book, and they were gone.

$$\pi$$

"Reality is Digital; Experience is Analog," Alice read aloud, then looked over the top of the manuscript clutched in her hands. She did a slow blink and stared blandly at Heather, as if waiting for the punchline of a bad joke.

A man sitting alone at a table across the mostly empty floor glanced up at them, as if the title of her manuscript had caught his interest, then sipped his drink and turned back to his paperback. Heather couldn't see the title from where she sat, but the cover art looked like generic thriller fiction art.

"It's about the dichotomy between quantum mechanics and classical physics," Heather said. She thought about telling Alice it was for her Physics 402 class, thought maybe if she said it was an assignment Alice would stop looking at her like a third eye had just opened in the center of her forehead. She decided it was too much effort. Alice had always thought she was a little weird, and Heather always tried to convince her she wasn't. She was tired of it. Maybe she was weird. Maybe she didn't care anymore.

That's what she got for dating a jock. Alice was hot, her body curvy, muscled and hard as a rock, but she was not the sharpest crayon in the box.

Truth was, Heather hoped to sell her paper to a journal. She had her eyes on *Reviews of Modern Physics*, but supposed she'd settle for the school journal. It would help her prospects for work after she graduated, but she was more interested in having her ideas validated.

If she thought she'd get that validation from Alice, she'd been mistaken.

"You said you wanted to read it," Heather said, feeling the heat of a blush spread across her face. She reached for the manuscript, but Alice pulled it back.

"I do. I just don't expect to understand it." She smiled at Heather, and began to read again, silently this time. Her brow furrowed; her lips moved as she tried to silently pronounce an unfamiliar word.

"Order for Alice," the barista called.

Heather rose before Alice could put the paper down and went to get their drinks. She didn't expect Alice to understand it either, but it meant something that she was reading it anyway.

That was when the the door opened, ringing the little bell hanging just inside, ushering the sounds of traffic, screeching tires, screams, panic. The man who blew in with those sounds of catastrophe was like something out of a nightmare, like the one she'd had the night before.

She'd been there, having a coffee with Alice before before warmup. Alice was playing that day, and though Heather knew as much about baseball as Alice knew about quantum physics, Heather would be there to watch her play.

And then the world ended.

Something like that.

She watched the approaching man-thing with a feeling of déjà vu and a growing sense of doom.

"*Five!*" Alice said, though Heather barely registered her voice.

Heather's eyes fixed on the gaunt man with the notebook open in one large hand. The fingers, spread apart like a skeletal starfish, were long enough to support the open book, to curl around its edges to hold it open. He scribbled in it with a tiny stub of pencil clutched in his other awkward hand. He moved without walking, his legs bent and trailing behind him, tapering into clutching clusters that could not be called feet.

"Matrix synapse error. You've corrupted yourself and everything you touch," Alice said. She didn't shout, but her voice rose in volume to drown out everything else: the panic of the paperback man scrambling over the back of his chair to put as much space between himself and the floating horror as he could, the screams and crashes from outside, the rising shriek Heather realized was coming from her own open mouth.

The man-thing looked up from his notebook to regard Alice, the grin that seemed somehow painted on the blank, mouthless flat of his face turned to static before resolving into an equally false looking sneer.

The hand/claw holding the mostly used up pencil lashed out toward Alice, cut deep but bloodless slashes in her skin. Where the flesh of her cheek flapped open, Heather saw the darkness of void, the nothingness behind the flimsy film of reality.

Alice seemed not to feel the injury. She caught the wrist of the claw-like hand and twisted it until the pencil fell from its grasp, rolling beneath their table. It tugged uselessly to free itself, but Alice's grip was unbreakable.

"Four!" Alice said. *"Parallax error. Each failed attempt only makes the next failure more certain."*

"My math is correct," the man-thing said. His voice was full of static, a poorly tuned radio. "I need more time!"

"Three! The finite mind cannot compensate for infinite variables." Alice grabbed his other wrist and twisted until it cracked. *"You have no more time."*

The man-thing wailed in his distant, staticky voice.

The notebook hit the floor next to the stub of pencil and closed.

"Two! Quarantine and removal of corrupting dynamic…"

The man-thing was gone.

As if he'd never been there.

As if he'd never *been*.

The bell above the door rang as another customer entered.

The paperback man looked up from his book to note the new arrival, an elderly woman in a peacoat much too warm for the weather, then sipped his drink and went back to his story.

Alice sat, reading Heather's manuscript, flipping the page and continuing with apparent—and to Heather, surprising—interest.

Heather was back in her seat too, though she didn't know how she'd gotten there. Whatever had happened outside seemed to have ended. The sounds of catastrophe were gone. Now it was the low, unexciting white noise of pre-rush hour traffic.

"You okay?" Alice asked, pulling her gaze from the manuscript.

Heather's hammering heart was slowing. Whatever had happened to scare her so badly seemed to be fading from her memory as it had from the world.

But there had been *something*!

"Heather?"

"Huh?" Heather found Alice watching her with apparent concern. "Yeah, I'm fine."

Alice seemed unconvinced, but went back to reading, nodding as if she agreed with something she'd just read.

"Order for Alice," the barista called, and Heather started in her seat.

She got this sometimes, the eerie feeling that she'd just doubled back and experienced the same moment twice. A strong sense of déjà vu, and an inexplicable fear while she waited for something bad to happen.

So far, the vague sense of approaching doom had never borne fruit, only faded into confusion, and later the excitement of having experienced something paralleling the supernatural, which she certainly did *not* believe in, though she wished she could.

Alice showed no signs of putting down Heather's manuscript to get their drinks, so Heather did.

On her way back she saw a notebook beneath their table, next to a blunt stub of pencil. It looked as if it had been carried around the universe several times, collecting all its secrets along the way.

She set her drinks down and bent to pick it up before sitting down.

Alice placed Heather's manuscript down on the table between them and picked up her drink, a large caramel mocha, extra shot.

"You're right you know," Alice said, tapping the cover page. "Well, mostly right."

"What?" Heather was reaching for her own drink when this unexpected communication caught her. "When did you learn quantum mechanics?"

Alice seemed to consider this for a moment before shaking her head.

"I have no fucking clue," Alice said. "You must be rubbing off on me."

"Dear diary," Heather said. "A strange thing happened at the coffee shop today."

She clutched the well-worn notebook and shuddered as that sense of déjà vu doubled back on her. Kidding or not, she was pretty sure something strange had happened.

Maybe it still was.

SOLVE FOR X

Wil Forbis

I never liked math. All those confusing equations and stupid formulae could drive a person bonkers. But when I was a kid, math changed my life.

Well, I wasn't a kid exactly. Having entered the ninth grade, I was a boy, a lad, a young buck on the cusp of being a man. I don't mean to bore you with pedantics, but as an author, I'm very precise with the words I use. Yes, I'm an author, and this is the point where people usually ask, "Oh, have I read anything you've written?" And, if I think they're cool, I'll say, "Have you read *Blood Orgy at Brenton Beach*, *Zombie Love Slaves*, or *Teen Werewolves in Heat*?" If they're not cool, I mumble something about how I write obscure literary works that seldom get read and barely pay the bills. At least the latter half of that sentence is true.

But I'm already losing the plot (something a writer should never do), so let me get back on track.

I'll start with the last time I saw Darleen Milford alive.

She was my math tutor and I'll be damned if I didn't need one. I was living in Twain Crest, a small town in Washington state about ninety miles from the Pacific coast. When it became clear I was on my way to flunking Algebra for the second time, my dad looked for a tutor who could come over on Tuesday nights and force all those numbers and equations to stick in my head. And that's just what Darleen, a senior at my high school, was doing.

"So, what's the value of x here?" She sat beside me at my bedroom desk, pointing at some incomprehensible scribbling she'd just introduced as an example of a linear equation.

For more than a minute, I dragged my trusty Faber-Castell No. 2 pencil over a piece of yellow notebook paper, in a desperate search for an answer.

"Six?" I ventured.

A disappointed sigh flitted from her lips and she pointed again at the original equation:

$$3(x - 2) = 2x + c.$$

"You're forgetting to calculate in the value of c. See, there's an extra constant c, which I set at fifty-six. So, x equals sixty-two."

"But if you wanted a fifty-six, why didn't you just write one?"

"Because this way, we can change the value of the constant to see what the equation will do under different circumstances. Maybe this equation models price for a business and they want to change how much profit is in their price without having to re-do everything else in the equation."

I groaned. "This sucks. Why do I have to do math, anyway? I'm going to be a rich and famous author, like Stephen King. Then I'll just hire peons to do my math for me."

"Maybe you will. But right now, your dad is paying me good money to make sure you pass the final in five weeks."

"Do you even know what a peon is?" I asked snarkily.

"I'm staring at one."

I reddened. Darleen might've looked like your average high school blonde, but if I'd learned one thing during our two-hour tutoring sessions, it was that she was super smart. Like Einstein level. Good with numbers and good with snappy repartee.

And, frankly, pretty hot. When she leaned over and wrote another equation on my yellow paper, the frilly edge of her blouse brushed against my shoulder and a burst of heat flared in my neck. And, umm, other parts.

"Can you do that one?" she asked. "Solve for x."

I creased my brow and got to work, running all the variables and calculations through my math-frazzled brain. Finally, I pointed at my answer.

Darleen frowned. "The constant, Andy. Don't forget to calculate in the c. The answer would be three hundred forty-seven."

"Goddamn shit-balls!"

"Don't swear. Look, you just have to take your time. Here's what I do when

I have a conundrum. I take three deep breaths and count to ten. Then I can focus and figure it out." She paused, then added, "It works for a lot of things, not just math."

"Yeah, like you have conundrums. You're a senior with a 4.0 GPA. You're guaranteed that Stanford scholarship. I bet your life is a breeze."

"I wish," she said almost absentmindedly. She looked at the aqua and pink monstrosity that passed for a wristwatch. Her eyes narrowed.

"You got a hot date?" I asked. "I'd hate to think I'm keeping you from something."

She showed a hint of a smile, then her face flatlined back to its usual serious mien. (Yes, it's a word. Look it up.)

"It's eight-fifteen," she reported. "My sister was supposed to be here at eight."

Ah, her sister. Everyone in Twain Crest knew Tessa Milford, the town's resident fuckup. Whereas Darleen was a brainiac who'd skipped seventh grade, Tessa was a nineteen-year-old high school dropout who drove around in a beat up '78 Camaro that smelled of pot and cheap beer. Seniors would point at her and say "she swallows" before descending into fits of sniggering.

"Huh," I said. "Well, maybe my dad can take you home." The old man was downstairs in his study.

Darleen looked out my window at the snow gathering on the sidewalks and streets under a night sky. She seemed lost in indecision for a moment, then said, "No, I don't want to bother him. It's not that far for me to walk."

"Are you kidding? You'll freeze your nutsack off out there."

"Don't swear," she admonished again. (Though, is 'nutsack' really a swear? Regardless, I still can't say why she chose to correct the profanity instead of the anatomy.)

I wish I'd tried harder to convince her. Like, I could have just demanded she get a ride from my dad. Or gone all-in and walked her home myself. Instead, I said nothing as she padded across the bedroom carpet and grabbed her puffy winter coat off my dresser.

(Oh, and in case you're wondering why she didn't just pull out her iPhone or Android and call her sister? This was 1990, and the only mobile phones in existence were the size of parking blocks.)

As Darleen stuffed her arms into her backpack straps, I returned my gaze to the notebook, peeking ahead to the quadratic equations we'd have to tackle next. They still looked like some foreign language, Greek or Klingon. "So, you really like math, huh?" I asked.

"It just comes easy to me. Always has. Numbers make sense. People, not so much."

I leapt at the chance for a meaningful connection. "Yeah, I hear you there. That's why I enjoy writing. I can just ignore the world, get lost in my head." I paused and looked over at her. "We're a lot alike, you know? I think you use numbers and math to tell stories the same way I use words."

Darleen chuckled. "Well, that's not quite right. Numbers are abstractions, they don't have semantic meaning. You can't use them to tell stories."

"*Au contraire, ma petite cherie*," I said, using a phrase I'd picked up from an old comic book. "Numbers can be used as code. I just wrote a short story where the hero Zaran the Bold uses numbers to send a secret message to the wizard Snarf the Magnificent."

"A number code? Like where 1 equals A and 2 equals B?"

"No, it's not that obvious," I flared. "Snarf has to subtract Zaran's age from the number. Zaran is twenty-three years old, so thirty-five is really twelve which is…"—I took a moment to think it through—"…an L."

I could almost hear Darleen's eye roll. "Sounds unbreakable. Where were you when we were fighting the Nazis?"

"Hey, I thought it was pretty cool. Zaran's first message is 27-24-37-30-28-41 which spells out 'danger.' Then he follows it with—"

She waved a hand to shush me. "Sorry, kiddo, but I've got to get going. If Tessa ever shows up, just tell her I walked. But I'll see you next week. And in the meantime, practice your equations."

"Yeah, okay." Disappointment pulled my lips towards a frown. I'd been pretty pissed when my dad said I needed a math tutor, but I liked spending time with Darleen.

And she seemed to catch that. She gave me a thumbs-up sign. "You're doing really well, Andy. You're smarter than you think. You know that, right?"

Frown averted. But before I could reply, Darleen walked out the door and turned down the hallway. Seconds later, I heard her boots clumping on the stairs.

$$\pi$$

Later that night, I lay in my darkened bedroom. In my mind, I was running through Darleen's steps for solving linear equations, how you had to do the same thing to both sides, account for those damned arbitrary constants if there were any, and—

Look, that's not what I was doing and we both know it. I was jerking off. About Darleen. Because she was hot and I was fourteen.

I was in mid-stroke, breathing ragged, when thumping came from downstairs. Someone knocking on the door.

Around my family's house, that never happened this late. My heart pumped in my chest. Well, more than it already was.

As I was yanking up my pajama pants, I heard my parents leave their bedroom. By the time I got down the stairs to the front hallway, they were hovering by the open door, talking with two men standing on our porch. The sheriff and a deputy.

Mom turned and looked at me, her eyes wide under brown bangs. "Oh, Andy…go back upstairs, baby."

She only called me *baby* when things were really bad. "What is it?" I looked at the sheriff. "What's wrong?"

Dad answered. "Your math tutor never came home. Did she say anything about where she might've been going when she left?"

My lower lip quivered. I explained how her sister had never arrived and Darleen was going to walk home. The sheriff nodded like he knew all that.

There was a bit more conversation, and the cops said their goodbyes. I moved to the living room window and watched them stomp across the snow-covered asphalt to a police cruiser parked under a bright streetlight. In the back seat, dark-haired Tessa Milford sat next to an older woman holding her face in her hands. Darleen's mother, I guessed.

Mom put her arm on my back. "Let's get you some hot chocolate, Andy. I'm sure the police are going to find her."

"I'm not a little kid, Mom!" I yelled, right before I ran up the stairs with tears welling in my eyes.

$$\pi$$

But they didn't find her. Not in the first forty-eight hours that they always say are the most important, nor in the weeks afterwards. The cops sussed out what Darleen's path home would have been, but all they could determine was that, at some unknown point, she disappeared.

Around town, people mused that maybe a wolf or coyote had gotten her and dragged her into the woods, but we all knew that would have left evidence. Others theorized she'd run away to Portland or Seattle. But why would anyone do that a year away from a Stanford scholarship?

The first Sunday after Darleen disappeared, I heard a few older ladies in church say in hushed tones that maybe she was just like her sister, that she'd gone off to "party" with some weirdo and that was the end of it. I wanted to march up and demand they retract their salacious (I'd picked that one up from a Dean Koontz novel) accusations, but instead I fumed in silence.

After three weeks, it didn't seem like there was any chance of finding her. It was like everyone in town, the sheriff included, just threw up their hands and said, "What can we do?" The "missing" posters stapled to bulletin boards and telephone poles grew tattered and faded. The gossip at school moved to whether Jake Twilla and Chevi Quinn were doing it, or if Rory Fitzgerald was gay.

And my dad was still shitting himself about that upcoming Algebra final. Here's the thing you have to understand about the guy: he'd been a whiz at math since he was a kid. Like Darleen, he had a photographic memory for numbers, and he'd parlayed that ability into a cushy job as a computer programmer. So he was damned if he was going to have a son who didn't know his way around polynomials, expression factoring, and functions.

Since there weren't any other student math tutors in town, Dad found the next best thing. He went to his old college buddy—my math teacher, Mr. Edmundsen—and talked him into giving me extra help after school. So, every Tuesday and Thursday at 2:30, I trudged into Edmundsen's office and let him blather on about math and algebra. He wasn't easy on the eyes like Darleen—he was overweight with sweat stains on his cardigans, and had a comb-over that looked like a roadkill ferret had crawled atop his bulbous head and died—but he did his best. And his best turned out to be good enough. After a couple weeks, I started feeling confident about the final.

That confidence put a nice swing in my step when I left Edmundsen's classroom after our fifth session together. I was so lost in my thoughts as I stepped past the fence that cordoned the school off from the surrounding neighborhood, I didn't even notice the approaching group of boys until they surrounded me.

"Hey nerd," said Troy James. "I want to talk to you."

My heart thrummed in my chest, but I tried to play it cool. "Hey Troy. What's happening, my brother?"

Troy lumbered towards me until the breast pocket of his denim jacket was inches away from my head. "I said I want to talk to you, nerd. I need you to do me a favor."

"Favors are my specialty, cool guy. You need someone to walk the dog? Mow the lawn? Take your sister to the winter prom?"

"Fuck that," Troy said. "I know you're hanging out with Edmundsen after school. I want you to get a copy of the math final. I gotta pass that bitch if I'm going to stay on the team." He mimed tossing a football into the end zone.

"Aw, man." I pursed my lips in faux-disappointment. "I don't think Mr. Edmundsen keeps that test in his office. We're in the '90s now, my brother. Everything is computerized, like on *Star Trek*. He probably has the test on his PC at home."

"What? He keeps it in his pee-pee?"

"His *pee-see*," I corrected. "Personal computer. He doesn't have the files in his school office."

Troy smiled like a happy reptile. "Well, then, I guess you just need to break into his house and get it for me." He took a step forward, pushing me back against the chain-link fence.

I chuckled as I tried to keep my bowels from emptying into my corduroy trousers. "Gosh, that is a great plan, buddy. But, you know, I'm just not much of a second-story man. Maybe one of your pals here can help you out. So I'll just be on my—"

"Nerd!" Troy held a fist under my chin. "Edmundsen knows you. He trusts you. You can get into his house. And you're going to get me that test. You dig?"

"Okay, okay," I whined. "I'll get the test. Can I go now?"

A flat palm slapped my cheek. "You think I'm an idiot, nerd? I know you're not going to get the message without some thwacks. Me and the boys are gonna leave a couple bruises on you, okay? But don't worry. We won't mess up your pretty face." That got a round of laughs from the surrounding gaggle of ninth-grade behemoths.

Wham! I crumpled over, Troy's fist in my belly. I was able to gasp for air a couple times before I felt a blow to my ribs. I toppled to one side and hit the ground.

"Get up, nerd. Take your beating like a man."

"Suck eggs" was what I wanted to say, but the deficit of oxygen in my lungs and my sense of self-preservation kept me quiet.

"Get him, dude," came a voice I recognized as belonging to Troy's second-in-command, Pete 'Stitches' Norwood. "Fuck that nerd up."

Troy rolled me onto my back and straddled my chest. "Just a couple more hits so you get the message." He jabbed his fist into my shoulder and I felt an explosion of pain. Tears dampened my eyes and warmed my cheeks.

A thunderous roar split the air, growing louder in the space of a few seconds. Tires screeched to a stop and a car door opened and slammed shut.

"Get away from him, you little shitbags!"

I turned and saw a young woman in a leather jacket, Metallica t-shirt, and torn jeans standing in front of a black Camaro. Tessa Milford was glaring at Troy and his gang.

"Buzz off, sister," Troy said. "This isn't any of your business."

Tessa reached down into her boot and pulled out a knife that belonged in a *Crocodile Dundee* movie. She smiled at Troy. "Your scalp is going to look great hanging from my rearview. And I bet your buddies will make a nice set of lamp-shades."

Troy gulped and tried to play it cool. He got off me and held his hands up in surrender. "Fine, you psycho slut. We'll lay off."

"Help him up," Tessa demanded.

Troy turned and extended his hand. As he pulled me to standing, he whispered, "This doesn't change anything, nerd. Get me the fucking test!"

The bully and his gang strutted off, leaving me with the knife-wielding sister of my missing math tutor. "Umm, thanks," I said. "You showed up at the right time."

Tessa dropped the knife back into her boot. She stepped forward and, for the first time in my life, I saw her up close. Curls of oily black hair dangled into her bloodshot eyes. Her alabaster skin had a few blotches of acne. But, while she didn't have Darleen's natural beauty, she was still attractive.

"It's not exactly a coincidence," she said. "I've been keeping an eye on you."

"Huh? What for?"

She looked at me like she was going to lay what people would soon be re-ferring to as *truth bombs* on me. Her lower lip curled into her mouth and she ner-vously chewed on it.

It was, as we said back then, hella sexy.

"Everyone knew Darleen had this talent for math," she said (and believe me, I took notice of her choice of *had*). "But I've got my own talents. I can sense things about the world. Sometimes I see, I dunno, shapes, colors around people that reveal their emotions."

"Auras," I said.

"Yeah, whatever. And right after our dad died two years ago, I could still feel him around us. I could still feel his love." Her eyes moistened.

"Wow. That's pretty intense."

Tessa shivered. "When Darleen disappeared, I felt like I could still sense her out there. She was frightened, crying, in a state of terrible fear. I could feel her mind reaching out for me. But I couldn't close in on it. I couldn't locate her." Her anguished tone made clear how much this tormented her.

With nothing to say, I just nodded. Inside, I was wondering if this chick was batshit crazy.

"Then it was like the signal disappeared. Suddenly I couldn't feel anything. That lasted a few weeks, until I started having the dreams. Everything was foggy, unclear, but there was a figure, someone I took to be Darleen. And she was trying to tell me something. But it just wouldn't come through."

"Do you know why? Why couldn't she connect?" I still wasn't sure I believed any of this, but I was curious.

She looked up at the white clouds filling the afternoon sky. "I don't think she's part of our world anymore. I think she's moved on. And wherever she is, it's hard to communicate. But she still has—"

"Unfinished business," I said, though the sentence practically spoke itself if you'd ever seen a ghost movie.

"Yeah. Unfinished business."

I blinked in confusion. "But why were you watching me? I don't know anything about this stuff."

"Darleen liked you," Tessa said. "I mean, not romantically or anything. She thought you were a dork, like everyone else in town, but—"

"Are you going somewhere with this?"

"She said you had a good heart." Tessa smiled. "And in my dreams, all I can get is that she's going to deliver a message to you. It's a message only you will be able to understand."

"A message? I haven't seen any message."

Tessa sighed. She reached into her jacket pocket and retrieved a pack of Marlboros and a lighter. Moments later, a lit cigarette dangled from her lips. Also pretty damn sexy.

"I don't know," she said. "Like I was saying, I'm not getting a clear signal. Sometimes I think I sense something and when I try to focus, it's gone. But just tell me you'll keep your eyes open. We need to find out what happened to her." She paused. "I should have picked her up that night." She rubbed her temples, her hand covering her eyes. Soft sobs quavered her chest.

"Why do you drink so much?" I asked. "Why are you always stoned?"

She stared at me. "I told you. I see people's emotions. I can tell what they're really feeling. Anger, sadness, fear, depression. It's not easy to have all that going off in your head. You don't know what part is you and what part is some-body else."

For a second time, I nodded. That sounded like a lot to bear, whether real or imagined.

I contemplated whether to ask my next question until curiosity got the best of me.

"People say you sleep with a lot of guys. Is that true?"

Her eyes clouded, like she couldn't believe what she had to put up with from this stupid ninth-grader. "Do you ever even see me with guys?"

I thought about it and had to admit I did not.

Tessa took a long drag from her smoke. "I don't have any fucking friends in this town, much less boyfriends or whatever." She looked to the side, avoiding my gaze. In a quieter voice, she said, "I'm a virgin, you dope."

I straightened to my full height, still a few inches shorter than her. "You know…I think I could help you out with that."

She blurted a laugh. "Man, you really are a twerp."

I have to admit, that kind of stung.

We wrapped it up from there. I told Tessa I'd look for any messages from the spirit realm, but my tone made clear I wasn't hopeful. She gave me her num-ber and told me to contact her if I saw anything. Then she drove me home in her Camaro, which was pretty cool, though she insisted on blasting these shitty tunes from some band called Nirvana she said was going to be a big deal.

π

As the days dragged on towards the Algebra final, my stomach tied itself in knots over Troy's demand I get him a copy of the test. I mean, how was I sup-posed to get into Edmundsen's house? And even if I did, would the test be on the computer? That was more of a guess on my part than anything solid.

With my head filled with visions of Troy pounding my face into a pile of crimson sludge, I had little leftover brainpower to use on Tessa's idea that Dar-leen would be contacting me from the beyond.

That changed the day of the pop quiz.

I was in a Tuesday math class, feeling the heat of Troy's gaze on my neck, when Edmundsen announced we were having a test. "To prepare you for the fi-nal at the end of the week," he said before he walked down the aisles and handed out a piece of paper with eighteen questions.

Now, like I said, with the baseline of Darleen's prep and Edmundsen's help on top of it, I was starting to get okay at this math crap. I worked my way through the problems pretty quickly and didn't think much of them until I got to the last question that involved using a calculator to find the decimal approximation of irrational solutions to equations. When I penciled the number onto the answer line, my heart pushed up into my throat.

Remember the story I'd told Darleen about, the one with Zaran the Bold? I was still working on it, though the hero was now called Zaran the Paladin because I thought it sounded more sophisticated. As a result, the numerical code Zaran used to warn Snarf the Magnificent of *danger* was fresh in my head. That series of numbers was 27, 24, 37, 30, 28, 41.

The answer to the final question on the quiz was 27.2437302841.

Spooky, huh? I thought so. I realized it could be a coincidence, but I was reminded of Einstein's quote, "Coincidence is God's way of remaining anonymous." Yeah, God—or maybe somebody else.

But what did it mean? What was I supposed to do with this? I had no idea.

I didn't have much time to think about it. After school, I had a session with Edmundsen, the last before semester finals started. On Wednesday, it was going to be all humanities tests, then math and science on Thursday. That meant I had less than two days to get the questions to Troy.

Just in case I'd forgotten that fact, Troy conveniently reminded me. I'd taken to leaving campus by sneaking through the teacher parking lot and it had worked like a charm so far. But after my test prep with Edmundsen, Troy and his goons were waiting.

"Where's my test, nerd?" Troy barked as he pushed me against Coach Phillips' 1986 Dodge RAM with the bumper sticker that read *If the van is a-rockin', don't come a-knockin'.*

"Troy, good buddy, where've you been? I've been looking all over—"

He cut me off with an uppercut to the solar plexus that knocked the wind out of me and crumpled me to the asphalt. "I don't have time for your bullshit, dork. I've gotta pass that test or I'm off the team. When are you gonna get it for me?"

"Umm, is tomorrow too soon?" I asked, though I had no idea how I would do it.

"I dunno. Is it too soon for me to break open your face?" he snarled.

"That doesn't really answer my quest—" Troy gave me a swift boot to the ribs. Then he and his buddies, to use a popular euphemism, kicked the shit out of me.

But I gotta give those guys credit. They didn't leave a mark on my face.

That night, my dad slapped me on the back, right where one of the bruises Troy had left was flowering purple. "How you feeling about that Algebra final, Andy? Has Mr. Edmundsen's tutelage been helping?"

I suppressed a groan. "I think I'm gonna nail it, Dad." I left out the addendum, *unless I get busted stealing it from the teacher's computer.*

Mom gave me a sorrowful look. "We know it hasn't been easy for you, honey. With everything that happened with Darleen. Maybe you can think of passing the math final as a way of honoring her memory?" She gave an awkward smile and added, "Even though I'm sure they're going to find her."

Yeah. Thanks, Mom.

After the lights went out, I lay in my bed feeling my guts churning like a nest of vipers. I had no idea how to get that test, and with my brain buzzing the way it was, I couldn't even begin to concentrate on the conundrum.

Conundrum. I heard Darleen's voice from all those nights ago.

Here's what I do when I have a difficult conundrum. I take three deep breaths and count to ten. Then I can focus and figure it out.

I tried it and damned if it didn't work. The scheme came to me in a rush. As Dad's snores filtered through the house, I crept into the bathroom and grabbed what I needed from the medicine cabinet. Then I snuck downstairs to Dad's office where his tan Gateway 2000 PC sat on a desk.

$$\pi$$

The first half of Wednesday sailed by. I had History and English Lit finals, which I nailed because I loved those subjects. As I walked off campus at noon, I ran into Troy. The bruises on my chest and back throbbed at the sight of him, but I flashed a smile. "Meet me at Dane's Park at three. I'll have your test."

"I'm gonna kick your ass, nerd."

"Do you seriously not understand why that's not an incentive?"

He scowled as I walked off, but I figured he'd gotten the message.

As a math teacher, Edmundsen didn't have any tests to deliver that day, so I guessed he'd be home. Sure enough, he responded quickly when I pounded on the door of his two-story Craftsman. "Andy?" he said with a confused look. "Can I help you?"

"It's the math final, Mr. Edmundsen," I squealed. "I just don't feel prepared. And if I don't pass, my dad is gonna kill me, sir. I'm just so nervous I can't—"

"Andy, Andy, calm down. I've seen your scores on the prep quizzes. You're gonna be fine."

"Please, Mr. Edmundsen. Could we just go over the equations one more time? I just want to make sure I got it." I held up a piece of plastic Tupperware. "I brought some slices of my mom's chocolate mayonnaise cake."

Edmundsen smiled. "Okay, fine, Andy, I can give you an hour." He waved me through the door and led me down a hallway into his office.

It was easy to see why Edmundsen was unmarried: the place was a pigsty. Books and magazines lay scattered over coffee tables, couches and chairs. In the center of the room, numerous ceramic mugs sat on a coffee-ringed oak desk that also supported a large computer and some weird marble statuette of an owl.

The window on the far wall had a nice view of his backyard, though. I'll never forget looking out there and seeing the giant bigleaf maple tree towering over the snow-patched dirt, its skeletal limbs covered with green lichen.

"Let's get started," Edmundsen said. "Should we review polynomials? The quadratic formula?"

"You wanna have the cake?" I asked. "Sugar is good brain fuel."

"Don't mind if I do." Edmundsen opened the Tupperware, picked up a frosting covered delicacy and shoved it in his mouth. "Mmmm, chocolate," he said as he chewed with his mouth open, another clue in the *why Edmundsen wasn't married* mystery. "There's two more pieces, Andy. Would you like one?"

"I'm diabetic, sir," I lied. "They're all yours."

As he devoured the remaining cakes, he explained—yet again—the coefficients of polynomials. One thing was obvious as he blathered on: Edmundsen loved math. I mean, he really seemed to enjoy the abstraction of numbers and formulae. I guess he was a lot like Darleen in that regard.

But it didn't take long before the laxative pills I'd melted into the chocolate started to take effect. His stomach burbled and he shifted uncomfortably in his chair. When he actually ripped a fart in front of me, he mumbled something about needing to take a bathroom break.

I worked quickly. Like I said, I couldn't care less about the math my dad loved, but I shared his interest in computers. So it was easy for me to navigate my way through the Windows 3.0 folder structure (fun fact: there was no password security back then) and locate the file marked "Algebra Final_90." I inserted the five-and-a-quarter-inch floppy disk I'd taken from my dad's office into the drive and copied the file. Edmundsen was still in the bathroom when I pulled the disk out and tucked it into my knapsack. I walked to the hallway and shouted, "How you doing, sir? Can I get you anything?"

He groaned something unintelligible in response. I chuckled and sauntered through his office looking at math geek stuff. My mission was complete, and I was just killing time.

I got to a large bookcase in one corner and started examining the photographs set on a shelf. There was one of a young Mr. Edmundsen and a group of people in a foreign country, like Spain or France or something. Then there was one of him seated with a couple of old people, probably his parents. Past that was a framed certificate for Twain Crest High School's teacher of the year award.

I paused at a picture of Edmundsen with twelve kids around my age standing behind a banner that said, "Student Mathletes, 1988." I gazed over the faces until my eyes froze in their sockets.

"See something of interest?" Edmundsen was in the doorway, staring at me.

I raised a trembling finger. "You knew Darleen Milford?" She stood in the picture, right next to Edmundsen. He had his arm around her shoulders and she looked really uncomfortable.

The floorboards creaked as the heavyset man crossed the room to join me. "Of course. She was one of the best students I've ever had. Truly a gifted mind." He turned to me. "I understand you were the last person to see her alive."

"Yeah," I said. "Except for…" I didn't finish the sentence. *Except for whoever killed her.*

At that moment, a strange look crossed Edmundsen's face. His lower lip quivered and the edges of his mouth turned ever so slightly towards a smile. His eyelids narrowed around his gray pupils and he stared at Darleen.

It was a look that chilled me to the bone.

Edmundsen shrugged. "Well, should we get back to the quadratics? We want to make sure you feel confident for that test."

My mouth went dry and my heart pulsed against my ribs. I reached for my knapsack and threw my arms into the straps. "You know, sir, I think I'm good. I've got it all figured out. Th-thank you."

"You sure? I could go another hour if you want. Now that I've cleared out the plumbing so to speak." He patted his round belly.

"Really, sir. I've taken up enough of your time already." I turned and took several steps towards the hallway.

A hand on my shoulder stopped me in my tracks. "Andy?" Mr. Edmundsen said.

I gulped and swiveled to face him. He looked at me with a grave expression, his eyes studying my face.

"Yes, sir?" I asked.

"Good luck on the final."

He smiled, released his grip on my shoulder and I made like a banana and got the flying fuck out of there. Back home, Dad wasn't in his office, so I was able to print out the test without any questions. I scarfed some microwaved pizza rolls and headed back out the door, arriving at Dane's Park at 3:15.

Troy and the boys stood by the empty basketball court. "You're late, nerd."

"C'mon, good buddy. Good things come to those who wait." I handed him the printout.

Troy unfolded the sheets and scanned the material. He looked like a bird had just taken a dump in his hair. "What the fuck is this?"

"It's the Algebra final, buddy. It's all the questions."

"I don't need the questions, retard. I need the answers. You're supposed to give me the answers."

"Jesus Christ. I gotta do everything around here. Fine, one of you jokers got a pencil?"

Ryan Suzuki reached into his pocket. "Umm, you mean like this?"

"Yes," I said. "You have, in fact, correctly identified a pencil." Ryan smiled at his victory and I sat down on a park bench and started running through the test. It was fifty questions total, so it took me just shy of an hour, but thanks to my new math expertise, I powered through the sonofabitch.

The last twelve questions were all linear equations that needed to be solved for x. They also each had several c values, which seemed a bit strange. After I finished, I paused and looked at the answers, none of which were over two digits.

Troy had been following my progress. "You done, dork?"

"Hold on." I ran each answer through Zaran's code, subtracting 23 from the number to arrive at a letter. As my breath stalled in my throat, I grouped the results together and got...

...absolute gibberish. The numbers didn't decode to anything that made sense.

"C'mon!" Troy grabbed the paper out of my hand and examined my work, as if he could make any sense of it. "Looks good." He punched my shoulder. "I guess we won't kick your ass again."

"Lucky me," I muttered, my mind racing to figure out what I'd done wrong. Maybe everything. Maybe the previous message in the pop quiz had been a fluke. Maybe Tessa's ideas about some sort of communication from Darleen were just the ramblings of a guilt-ridden sibling trying to make up for abandoning her sister.

Troy and his buddies were walking off when it hit me. What had Tessa said? *It's a message only you will be able to understand.*

"Wait," I yelled. Before Troy could make a full turn, I ran up and grabbed the test out of his hands.

"You fucking dork!" He pulled his fist back, animal rage flashing across his face.

That faded when he saw the look in my eyes, a look that told him if he fucked with me I would go down fighting dirty: gouging eyes, biting flesh, squeezing testicles until they popped like grapes.

"I just need a couple more minutes," I said. "Then you'll get your test."

He wiped his nose and gave a curt nod.

I returned to the bench and ran through the questions again. But this time I didn't account for the *c*-values. I made the same mistake I'd kept making that last night Darleen was at my house. Then I ran Zaran's code and gaped at the words written at the bottom of the page:

BIGLEAF MAPLE.

$$\pi$$

"I've got it!" I barked into the phone.

"Whaddaya mean?" Tessa replied. She sounded drunk. But I explained how I'd figured out the message and all we needed to do was tell the sheriff. Edmundsen would be cooked.

Tessa laughed. "Yer gonna tell the cops that my dead sister sent you a secret code in a math test that tells you she's buried in some guy's backyard? Good luck with that."

Hmm, she had a point. "Meet at my house tomorrow at noon," I said. "We're going to end this."

$$\pi$$

The Camaro growled as Tessa pulled up to the curb outside my house. Before she could get out, I opened the passenger door, tossed a shovel on the back seat, and got in. "Let's go. We're headed to Edmundsen's."

"What if he's home?"

"He's not. He's proctoring the Algebra final."

"Umm, shouldn't you be there?" she asked.

"Fuck math."

Minutes later, we pulled up near Edmundsen's house. Tessa looked up the tree-lined street, her face paler than usual. "I just realized," she said. "If Darleen was walking home from your place, she'd pass right by here."

I gave a grim nod.

We rounded the side of the house to a seven-foot-tall wooden gate. Tessa pushed me over the top, then I opened it from the inside and let her in. We walked over to the tree.

"Bigleaf maple," Tessa said, quoting Darleen's message.

"Yep. The only question is: where? This tree's got a pretty wide expanse. We could be digging for hours."

Saying nothing, Tessa walked under the decrepit branches, her face fixed with intent, like she was listening for something. Finally, she stopped at a patch of dirt near a wide root. "Here," she said softly. "She's here."

I started digging with the shovel, piling the displaced earth off to the side. I'd dug a hole that was about three feet wide and two feet deep when I had to take a break. Tessa took over, expanding the width by a foot and getting another foot down. She stood in the pit, sweat beading on her brow despite the chilly winter air. "I dunno," she said. "Maybe we got something wrong. Maybe I'm full of shit."

"No," I said. "Take a rest. I'm ready to dig again."

She walked over to the steps that led up to Edmundsen's back porch and sat down. I got in the hole and resumed driving the shovel into the earth. After five minutes of effort, the shovel hit something harder than dirt but softer than rock. I looked down at what could have been a stray root. Or something else.

I tossed the shovel, knelt in the hole, and wiped the dirt away with my fingers. Within seconds, I was staring at a small human hand.

"Tessa," I said. "Come here!"

There was no answer.

"Tessa?"

I stood and turned. Across the yard, Edmundsen stood behind Tessa, pressing a silver kitchen knife against her throat.

"Goddammit, Andy," my math teacher said. "I thought you were acting funny when you came by the house. But it wasn't until you skipped the final I figured out what you were up to." He clucked his tongue. "Such a disappointment. I had to flunk you by the way."

"Any chance of a makeup?"

He didn't laugh. "Get out of the hole." Keeping the knife against Tessa's neck, he marched her to the middle of the yard and stopped a few feet in front of me.

I furtively cast a side eye at the shovel. Maybe I could—

"Don't," he said. "I'll slit her throat like I did her sister."

My teeth clenched. "So you did it. Why? Why'd you kill her?"

Edmundsen exhaled, the sound coming out as a whistle. "You don't meet many girls like Darleen. So smart, and so beautiful. I was in love with her the minute she joined the Mathletes. But I had to keep it secret, you know? I had to just hope the feeling would pass."

Tessa growled like a wounded dog. "You're a sick fucking fuck!"

"I probably am," Edmundsen mused. "But those feelings never went away. And then, when I heard that Darleen would be leaving for Stanford next year, it just made me want her more. So it was almost a dream when I looked out the window that night and saw her walking in the snow. Like some kind of angel."

A grief-stricken moan escaped Tessa's throat. She'd been reminded, once again, of her failure to pick up her sister.

Edmundsen's finger tightened on the knife handle, his knuckles turning white. "I stepped out on the porch and called to her. She waved, and I invited her in. She was reticent, but I offered her some hot chocolate and, well, I can be pretty convincing when I want to be. When I got her in the office, I grabbed her and tried to kiss her but she wasn't having any of it. She started shrieking, and I had to knock her out with my owl statue."

Tears streamed down Tessa's face. Mine too. We didn't want to hear, we didn't want to know what would come next.

"I kept her tied up in the bedroom for three days," Edmundsen said. "Oh, we had some grand times. Made memories that will last a lifetime. For me anyway." He chuckled. "But it was obvious I couldn't let her live."

He leaned closer to Tessa's ear, and I heard him whisper. "She went quickly though. Just as you will."

He pressed the glinting silver into the side of her neck and blood ran down her flesh. As he swiped the blade sideways, she raised her knee and reached into her boot. He'd cut halfway across her throat when she jammed her knife into his gut.

"Shit!" Edmundsen screamed and released Tessa. She staggered forward, coughing, blood spattering her jacket. I wanted to grab her, to hold her, but Edmundsen wasn't slowing down. He marched at me, the Crocodile Dundee knife protruding from his belly. I hunched, picked up the shovel and swung low. There was a crunch as the metal blade connected with his knee. He screamed and toppled backwards to the ground where the hole we'd dug swallowed his upper body.

I knew we weren't out of the woods yet. Edmundsen would climb out, and despite that knife sticking out of him, he seemed to have a lot of adrenalized rage.

Only, he didn't get up. He just lay there like an overturned beetle, his spasming legs sticking out of the hole, the rest of his body obscured by dirt. "No!" I heard him cry out. "It can't be. You're dead! You're dead!"

There was another crunch, this one laden with a soul-rattling air of finality. Edmundsen's legs fell flat against the earth.

I ran to Tessa. She was holding her palm against her neck, blood seeping through her fingers. "I'm all right," she rasped. "I can breathe. He just cut the skin."

I winced. "But you need an ambulance. I shot up the porch steps, tossed a potted plant through the window, and raced into the office to call 911.

When I returned outside, Tessa was staring into the hole. She held one hand tight to her bleeding throat and waved me over with the other. "You need to see this," she whispered.

I crossed the yard and joined her at the edge. Edmundsen lay flat on his back, his wide eyes staring up at the bigleaf maple's barren limbs. The gray-skinned hands of Darleen's corpse coiled tightly around his impossibly stretched neck. Her head rested to one side, dead eyes gazing at the man who'd murdered her, a satisfied smile across her lips.

$$\pi$$

You know the drill from here. The cops and medics came. Tessa was taken to the hospital for what proved to be minor cuts. I explained to the sheriff what had happened though I breezed over the paranormal stuff and just said I had a hunch Edmundsen was the killer. With Darleen's body buried in his backyard, it was pretty obvious.

For the rest of my high school days, Tessa and I hung around a bit. After all, we'd been through some pretty heavy shit together. But it was obvious she was spiraling, roiled by the guilt of what had happened to Darleen. After a while, the booze and pot turned into heroin and coke. She got a bunch of DUIs, and the cops impounded the Camaro. Some days I'd see her hanging out with homeless dudes under the 12th Street Bridge. I'd wave at her and sometimes she'd wave back, but other times it was like she didn't even recognize me.

I wanted to save her, I really did. And I suppose some of you will fault me for not doing more. But Jesus, I was just a kid. A boy, maybe a lad, certainly no-where fucking near a man.

And then, one day, she was just gone. I realized I hadn't seen her for a while, not shuffling down the street, not hanging under the bridge, not staggering back from Minty's Saloon. She'd disappeared.

But, like it always does, life went on. I attended college, ran up a ton of debt on a worthless Creative Writing degree and ended up working double shifts at a shipping warehouse in Seattle to afford my insanely high rent. Dad died of a heart attack, and Mom moved to Vermont to be with her sister. I dated, had relation-ships, but nothing ever stuck. Gained weight, lost weight, gained a lot of it back. My twenties moved into my thirties and headed towards my forties.

But I kept writing, posting shit online, where I was largely ignored. Until one day I discovered my story "Vampire Suck-Fest" had three hundred thousand views. I expanded it into a novel, knocked out a couple sequels and soon I was (barely) making a living off writing. When I added in the *Chainsaw Lovers* and *Ec-toplasmic Ecstasy* series, fringe bookstores and comic shops started calling and ask-ing me to come by and do signings.

And that's where I saw her again. I was so focused on signing copies of my latest, *She-Squirters in the Slaughterhouse*, that I was barely looking up from the ta-ble. A figure handed me a book and said, "Can you sign it to the girl who was into Nirvana before it was cool?" It was Tessa. Older, of course, but she looked good. I mean really good.

After the signing, we grabbed coffee, and she explained that after she left Twain Crest, things got really dark for her. More drugs, gangs, some prostitu-tion, a hep-c infection. Somehow she stayed alive. She rehabbed a bunch of times but it didn't stick until she found herself in a ranch in Mexico's Sonoran Desert. Something about the open landscape and the endless dry days taught her how to quiet the voices in her head. Or at least turn down the volume.

We started dating, eventually moved in together, and within a couple of years, our son Kurt came along. He was followed by Andrew Jr. And thank God my *Mummies in Lust* series took off because not long after him we had our daugh-ter, Mayflower. She's only four now but she can already count to a hundred and asks me questions about geometry that blow my mind. I just tell her "Daddy's working" and to go ask her mother.

Tessa and I still talk about what happened all those years ago. We lie in bed late at night and wonder how Darleen was able to manipulate the test questions from beyond the grave, or what happened to Edmundsen in that pit. The best that we can come up with is that there's another world out there, something out-side of our understanding. And the people that we love, when they die…well, they're still part of our lives somehow.

Obviously, Tessa's always known that.

And me?

I guess I've come around.

A PRESENCE BEYOND THE SHADOWS

David Lee Summers

Barbara's voice came over the phone in a breathless rush. "I swear, the door creaked open at the end of the hall and then something cold brushed past me."

Nick sighed as his eyes drifted around his office in the math department. Looking out the window, he noticed trees moving in the wind. "I'm sure it was just a wind gust. It's an old house. Somehow it found its way inside."

"I wish you'd bring those glasses you invented home." Barbara huffed. "You might learn something about whatever's haunting this house."

"They're goggles and they're for research. I can't just bring them home because my wife thinks there are ghosts." Nick rubbed the bridge of his nose. "It's because I'm department chair that we can afford the lovely old Victorian house you wanted. The last thing we need is for someone to decide I'm using department resources inappropriately."

This time, Barbara sighed. "Look, you've only really used your dimensional goggles around campus. Doesn't it make sense to take them further afield and see how the results change?"

She had a point. As a mathematician, Nick Levy specialized in applying vector analysis to four-dimensional topology. A few years earlier, he'd been working with a colleague in the university's physics department when they figured out a way to detect a fourth physical dimension, perpendicular to the usual three: left-right, forward-back, and up-down. Nick's physicist colleague, Rod Koenig, built a sensor and Nick worked with programmers in the math department to map its readings into images the human brain could interpret, record them, and transmit the images to a server. These were assembled into a special pair of goggles. They had been testing the goggles around campus recording and noting their results, but they hadn't gone further afield.

"Nick, are you still there?"

"Uh, yeah, sure," he sputtered. "I think you may be onto something. I'll check with the department secretary and discuss the appropriate procedure for bringing the goggles home."

"Thank you." Barbara sounded relieved.

"Look, I'm not saying I believe our house is haunted…I just think there may be value in testing the goggles out in the field, away from the more controlled university environment. If we happen to see something, that would be great, but I'm betting good old-fashioned infrared goggles would do more to track down air flow through the house that pushes doors and gives you chills."

"What about that time something sat on the edge of the bed in the middle of the night?" Barbara prompted.

Nick shuddered at the memory. He remembered waking up when a weight had settled on the bed. If they'd had cats or dogs, he might not have thought anything of it. When he'd turned on the lights, something did indent the blankets for a moment. When he reached over, he could feel nothing. The incident made him think this little experiment might not be a complete waste of time. "We'll discuss this more when I get home," Nick said. "And no guarantees. I need to make sure I'm not violating any rules by bringing a new device home. I also want to make sure the Wi-Fi transmitter will connect to our router, so I can record any observations."

He ended the call after a few pleasantries, then sat back. Theoretical physicists had been postulating extra dimensions for some time. Einstein used four in his equations of general relativity, which were fundamentally tied to gravitational theory. String theorists worked with as many as ten dimensions—even more in some variations. He found the topological problem of additional dimensions fascinating. When human perception is limited to three dimensions, how do you prove the existence of others and map them? How do you translate mathematical abstractions into perceivable reality?

He reached over and pulled the case containing the goggles toward him. He opened it, put them on, then looked around the room. Left-right and forward-back were the same dimensions as always, but "up-down" had been mapped into the fourth dimension the goggles detected. As he moved his head around, he could see the occasional shadow, or the ghostly echo of a flat surface. The new up-down resembled a flowing medium, like a meandering river or stream that broke and swirled around the flat objects he could see. Unlike a river or stream, the program painted these eddies and swirls in shades of orange, yellow, green, reminding him of the psychedelic imagery of the 1960s. Koenig suggested these eddies and swirls might be related to gravity because of Einstein's equations. All Nick knew for certain was that he got a headache if he wore the goggles too long.

He turned the goggles off, removed them, and sat back, rubbing his eyes. It would be interesting to see if the ripple effect was any different away from campus. He called the department secretary to determine the proper procedure to take the goggles home.

$$\pi$$

Nick drove home after work. He stepped from the car and looked up at the tasteful gray, two-story Victorian house with its gables, columns, and even a round turret off the upper floor. Even as a department chair, he could barely afford such a house in the Bay Area, but his wife also had a good income as a programmer. It often baffled him that his wife, who had a similar background to him, was so willing to believe in the supernatural.

Still, he wouldn't be surprised to find something going on in the house. As his wife reminded him, there had been the incident where something seemed to have perched on the bed. At the time, he'd suspected a lingering dream or maybe that Barbara had somehow planted the suggestion of something settling on the bed while he'd been half asleep. However, the idea that he might discover even a minor gravitational anomaly with his goggles could be a major coup—the kind of thing that won awards. He hoped such thoughts weren't pure fantasy.

He took a moment to slip on the goggles and look at the house. He flipped a small lever on the top of the goggles, confirmed that they connected to his Wi-Fi router, and recorded his readings. He looked around. The house had so few planar surfaces aligned with the ground, he could make out little other than the psychedelic, wavy-line wilderness that characterized most views. Perhaps those waves were a little denser toward the house than away from it. Glancing down the street toward the setting sun, he distinctly saw the waves get closer together and become denser, almost as though they emanated from the sun itself. That would seem to support Rod Koenig's hypothesis that the waves were somehow related to gravity.

Nick removed the bulky eyewear, returned the unit to the case, and went inside. His wife emerged from her home office. They embraced and exchanged a brief, chaste kiss. She glanced over at the clock. "I lost track of the time. I still have a project to wrap up. Did you want to make dinner, or should I get something delivered?"

"Let's go for delivery," Nick said. "Now that you've put the notion of looking around the house with the goggles in my mind, I want to get a baseline while things are quiet."

"All right, I'll call it in. Chinese all right? The usual?"

Nick acknowledged the query with a non-committal grunt. He removed his coat and tie, then hung them up in the closet. He considered mixing a drink, but decided the goggles were mind-bending enough. He'd toast any interesting finds he made after he looked around.

He went upstairs, stood at one end of the hall, and made a plan. He'd walk along the hallway with his hand on the wall and look into each of the three rooms on the left in turn and record his findings.

Inside the house proved a bit more interesting than outside. He saw more shadows and more translucent ripples where flat surfaces should be. Occasionally the vertical ripples made an unexpected jag. Neither he nor Rod could explain those…yet. He looked in the first room—the guest bedroom—and noted little of interest. He moved on to the next room, which was the bedroom he shared with Barbara.

There, he noticed something unexpected. A large shadow formed by their queen-sized bed dominated the floor. Some planes—the vanity and a dresser— hovered beyond the shadow. Embedded in the waves swimming around the bed's shadow drifted a darkness, deeper than the usual two-dimensional shadows and not wavering, almost like a hole in the waves' midst. He tapped a button on the goggles, which set a bookmark in the recording, then lifted them.

The empty, dark bedroom stood before him. Nothing unusual.

He placed the goggles back over his eyes and stared into the dark void. As he watched, two glowing, green orbs faded into view.

Nick shuddered. It seemed like a creature stared at him, evaluating him.

He took a step closer. Did the orbs squash? He almost sensed a narrowing gaze.

"Whacha up to?"

The voice of Nick's nine-year-old daughter, Elisa, made him squawk involuntarily. Just as he lifted the goggles, he noticed the orbs had vanished. He lifted the goggles and whirled on his daughter. She must have crept out of her room across the hall.

"Can't you see that Daddy's working?" Nick snapped.

Elisa smiled, held her hands and rocked back and forth on her feet. "What are you working on?"

"It's my experiment understanding other dimensions."

"What's that on your head? Can I see?"

"No," he snapped, harsher than he intended.

Elisa recoiled, almost as though she'd been slapped. She snuffled and her eyes grew moist.

Nick knelt down beside her. "Look, this is expensive equipment and I need to make sure it makes it back to the department in good shape. It's my responsibility." He thought fast. "It's like last year, when you brough the class hamster home."

She nodded and rubbed her eyes. "I let you hold the hamster."

Impatience prickled at Nick and he struggled to keep an even tone. "Maybe we can look at these goggles together later."

Elisa nodded, seemingly unconvinced. She turned and sulked back into her room.

Nick sighed, then stood and faced his own bedroom again with the goggles back in place. The anomaly remained and the glowing orbs had returned, still slightly squashed. He stepped back involuntarily.

The doorbell rang and he nearly toppled over, disoriented as he was looking through the goggles. He lifted them, rubbed his, eyes and went downstairs for dinner.

$$\pi$$

Over the next three days, when not at work, Nick continued to examine the house with the goggles. The orbs and void only appeared upstairs. They tended to hover in the bedroom, but occasionally, he spotted them down the hall. He thought he noticed them drifting away from him at one point, but the perspectives in the extradimensional view were so disorienting, he couldn't be certain.

He visited Rod Koenig at the physics department and described his observations.

Koenig shrugged. "Sounds like you're seeing something real. My guess is a field of some kind. I'm guessing it must exist, at least partially, in at least two of our dimensions for you to see it so clearly. It would be nice if we could pin down something besides the visual detection through the goggles." He snapped his fingers, then stood and beckoned for Nick to follow. He led Nick to the physics stock room where they checked out a half dozen electromagnetic field detectors.

Nick narrowed his gaze. "Do you think the anomaly is electromagnetic in nature?"

Again, Koenig shrugged. "You're in an older house. Could be something funky with the wiring."

Nick frowned, disappointed. "That doesn't sound like it would be a Nobel Prize-level discovery."

"Probably not." Koenig winked. "But it would still be interesting. We don't expect electromagnetic phenomena to have a fourth dimensional component. If it did, it would be interesting."

"And if the orbs don't register on the meters?"

"Then we need to come up with another hypothesis." Koenig loaded the meters in a box and thrust them at Nick. "Let's try one thing at a time. Electromagnetism is easy to measure. Quantum and gravitational fields are more challenging out in the field."

Even though it was only early afternoon, Nick went directly home to give the experiment a try. Elisa would still be at school and Barbara would be working, so it would give him some quiet time to see what he could learn.

He set up the detectors, then examined the bedroom and the upstairs hallway with the goggles. Not seeing anything, he waited. Time wore on. He lifted the goggles and began answering emails on his phone, then started to worry that Elisa would get home from school and interrupt his experiment again. Just then, the meter across from him in the bedroom began to woggle. He put the phone aside and lowered the goggles. He punched the air when he noticed the orbs. Whatever they were, they registered on an electromagnetic meter.

Still, as he watched, the weird "hole" in the fabric of reality associated with orbs seemed to grow larger. He shivered.

"I thought I heard someone up here."

Barbara's voice startled him. He yelped and lifted the goggles.

"Sorry, I didn't mean to sneak up on you," she said. "I just didn't expect you home this early."

Nick glanced from Barbara to the meter. It still seemed active, but the dial began to drop.

She shivered. "Did you feel that?"

Nick shook his head. He put on the goggles. The orbs and the "hole" had moved past Barbara and now hovered in the hallway.

Barbara's brow furrowed. "Have you been seeing something with the goggles?"

Nick chewed his lower lip for a moment before responding. "I have, but I'm not sure what…maybe an electrical field or something."

"Then you don't think the house is haunted?" She seemed disappointed.

Nick snorted a laugh. "No, I don't think it's haunted, but I think I may have found something that explains at least part of what we've been experiencing." He had to admit, he didn't know how an electromagnetic field might explain a weight on the bed, but that did have other possible explanations.

"You know," Barbara said as she eased closer to the bed. "It's been a while since the two of us have been alone in the house without Elisa. There's still about an hour before the school bus gets here. Maybe we could have a little adult recreation."

Her weight settled on the bed beside him—no uncertainty there.

"I need to make some notes," he said.

She lifted the goggles from his head. Nick blinked and his head swam as the view swapped back to the ordinary world. He looked at her.

"Your notes can wait." She unbuttoned the top button of her blouse.

Nick reached over and put on the headset for a moment. The orbs had vanished. He turned off the recording device. It didn't need to record anything that happened for the next hour.

π

The next day, Nick sat in his office at home, writing up his observations. He hypothesized that the void and glowing orbs were the goggles' way of visualizing something like a vector field. The void would be a field following a vector directly away from him while the orbs were fields pointed right at him. The hypothesis didn't explain why the orbs seemed to change shape or size, but that could be how the field reacted to external forces, or it could just be related to the psychedelic visualization. After all, the goggles used AI algorithms to try to map structures into shapes the human brain could interpret. However, machine learning algorithms had no more experience with fourth dimensional reality than humans did. He suspected the fourth dimensional topography he saw wasn't well mapped.

As he pondered all that, the doors flew open, and Elisa plodded into the room. She dropped down onto the chair opposite her father, looking dejected.

"Dad, can I have help with my math homework?"

She placed a worksheet on the desk in front of him. He stared down at the sheet of multiplication and division problems. He could do the problems in his head. "Did you even try these?"

"I don't understand how to do the problems," Elisa whined.

He tried switching gears and thought of his own students. "Did you do the reading?"

She blinked at him. "Dad, we have to keep our books at school. The teacher explained how it works and I thought I understood, but now I don't get it."

Nick growled low in his throat, growing impatient and wanting to return to his own work. "All right. Let's take a look at this first one. Three times five. How do you do it?"

Elisa shrank back, a little intimidated by her father's forceful approach. She shook her head.

"Look, it's simple, it's just five three times." He held up his hand and counted by fives. "Five, ten, fifteen. That's your answer."

"But what about the division problems?"

"Same thing but in reverse," he grumbled. "Go give it a try and then we can talk about it."

"But I don't know what you mean about same thing but in reverse. That doesn't make sense." She jumped to her feet, frustrated tears sprouting in her eyes.

"Give it a try. You need to be able to figure some things out for yourself, or you'll never amount to anything."

Elisa sniffed, jumped up from the chair, and sprinted from the office.

Nick snorted. He remembered how his own father had also told him to figure things out for himself. He'd hated it at the time, but it had set him on the path to getting his doctorate, earning tenure, and finally being named department chair. He went to the door, closed it and locked it, just to make sure Elisa didn't bother him again.

When he turned around, he noticed the paper on the desk. He'd take it to Elisa when he finished. Just as he sat down, a low growl sounded, not unlike the one he'd made when he'd grown frustrated. He looked around, trying to figure out which direction it came from. It seemed to come from everywhere and nowhere.

π

Barbara worked on her computer as Elisa entered her office. Her daughter snuffled and dropped onto a chair.

"What's the matter, honey?"

"Dad won't tell me how division works."

As she spoke, Barbara noticed tears leaking from the little girl's eyes. "Your dad's a very busy man." Even as she apologized for him, she grew more than a little irritated that he believed himself too busy to even help his daughter. "He sometimes gets caught up a little too much in his work." *And his own self-importance,* she thought, but didn't say that last part aloud. "Show me your homework sheet and I'll see if I can help you."

Elisa gasped. "I think I left it on Daddy's desk."

"Don't worry, let's go get it." Barbara stood and took Elisa's hand. They walked to Nick's office. She tried the door. He'd locked it. She knocked.

Instead of an answer, a scream sounded from the other side.

"Nick? Nick! What's going on?" Barbara tried the door again.

Another scream sounded, this one wet and gurgling. She took Elisa's hand and ran back to her office. "You sit right here and don't move."

"Is Daddy okay?"

Barbara shook her head. "I don't know, sweetie. Let me look. If I shout for you to run, you go right to the neighbors, okay."

"What's wrong? I'm scared."

Barbara nodded and wanted to reassure he daughter, but she also knew she needed to get moving. She opened her desk drawer and grabbed the spare key to Nick's office, then ran back. She unlocked the door, threw it open and saw… nothing wrong.

Except Nick wasn't there.

She walked over to the window. It was latched.

She looked the room up and down but couldn't find her husband.

"Nick, where are you?"

He could have left the room, but if he did, why did he lock it behind him? She sprinted from the office and made a circuit of the house, calling for Nick.

"Nick, if you're playing some childish prank, I'm going to kill you!"

When she reached her office again, Elisa stood by the door. "Mommy, I'm really scared."

Barbara couldn't lie to her daughter. She licked her lips and nodded. "To tell you the truth, I'm pretty scared, too."

She told Elisa to wait, then returned to Nick's office and looked around again.

He'd left his computer turned on, the file with his notes open. On the desk stood the case that held the dimensional goggles. She took them out of the box and turned them on. The view disoriented her. At first, she thought she'd moved into some kind of flowing river, except she couldn't feel the water. After a moment, she began to discern shadows and flat surfaces. As she turned around, she noticed red blobs and gobbets like chopped meat. She took a step toward the phantoms and reached out. Of course, her hand touched nothing. She could only see into this dimension, not feel it.

Then, out of the corner of her eye, Barbara noticed a presence beyond the shadows. She thought of the reason she'd asked Nick to bring the goggles to the house in the first place. She thought of ghosts and malevolent spirits. A cold sweat broke out on her forehead as she turned to face whatever was in the room with her.

It was a dark void, almost like a hole in the fabric of reality. Two glowing orbs hovered on either side of the void. The form moved closer and closer. She stepped back and bumped into the desk. As she did, the void seemed to pass right through her.

She shuddered from a chill. A rank odor wafted to her nose, like one she'd smelled near a meat market once.

She turned and looked at the form. A crescent appeared below the void. Perhaps there had been a rupture in the field Nick had been talking about.

As the rupture widened, she could discern teeth.

An involuntary laugh erupted because it reminded her of the Chesire Cat's smile.

She swallowed the laugh when she noticed the teeth were coated in blood.

THE GHOSTS OF THE SPIRAL

Maxwell I. Gold

I saw ghosts where none existed, at the beginning, trapped in a continuous mass falling towards spectral nothingness. Chains and bones rattled the voids, whose music stole my courage, until the night was robbed completely of stars.

One by one, the lights went out, such spectacular heat-deaths ignited throughout the pathetic abysms of a thankless, empty universe.

Soon, I felt myself tumbling through the inevitable, a twisted column of light

shrinking fast, filled with cackles of thunder from old ghosts.

Space closed around me; I can't breathe.

Spiral Ghosts—*they're here!*

Dear god, no!

I'm trapped

at

the

close.

π

Opening again, breathing like some awful monster, twisting and writhing at the bottom, I was pulled up and out again through the infinity of a dark and terrible dream towards Entropy's wide, gaping maw. The end

was a lie painted in false equations, and laughing specters who, like tatters of pixelated what-ifs manipulated my tired brain

until up was down, and all shape had no meaning inside a twisted column of light.

Shrinking fast, filled with cackles of thunder from old ghosts,

Space closed around me; I can't breathe.

Spiral Ghosts—*they're here!*

Dear god, no!

I'm trapped

in

the

Dark

...

ABOUT THE CONTRIBUTORS

Robert (Bob) Lewis is a Colorado-based author, editor, publisher, magician, scholar, podcaster, YouTuber, entrepreneur, and more. He holds degrees with Latin honors in Biology, English, Mathematics, and Psychology from the University of Colorado Denver (where he also took an Astrophysics minor) as well as a Master of Education in Science and the Public from the University at Buffalo. A dedicated polymath, he likes to tell people that his hobby is to collect new hobbies. Among his current favorite pastimes are chess, cooking, woodworking, tinkering in his workshop, collecting bizarre artifacts and curiosities, and (re)learning his musical instruments. By the time you read this, he'll assuredly have added some more to the list.

Professionally speaking, he is the founder, owner, and executive editor of Polymath Press, host of the YouTube channel *Phobophile*, co-host of the *Do You Like Scary Movies* horror podcast, member of the Rocky Mountain Paranormal Research Society, and performs as a magician at Bob Lewis Magic. He's the co-author (with Bryan Bonner) of the *Case Files of the Rocky Mountain Paranormal Research Society* series and the editor of *In the Woods: A Fiction Foundry Anthology*, both of which are available from Polymath Press. By the time you read this, there's a good chance he'll be in the process of adding something to this list as well.

π

Elizabeth Massie is the author of novels, novellas, short fiction, media-tie ins, poetry, and nonfiction. Her novels and collections include *Sineater, Hell Gate, Desper Hollow, Wire Mesh Mothers, Homeplace, Naked on the Edge, Dark Shadows: Dreams of the Dark* (co-authored with Mark Rainey), *Buffy the Vampire Slayer: Power of Persuasion, It Watching, Afraid, Madame Cruller's Couch and Other Dark and Bizarre Tales, The Great Chicago Fire*, and many more. She is also the creator of the *Ameri-Scares* series of middle-grade novels. Elizabeth's short fiction has been included in countless magazines and anthologies, including several years' best publications. She lives in the Shenandoah Valley of Virginia with her husband, artist/illustrator and Theremin-player Cortney Skinner. Elizabeth is a two-time Bram Stoker Award-winning author and recipient of the 2022 Horror Writers Association Lifetime Achievement Award.

π

Miguel Fliguer (b. 1961) lives in Buenos Aires, Argentina. His self-published first book, *Cooking with Lovecraft* is a collection of gastronomical weird tales. His short stories and collaborations are featured in the *Ancestors & Descendants, Weird Tails, Portraits of Terror, Corridors*, and *The Pickman Papers* anthologies from Innsmouth Gold Press. He is also published in *Circulo de Lovecraft* (Spain), *Vastarien Literary Journal* (Grimscribe Press), *Strange Aeon 2022*, and Red Duke Games' illustrated culinary grimoires. He dwells on Twitter as @cookingwithHPL and as @cookingwithlovecraft on Instagram.

π

Mike Slater rose from the stygian depths of corporate America at about the same time Viagra and Google came to be. Irish Astrologers and Iron Maiden fans remain divided as to whether or not these events are related. Mike is the author of *The Necronomnomnom, LoveCraft Cocktails, The NecroMunchicon*, and several horror tales scattered about the dark literaturescape, and a designer of games of all sorts for Red Duke Games. He is a lifelong fan of Things Not of This Earth.

π

Patrick Freivald is the four-time Bram Stoker Award nominated author of eight novels and dozens of short stories, including his collection *In the Garden of Rusting Gods*. A physics teacher by day, he is also an avid beekeeper and the owner of a hot sauce company and writes about whatever interests him, including nonfiction (physics, mostly), horror, science fiction, and fantasy. Growing up on a steady diet of *The Twilight Zone* and *Tales from the Dark Side*, he's always had a soft spot for the monstrous and weird. He and his wife live in the hinterlands of Western New York with dogs, cats, chickens, parrots, and several million stinging insects. You can find him online across social media and at patrick.freivald.com.

π

Liz Kaufman is a Toronto-based writer who has always loved a good scare. She enjoys reading and writing horror, romance, and speculative fiction, and most enjoys mixing elements of all three. In her spare time, she loves going on long walks and fantasizing about moving to a remote cabin in the woods. But, for now, she lives in the city with her husband and large orange cat. You can read more about Liz and her work at lizkaufman.com.

π

Damon Nomad is the pen name of an author of numerous short stories and essays, several of which have won competitions at Writing.com. He is educated and trained as both an engineer and lawyer and has lived and worked all over the world. Speaking Volumes has published his two novels, *Phantom in the Desert* (July 2022) and *A Dangerous Test* (September 2023). His short story "Death Trap" is slated for publication in Jane Nightshades' *Serial Encounters* anthology in early 2024.

π

Sarah Lazarz has loved stories ever since she found a secret cache of fantasy novels in her grandparents' cabin as a child. Besides writing, she adopts cats, teaches middle school, and drinks coffee. She lives on the bank of the Mississippi River with her spouse and hopes to get over her fear of heights someday.

π

Martin Zeigler writes short fiction, primarily mystery, science fiction, and horror. A number of his stories have been published both in print and online. His work can be found in *Mystery Magazine*, *Mystery Tribune*, *Shotgun Honey*, *Yellow Mama*, and in a whole slew of other magazines and anthologies. Many of his stories can also be found in two self-published collections, *A Functional Man and Other Stories* and *Hypochondria and Other Stories*.

When he is not writing, Marty is quite possibly outside taking a long walk or inside dabbling on the piano or struggling valiantly with a classic unsolved problem in number theory. He makes his home in the Pacific Northwest.

π

Josh Snider is a multi-genre author from a family of writers and editors. He has participated in professional writers' groups for his entire life, being the youngest member of his first group, the award-winning Colorado Springs Fiction Writers Group, and a founding member and former president of Fiction Foundry. He has a background in poetry and has since moved into prose. His work has previously appeared in *In the Woods: A Fiction Foundry Anthology*, from Polymath Press.

π

Rivka Crowbourne is an aspiring poet and writer who wishes you infinitely well.

π

Joe Stout is an east-Tennessee based writer who focuses on short stories and flash fiction. His work has been published by the *NonBinary Review*, Psycho-Toxin Press and CafeLit. When he's not writing, he enjoys exploring the mountains and spending time with his children. You can follow him on Facebook at Joe Stout Writing or Instagram @joestoutwriting.

π

Brian Knight lives in Washington State with his wife and the voices in his head. He has published over a dozen novels and novellas including *Feral*, *Hacks*, and the *Phoenix Girls* trilogy, as well as two short story collections in the horror, fantasy, and crime genres. Several of his short stories have received honorable mentions in *Year's Best Fantasy and Horror*. Learn more about Brian and his work at www.brian-knight.com.

π

Wil Forbis writes horror and suspense fiction that simmers with tension before exploding into action. He's placed several short stories in anthologies and his novel *What Waits in the Shadows*, a tale of the monsters that dwell in the mind (and elsewhere), was published in 2024. Visit www.thehorrorofwilforbis.com for free stories and updates.

π

David Lee Summers is the author of a dozen novels and over ninety published short stories. His writing spans a wide range of the imaginative from science fiction to fantasy to horror. David's novels include *The Solar Sea*, which was selected as a Flamingnet Young Adult Top Choice, *The Astronomer's Crypt*, which is a horror novel inspired by his work at an astronomical observatory, and *The Brazen Shark*, which was voted best steampunk novel in the 2017 Preditors and Editors Reader's Poll. His short stories and poems have appeared in such magazines and anthologies as *Realms of Fantasy*, *Cemetery Dance*, and *Straight Outta Tombstone*. In 2010 and 2016, he was nominated for the Science Fiction Poetry Association's Rhysling Award and in 2017, he was nominated for SFPA's Dwarf Stars Award. In addition to writing, David has edited five science fiction anthologies including *A Kepler's Dozen*, *Kepler's Cowboys* and *Maximum Velocity: The Best of the Full-Throttle Space Tales*. When not working with the written word, David operates telescopes at Kitt Peak National Observatory. Learn more about David at davidleesummers.com.

π

Maxwell I. Gold is a Jewish American multiple award nominated author with half a decade of writing experience who writes prose poetry and short stories in cosmic horror and weird fiction. He is a five-time Rhysling Award nominee and two-time Pushcart Award nominee. Find him and his work at www.thewellsoftheweird.com.

If you enjoyed reading *Arithmophobia: An Anthology of Mathematical Horror,* please consider leaving a review online and telling your friends about this book. Independent publishers rely heavily on word of mouth advertising. You have our thanks in advance.

Also available from Polymath Press

In the Woods: A Fiction Foundry Anthology
Edited by Robert Lewis

Strange things can happen in the woods.

Sometimes they're frightening.

Sometimes they're funny.

Sometimes they're just plain weird.

The authors of the Fiction Foundry writers' critique group have taken it upon themselves to explore all the strange things that happen in the often majestic and yet often harsh woodlands.

Fiction Foundry, established 2012, is a group of writers dedicated to helping prepare one another's work for professional publication. In this anthology, the group's authors show off their eclectic visions of life among the trees.

Featuring contributions by John H. Howard, Sangita Kalarickal, Josh Snider, Carolyn Kay, Robert Lewis, Charli Cowan, Henry Snider, Shiloh Silveira, Kari J. Wolfe, Christophe Maso, and Hollie Snider, this anthology brings us out of urban life and shows a world of forest spirits, haints, mental illness, parasitic spiders, werewolves, out of control plants, evil forces, reincarnation, humans with animal ears, witches, and Lovecraftian horrors.

And all of them can be found...*In the Woods*.

Case Files of the Rocky Mountain Paranormal Research Society Volume 1 by Robert Lewis & Bryan Bonner

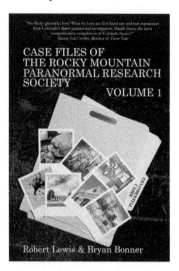

Do you enjoy a good ghost story?

"Forget everything you've seen on T.V. or movies about paranormal investigating - this book is the real deal, and it's smarter and scarier (and sometimes funnier). The Rocky Mountain Paranormal Research Society's case files are detailed but also exciting, written not just with a scientist's quest for truth but also a novelist's attention to pacing and background. This is a book that I suspect many of us will return to over and over in the years to come." - Lisa Morton, author of *Ghosts: A Haunted History* and *Calling the Spirits: A History of Seances*.

For nearly a quarter of a century, the Rocky Mountain Paranormal Research Society has investigated ghosts, aliens, cryptids, and all manner of bizarre claims and happenings in Colorado and beyond. Combining historic and scientific research with a love of the weird and scary, they've researched and documented some of the best paranormal stories in the world. Now, Colorado's first and only forensic paranormal investigation team is proud to present this inaugural volume of their collected case files.

Within these pages, you'll learn not only the ghostly and paranormal stories, but the histories of the allegedly haunted locations and the methods Rocky

Mountain Paranormal uses to get to the bottom of some of the world's strangest phenomena.

Included in this volume:

*How Rocky Mountain Paranormal involved multiple departments of the United States Federal government in a paranormal investigation
*The haunting of an active nuclear military base
*A paranormal investigation inside a jail
*A paranormal investigation deep inside a cave
*A location that is still home to thousands of unidentified human bodies—and how Rocky Mountain Paranormal worked to tell their stories
*Colorado's own vampire legend
*The time one of our investigators got slapped by an unseen entity
*The inspiration behind a classic horror movie
*And many more!

Some of the cases are solved and others remain deep mysteries, but all are both entertaining and informative. Whether you like ghosts, aliens, monsters, history, science, or all of the above, these case files have something sure to please, and perhaps even to bring a chill to your spine.

(And look for Volume 2, expected September, 2024!)

Get your copies of these and other Polymath Press titles online at www.polymathpress.com or wherever fine books are sold.